Are You Game?

By

Douglas Brain

This book is a work of fiction. Names, characters, places and incidents are either the product of the author's imagination or are used fictionally. Any resemblance to actual persons, living or dead, or to actual events or locales is entirely coincidental.

Copyright © 2018 Douglas Brain.

All rights reserved.

ISBN: 9781912939152

For Kevin; always missed, never forgotten.

Preface

Sitting on my grassy deathbed, I look to wondrous nature.

Penning my final words as my breath betrays me.

Not once in my glorious life did I expect death to arrive so;

not as man or spectre, but an abomination, defiant of nature.

Pure grass, trees and rock; mountains touching rich blue sky.

I behold them as beauty and truth.

*

The lie arrives; manufactured.

It will kill me, eviscerate my matter.

Not before, once more, I rage against it.

I cannot save myself, but I will avenge my premature end.

Farewell.

*

If you find this note; know that I fought,

tooth and nail,

for you...

Creation

We called it Gām. It was a simple concept; just a new idea for some outdoor fun. One that could provide entertainment with purpose. How quickly it became much more than that. But first, let me explain the moniker. You may well have noticed the line over the letter 'a' in its title. This is a macron, a type of diacritical mark used in poetry and phonetics. Here it's used to denote a lengthening of the letter, making 'gam' to be pronounced as 'game'. That's all; a simple device to make it easier to search for on the Internet. It seemed that even in the creation of the title, the game wanted to be more than it was intended. I wonder if it's creators knew what the results would be when they started, would they have continued? I think they would have; its construction seemed inevitable.

*

We all subconsciously create that which destroys us, for only in confronting death, can we truly experience life.

Meeting

They met in the first-class lounge of Vancouver Airport where they were pleasantly surrounded by understated opulence. Although they each arrived separately, having taken different flights, they quickly gravitated towards each other as they inevitably would. Each happily made use of the comfortable chairs, free drinks and snacks like children at the Christmas table. There were eight of them in total; all good friends from twenty years ago where they had met at university. They had drifted apart but the bond, that was forged all those years ago, remained despite the intervening years.

They greeted each other with warmth as feelings of familiarity washed over them, displacing any doubt they might have had over their friendships after such a long time. Now, each at forty years old, or thereabouts, they thought of themselves as different people. As they hugged and greeted each other however, any onlooker could see the through the façade; they were the same as they ever were. At first the contact was tentative then, growing to firm, it became a need. Back then, at university, they believed themselves to be adults; as if such a thing ever existed. Older than children then, older more so now, they were no different; each needed the other to make them happy still.

There were hugs between all, kisses for the women and friendly claps on shoulders for the men. As the final guest arrived however, a cloud seemed to pass across their sun as the mood gradually became sombre. They were here, not for happy memories, but because where there were eight, there once would have been nine. It was Felicity, the host, who announced the absent member of the group.

"A toast," she announced to the silence, raising a complimentary glass of champagne, "to Lucas."

The name was muttered in sad voices as glasses clinked and sips were taken. Seven standing people sat back down in seven comfortable armchairs spread around a low table. The eighth member of the group was already seated, having never risen. The attached wheels either side of him preventing his joining properly in the toast.

"I was sorry to hear about your accident, Bertrand," Felicity commented after sitting, gesturing to his wheelchair, "I would have come and visited, but--"

He dismissed her forthcoming explanation with a casual wave of his hand, "it's fine. I didn't want anyone to..." Seeing that more explanation was expected, he placed his now empty glass on the table and took a deep breath before continuing. "It took me a long time to get used to being in the chair, but I'm better now." He expelled his growing unease in a long slow breath. "I am... resigned. I suppose is the right word."

No one knew what to say so looked away to random locations around the room, suddenly able to find interest in anything other than each other. "Well, you look great," Randal, ever the joker of the group, suddenly interjected in his distinctive New Orleans accent, "shorter than I remember maybe."

The inappropriate joke broke the tension as quickly as it had built and they all politely chuckled with the sudden release.

"Man, do I miss an English audience…" Randal added with a beaming smile.

However, any further conversation was interrupted by the arrival of a stranger. He had risen from the bar where he had been waiting as they'd laughed and relaxed, approaching them with a confident stride. This was Oliver, their pilot and guide for their adventure. Tall at six feet four in height, he cast a long shadow across the table as the sun once again flooded into the room. Felicity was the one to enquire what he might desire with an inquisitive lift of her eyebrows.

"Are y'all the Lucas Campbell group?" He asked assertively with a booming voice. Felicity nodded and, without waiting for permission, he pulled a chair over to their table while they dutifully shuffled theirs around to make room. "I'm Oliver," he stated loudly, "I'll be your pilot to take you to the park. Whenever you're ready of course," he informed them with a friendly smile as he awkwardly folded his giant frame into the small wooden chair.

He started to get comfortable as he looked around him for a waiter, but none of the group wanted to wait. They all finished whatever drink they had remaining and rose to their feet amongst the discordant tune of their glasses hitting the table-top. Felicity paused to help Bertrand, but he pushed hard on his wheels, forcing himself away from her and to the front of the queue. Immediately he started questioning the imposing figure of their pilot who, taking his cue from the friends, was quickly striding towards a subtle side-exit.

"So, Oli… what can you tell us about this game?" He called loudly to the pilot, his head being such a long way from the giant's, as he rolled along in his chair.

"Sorry, Bertie…" Oliver replied, tilting his head down and casually abbreviating Bertrand's name as his own had been. "No idea myself. I was hired to fly. I know you're going to trial some game but that's all."

"But you're our guide!" This was Felicity. She was stepping along quickly to keep up, complaining with a slight whine to the pilot.

"Apparently that's a part of the game, miss." He replied happily, not turning around as he strode onwards. He lifted his head a little as if talking to the sky, easily projecting his voice to the group behind him. "Mystery and discovery. Excitement and exhilaration in the great outdoors. The gām to end all games." He'd spread his arms out to emphasise the point and, as he lowered them, his voice changed to a more friendly tone, "at least that's what I was told."

As they arrived at the exit, he shoved it open for the eight friends. He turned to them all and gestured that they pass through to a large expanse of concrete. Upon the uniform grey surface beyond the portal sat the squat form of a huge black helicopter. Backed by a large grey wall, the combined effect suddenly drained everything natural from their world. The contrast from the opulence of the first-class lounge to this industrial setting with the massive machine pride-of-place, stopped them in their tracks. Felicity looked to the sky where the sun had once again retreated behind a dark cloud. The sheer size of the helicopter was overwhelming, the imposing vehicle dwarfed everything around it. "Your bags are all on board, if you would kindly make your way to the chopper..." Oliver called to them, oblivious to the change in mood. Obediently, mutely, they all walked to the giant black machine leaving only Bertrand, who had paused in his chair.

"I was told there would be provision for my... predicament?" He worriedly asked the pilot, finding his voice.

"Don't you worry, buddy," Oliver boomed back with incongruous boisterousness. "That I have seen, and you'll not be disappointed. Sorry for the temporary inconvenience but I'm going to have to carry you to the chopper myself, hope you're okay with that?"

Without giving him a chance to complain or agree, Oliver simply stooped down and lifted Bertrand from the chair into his arms. Bertrand had no choice but to wrap his arms around the friendly giant as he was carried across the concrete apron, quickly catching then overtaking the others. Oliver lowered Bertrand into the co-pilot's chair, gently placing his massive hand on Bertrand's shoulder as he did. "You get the best seat, for being so cooperative. Now buckle up," he said with a wink. Bertrand smiled back, appreciating the touch of the likeable stranger. Oliver rewarded his friendliness with a smile of his own and a wiggle of his eyebrows as he firmly closed the heavy door on his passenger.

Lucas

Lucas was an awkward child. That's what his mother had always told him, and he found himself living up to the proffered information later in life. He was intelligent, his parents had always told him so, but then what parents wouldn't? It took him an inordinately long time to realise the truth himself, however. He just thought that people made a fuss. When others struggled, he used to tell them, "but you just...". Life wasn't hard, he thought, people just made it so. It made him lazy, his intelligence. Maybe not lazy, but certainly relaxed. He didn't need to try, so why bother. So instead he indulged his awkwardness. He disrupted classes in school, having finished the work early each time. He frustrated his teachers. He wasn't bad, just 'difficult'. Teachers didn't know how to handle someone so clearly excelling at work but, at the same time, not trying.

Often in these cases, some children might become trouble-makers, bullies or just generally naughty. Lucas, instead, indulged his sense of humour, making jokes and generally amusing himself. People at school would say; "Lucas? Yeah, odd...". That was the word people would use to describe him. Either that or 'weird', or 'strange'. Such was his sense of humour; he stood alone outside, looking in. Even his name was strange, he was the only Lucas he knew, the only one any of his friends knew. He was going to be called Laurence, his mother had told him once. Were it not for his brother calling him Florence one day by mistake, he certainly would have been. Lucas knew no Laurence's either; he was destined, it seemed, to be unique.

Another feature of Lucas was that he was a nerd. To his core he was interested in engineering and science, never sport or music, girls or mainstream television. However, his nerd nature was not a trait he was eager to embrace. Instead of admitting that he was an avid Red Dwarf fan, he rode a mountain bike. Instead of telling people that he liked to watch documentaries on television, he went out with friends. Instead of wearing the Australian army hat he owned and loved, he wore cooler clothes with sporty labels. The main thing, however, that saved him from obscurity and Dungeons and Dragons parties, was that people liked him. His oddness was endearing, it was fun. He was fun. He was 'a nice guy.' That was something else people said about him. That, he grimly considered, was why he arrived at university without a girlfriend, definitely still a virgin.

It didn't bother him, his lack of sexual experience. It should have at the age of nineteen, but it didn't. He knew it would happen, he would just wait for it like he had with everything else in his life. Life happened to him, Lucas thought, and he might as well enjoy it as it did. He hid his growing sexual frustration with humour and being nice as always. When he'd had a few drinks, he was over-attentive to girls, but what nineteen-year-old male wasn't. He had arrived in the city of Liverpool at university and he had resolved to change. He was here to study psychology, a subject he enjoyed and one he could not drift through. Science and Maths, they were easy. You worked out the answer and wrote it down. Psychology was different, you had to remember things, learn names and theories; it challenged him. He only took it at college because it fitted around the maths and computer science courses he actually wanted to do. He was amazed to discover, however, how much he enjoyed it. The results of the experiments and studies surprised him. This was new: all the other school subjects were basically the same. They were predictable, you thought you knew how something should work and weren't surprised when it did indeed work just like that. People were different, they didn't work like they thought they did. They all think they are in command of their thoughts and behaviours; they are not. That's what psychology taught Lucas and he found it fascinating.

One valuable side-effect of a psychology degree, to Lucas anyway, was the ratio of men to women. With a subsidiary in computer science as a backup, he had signed up to study a degree in psychology and from his very first lecture he was not disappointed. There were colourful coats, hemp skirts, boots on the girls and tight trousers on the few boys. Nervous, lonely faces surrounded him. He had arrived. People here were as strange as he was. He sat back on the hard bench in the massive lecture hall and smiled. To the left, to the right, in front and behind him, were girls. Fidgeting nervously, looking around the huge room themselves. Surely one would want him, he thought. He was scared, this was new and honestly, frightening. But within, behind the fear, he was happy; he had arrived where he belonged.

Later, for his first tutorial, he sat next to the only girl who was on her own. Gathering the courage to ask if the chair was occupied was the hardest thing he had ever ventured to undertake. He introduced himself and started the arduous task of chatting her up. He told her all about himself, not forgetting to ask questions about her and to tell a few jokes. By the third tutorial, she had left, gone home having quit her studies. So that day he moved to sit next to someone else. She was also sitting on her own, her previous study partner not bothering to attend that particular tutorial. That was Felicity, his saviour. He smiled at her and she at him. She didn't tell him, but she had liked him from the first day he had walked into the small tutor group. She had been noticing him since, watching from afar in their larger lectures. Now he was sitting next to her. Unbidden, he had walked over and asked if he could sit. She was excited as she gestured that he should join her. They talked, they exchanged information about each other's lives. She laughed at his strange jokes. They became friends.

It wasn't through a lack of attraction that they never got together, it was through their mutual need for a friend. She was as alone as he was. She did know someone, her ex-boyfriend also attended the university, but she thought that he would be busy with his new life and wouldn't make time for her now. Felicity and Lucas both felt completely alone in this frightening place and this bound them together almost instantly.

For Lucas, his loneliness had started as an attempt to leave his old self behind. He had purposely chosen to attend a university far from home, far from the awkward lonely Lucas he no longer wanted to be. He was here to reinvent himself, he no longer wanted to hide behind jokes and lies. He wanted to be himself, and for people to like him for it or be damned. He quickly discovered, however, that his true self didn't like being lonely and didn't make friends easily. So, when a girl started talking to him, laughing at his jokes, asking him questions, inviting him out to a party, he leapt at the opportunity. He leapt at the opportunity to make a friend. He leapt at Felicity.

Lucas went to that party, hosted by Felicity's ex-boyfriend, Jasper. He met more people, other new friends that Felicity already knew. In just a few days he was part of a group; a gang. Felicity was the pivotal point, having also brought Elizabeth and Bertrand from her English literature classes that were part of her joint honours degree. It changed his life. Jasper, Felicity, Elizabeth and Bertrand changed his life. The support of these four people around him gave him the confidence to stay in Liverpool instead of returning home. They gave him the confidence to be himself. They liked him. He liked them.

The group subsequently opened up a world that had been hidden to him before. Jasper took him to clubs where they danced the night away. Felicity sat with him in psychology classes where they joked and played silly games. They moved as a pack; friends in a world in which they belonged. In the second year the whole group moved into a shared house together, it was inevitable that they would. He had made it, he was a university student living the life he had been dreaming of for so long.

Their house was a large red-brick Victorian terrace that was identical to all the others in the dead-end road. Narrow at the front and extending back a long way to a tiny garden as they all did. Lucas took the largest bedroom because he didn't mind that it was on the ground floor, facing the road. The others were afraid of someone breaking in. It hadn't occurred to Lucas and the realisation didn't frighten him; he thought it unlikely in the quiet no-through road. He decorated it with posters of movies, nineties bands, and Homer Simpson eating a donut. He put his television on a low table in front of the window and connected up his PlayStation. Starting up Tomb Raider, he listened to the familiar chord of the console and smiled, he was home. This was his first that was not his parents, he finally felt like a man.

In his first week of living in the new house there was a party at some friends of Jasper's. That night he decided to finally complete his journey to manhood by resolving to have sex. He put on a new white shirt and red velvet trousers he had bought for the occasion. He even applied a mist of aftershave to his freshly-shaven neck. He was ready. By the time he had walked with Jasper to the party, it was heaving with people. They had crammed themselves into the house at the end of the road. The alcohol was flowing and the music blaring. He found a bottle of beer and started to walk around, looking for her. It was not any specific 'her' he sought that night. At that point, any 'her' would have done. Because of this flexibility, they soon found each other.

Lucas came across her sitting on a sofa in the lounge, an empty bottle in her hand. She had a mop of blond hair perched on top of her head in a mass of curls and was wearing a very short dress. He looked at the dress and admired the way it was held by just two thin straps over her shoulders. The delicate structure being the only barrier between him and her chest stirred his soup of hormones. They had met before, he remembered; she was called Julia, a friend of Elizabeth's. He approached with another bottle matching hers, silently offering it to her. She accepted, and to his surprise, patted the empty space on the sofa. He sat, nervously sweating into the man-made fibres of his trousers. He shouted some question over the music and she shouted some answer back. Awkwardly they swapped the trivial details of their lives at university. Having exhausted the common questions he asked of everyone, he drank from his bottle and picked at the label. She sipped the sticky sweet alcopop from hers through dark red lips. He had no idea what to do at this point, so he looked around him for inspiration.

She, however, did know what to do. Lucas was not unattractive, in fact he was a good-looking young man. He was nervous, sure, but he was also very charming and gentle. Knowing this, she wanted him tonight just as much as he wanted her. Seeing his discomfort, she placed a hand on his knee, remarking how the fabric was pretty. He thanked her for the compliment, showing her how the velvet felt smooth in one direction and rough in the other. As he traced a pattern in the trousers with his finger, she laughed. His quirky humour and strange topic of conversation amused her. She copied his movements, dragging her hand up the red material of the trousers, remarking that indeed it was rough when you moved up them.

Her hand ended between his legs, having traced a long line through the velvet up this inner thigh. Her fingers were stroking the inside of his leg, very close to his discomfort. Lucas coughed, unsure what to do next. His was at a party, drunk. The music was blaring, and this girl had his complete attention. He made some comment again about the material of the trousers, asking if she liked the feel of it. He winced, his comment sounding like a line from a bad pornographic film. She laughed, however, rising from the sofa. She pulled her dress back down over her legs where it had risen high on her own thighs. Lucas just sat there, watching her, frozen. Julia reached down and took his hand, pulling him from the sofa. Without words, she took him upstairs to a bedroom where they had sex. It was quick, it was clumsy, it was a seminal experience of his life.

It was an important night beyond being merely the commencement of his sexual journey. They had sex a couple more times after that night but never became girlfriend and boyfriend; that wasn't meant to be. However, the experiences meant that they did become friends. Julia also became friends with Lucas' friends and a regular visitor to their house in Penny Lane. The truly important event seemed so inconsequential at the time; she invited him to a political discussion group of which she was a member. Lucas took the opportunity as any nineteen-year-old might and immediately started chatting up the other girls from the discussion group. It was their political discussions, however, that changed him. These regular meetings in the student union helped him grow into someone new. He transformed over the course of a few months from a quiet, confused attendee who was only there because of the chance of more sexual encounters, to the vocal leader of the group.

Initially he started contributing because to do so was fun. It felt like an extension of his behaviour at school. People liked him for it, they found him funny. He found it most interesting to take the opposite stance of whatever topic they were discussing. The mental acrobatics of arguing a point you barely believed, and had no knowledge to back-up, exercised his mind. Discussions about democracy lead to him arguing the virtues of communism or a dictatorship. When they talked of the evils of war, he would extol the scientific and engineering achievements and the general reduction in population they brought about. People's fears about Y2K he dismissed as conspiratorial nonsense, while he created theories of his own that were off the wall and hilarious because of their ridiculous complexities. Initially he worried that his off-beat opinions would aggravate the group. Instead it had a polarising effect. It made them argue harder, finding reason to refute his arguments rather than simply agreeing with each other as they had done before his arrival. It helped that it was obvious to them that he didn't really believe what he was saying. He was their Devil's Advocate and it energised them as much as it did him.

Buoyed up by the encouragement of this discussion group, he started writing essays and manifestos. Some were real, most were complicated jokes hidden deep in rhetoric. The group took to printing them out and pinning them to notice boards around the campus. Quickly they became a popular read for the students of Liverpool and weekly printouts could be found in most buildings across the campus. The most popular were his tirades on the accepted lies that people believed to be true. 'Love in the movies strikes you with overwhelming passion', he wrote in one essay. 'This is rubbish, the passion you are feeling is the overcompensation for the fact that you don't really like the person to whom you are attracted'. In another he blew apart the idea that anal sex between a man and a woman was a pleasurable thing. 'When there is a receptacle just an inch away that was designed for the purpose, why do men want to use the uncomfortable one?'. He challenged people to think, suggesting that; 'the only reason I can think of, is that either you are too small for the other, or you want one inside your own'.

That particular article, for they were properly printed and distributed now in the student paper, attracted a great deal of attention from the student body. Within the responses to the article, there were two offers that Lucas was brave enough to accept. One to use the alternative entrance offered by a young lady and one to receive the same treatment upon himself from an experimental friend of Jasper's. He set up the two offers to occur at once, with all three parties attempting to sample each of the experiences available to them. In publishing the results of this experiment, which confirmed his thesis that the anus was an inferior substitute for the female anatomy, he attracted the unwanted attention of the Dean and the subsequent cancelation of his articles.

Lucas accepted his censorship as an inevitable conclusion to his writing. Despite the protestations of Elizabeth and the rest of the group, he withdrew from his dalliance with writing and journalism. To placate an infuriated Julia, he created one final essay on the topic of censorship that they pinned to noticeboards. He happily gave up his foray into extra-curricular writing as he crossed into his third and final year, deciding that maybe concentrating on his degree might finally be a good idea. Jasper was to travel abroad for his third year to continue his law studies in French so Lucas and Felicity moved into a shared house together within the university campus. Here they met Charlie; their Malaysian housemate. Along with him, there was also Jessica; their new American friend. Charlie was there to study engineering and Jessica was on her own year abroad. Through her, Felicity and Lucas also befriended Randal, who attended the same 'International Students' support group as she did every Wednesday. Jasper also visited frequently that year, seeking respite from his year abroad with his former girlfriend, and his new friends. Thus, along with Julia, Elizabeth and Bertrand, the group of nine was formed. The bond formed between them would last the rest of their lives.

Other people inevitably came to the group throughout their time in Liverpool. Felicity had a boyfriend for a while who joined in a number of nights out before fading away. A married mature student, Elizabeth's husband was happily tolerated, although he never really fitted in or wanted to be a part of their group. Jasper had various boyfriends throughout the years, but they too came and went. Each addition was welcomed, liked and included. Each promised to keep in touch as they broke up, but none followed through. That was life at university. People make friends that are the core of their group. Others come and go like birds on a feeder, but the centre remains. This centre rotated around Felicity, she had brought them together and she kept them there. Her efforts, along with Elizabeth's and Jasper's eagerness, maintained the contact required to keep them united.

Lucas was an important part of the group but remained a member off to one side. Felicity's friendship with him, and his close friendships with Jasper in the second year, and Jessica in the third, kept him a part of the group but somewhat distant at the same time. Lucas' separation was a direct result of his reluctance to become dependent upon them. In meeting Felicity, he had made the friend he had needed so desperately. As he had done so, he had quickly realised that his need for her was too important. He knew within weeks of knowing her, that losing her would be a devastating blow to his fragile confidence. He could little afford that, and he was unwilling to risk more friendships that were destined to end when university did.

He knew from school that you couldn't depend on friends; they let you down. Through them changing or changes forced upon them, they always leave. He could depend on himself and no one else, this he knew and had accepted. He had broken this rule with Felicity as he had needed her so desperately. In order to mitigate the chances of further dependence and greater loss, he subsequently kept himself a small distance apart from the others. He had an eye on the future, and in that future, they would soon go their separate ways. He wanted to be able to manage that.

Just as he knew they would, they all eventually departed Liverpool. Promises to remain in touch were made and addresses exchanged along with hugs and kisses. These promises were kept by Felicity, Elizabeth, Jasper and Jessica. These gregarious members communicated between themselves and the wider group frequently. The others received and responded to these communications but inevitably drifted apart as they moved away. As such the connections of the friends were maintained but quickly withered to occasional polite emails and annual Christmas cards.

As he left university, Lucas finally gave in to his nerdish tendencies and proceeded to post-graduate studies in Birmingham. There he converted his interest in psychology to his calling in computers by studying Cognitive Science. Here he flourished, using theories of psychology, philosophy, and the other 'soft' sciences he had learned; applying them to the world of computers. The course could have been made for him, using the social sciences to engineer new ideas with computer software. From there, he moved to Bristol to work for a defence company. Not coincidentally this is where both Jasper and Felicity were also now working. He as a junior lawyer and she as an accountant. Lucas now had a good career and two old friends he could call on for support. Once again, he was happy, once again he considered his life complete.

This is where life for Lucas took a downward turn. First his brother died, then his father. In response, he retreated from his grief into work, moving apart even from Felicity and Jasper. He left the remainder of his family back at home in the country and threw himself into his computers. His social life suffered as much as his bank balance swelled. He maintained a connection with Felicity in particular as she would not let him fully retreat, but beyond the occasional coffee and a movie or two, he lived a life alone.

He excelled at his job, his work was his focus and it showed. He created new constructs of artificial intelligence and human-like behaviours in computer systems. Much of what he completed, he told no one of. He shrugged off the questions people had about his creations, citing that it was secret, for military purposes, and boring anyway. After ten years of working for various military firms in Bristol, he left the industry completely. Telling what friends he had, and his mother at home, that he was now working for himself. As a consultant, he obviously made a lot more money as he quickly moved into a penthouse flat in the harbourside.

Here he lived alone, watching out over the city. He attended parties, walked to the local coffee shop to work each morning, and the library each evening. He sought out contact with people, but only on a superficial level. He would meet and chat with old work colleagues occasionally but essentially, he lived a life apart. He was never totally alone, however. Felicity would not permit his total retreat from society. High in his flat, looking out through the expansive windows, he hosted Felicity once a week for coffee, biscuits and to watch whatever series was currently on Netflix. They would talk of old friends and new people in her life and her work. They would discuss politics, people, television, and the trivial things of life. They were friends. She was Lucas' only real friend.

Then, as Lucas passed his thirty-ninth birthday, something changed. That something was that Felicity left her husband of eleven years. It was six months after the completion of the divorce proceedings and she was sitting on the sofa next to him in his apartment. They were watching 'The Bridge', a Danish and Swedish drama collaboration. It was the fourth episode they had watched that night and as it ended and the next started, she pivoted on the sofa and put her legs across his lap. He was essentially ready for bed and wearing a loose black tee-shirt and a pair of thin tartan shorts. He could feel the soft material of her tights across his bare legs. She had aged well, he thought as he looked across to her. She had her hair down and loose curls of dark brown hair flowed over her slender neck. They naturally drew his eyes to her cleavage which stirred something in him. He casually tried to look up her short skirt but failed, her toned and muscled thighs were closed tight; creating a respectable barrier to his lazy attempt.

Felicity looked at him looking. Thinking for a second, she decided to inform him of something she had kept secret for almost twenty years. She told him that she had fancied him the first day she had seen him. The secret finally released, opened something in her. Felicity told Lucas how much she had liked him when he had walked into that psychology tutorial. She remembered that he had been wearing a colourful coat that was both strange and endearing. She recounted that, when he had sat next to some other girl, she had been very disappointed.

They talked for some time about her attraction to him and his need for her as a friend. As their discussion talked of ageing and how they had changed, he refuted her claims about the loss of her looks. He quickly complimented her on her current appearance and her body in particular. As he did so he stroked her leg, examining the tight muscles in her calves. Their eyes met once more and she could feel his arousal against the back of her leg. There was some unspoken signal; a silent arrival at a common conclusion. They kissed; old friends finally romantically connecting. There was an immediate escalation. Again, without discussion they both knew what was going to happen. They caressed softly, removing their clothes with care, they paid attention to all of each other. The sex was tender, it was long and gentle, it was sensational.

Their relationship lasted a month before coming to an abrupt and unexpected end. There were long walks in the park and casual drives to the coast. There was a special stay in a Cornish resort hotel with private hot-tub and a view of the ocean. Then, Lucas died. His father had died of leukaemia, his brother of skin cancer. He had always felt the lucky one, the healthy man in the family. It was perhaps inevitable therefore, that he was hit by a taxi. Crossing the road, not paying attention, looking at his mobile phone, he was run down. The unexpected impact drove him to the ground, hitting his head sharply on the curb. He was killed instantly. He would have died before he would have known about it, the doctors reassured Felicity at the hospital.

Most of the friends attended the funeral, only Bertrand was absent. They cried, hugged, and consoled each other. Felicity never told anyone of their romantic development, that was hers and hers alone. She cried as much as most of them, more than others. Her grief, however, descended to a depth that she didn't believe theirs reached. Looking to Lucas' mother, stood some distance from her, their eyes met and she could see the pain reflected in her eyes. She smiled grimly and nodded, acknowledging their shared emotional bond. Lucas was one in a million, special. Special to them, anyway. He would never be replaced.

Flight

As everyone strapped themselves into their seats, Oliver flipped the switches and turned the dials that brought the massive helicopter to life. With a loud bang and a building whine, the drooping rotors slowly started to turn. The massive fingers quickly picked up pace as the engines started screaming with the Herculean effort. The high-pitched shriek of the engines, combined with the deep thumping noise of the rotors spinning around the occupants, quickly overwhelmed all of their senses. Each scrambled to fit the headphones hanging beside them in an effort to defend against the assault. It felt like being inside a washing machine as they all started to shake and shimmy with the vibrations. Just as the movements reached a crescendo, Oliver pulled back on a large stick tightly gripped in his right hand and the whole contraption lurched into the air.

Once airborne, the experience quickly mellowed. The noise abated to something far more civilised and the violent vibrations settled down into the more soothing hum of well-maintained engineering.

"Sorry for the abrupt lift-off," Oliver said clearly through their headphones, "but we were about to lose our window and when that happens it's a shitty thirty-minute wait on the tarmac." Shaken by the experience, none seemed able to complain or even comment as Oliver offered his explanation for the rapid ascent. They knew where they were going, all having read the letter of invitation, so they flew in silence. The noise of the helicopter seemed to leave little choice in the matter.

Sat in the co-pilot's seat, Bertrand cut a somewhat pathetic figure of a man. Never large to begin with, his confinement to a wheelchair had wasted away what little muscles he'd once had. Looking anxiously out of the window now, he felt less than half the man his friends had known. His southern-European complexion, once his most handsome feature, now seemed only to highlight the permanent dark expression on his face. His jet-black hair atop his head was like a storm cloud hovering over him; casting a shadow over his dark eyes. In the airport he had been happy for a short time; talking to his old friends had reminded him how his life used to be. Now he was alone again with his thoughts, they quickly turned sour. He frowned as he stared at the buildings sliding past below, lamenting the loss of happier times. The noise of the helicopter had forced the group to sit in silence as it flew over the city and he was more than content with this. Brooding had become his pastime and he was relieved by the enforced break from joviality.

Many hours passed, the city and towns long since disappearing from view to be replaced by seemingly endless trees and lakes. The absence of conversation was finally broken by Bertrand. His trembling voice broadcast through the headphones of the occupants resting in the back.

"What's that?" He was pointing ahead, through

the windscreen. His sudden, unexpected exclamation made the entire group jump and sit up in their seats.

"Ah you noticed that, did you?" Oliver cheerily asked, ignoring the growing concern of his passengers.

"The huge silver UFO? Yes, I noticed it," persisted Bertrand, his fear mounting as he straightened himself in his seat.

Oliver smiled and turned to look at the rest of the group. The few in the seats facing the rear were twisting themselves around while the others craned forward to get a look at the floating object ahead of them. "That, my friends, is your first little adventure." Oliver flipped some switches and the helicopter slowed as he lined up with the silver object that glinted in the sun. They were closer now and could see that it was, in fact, a massive cigar-shaped balloon sitting as still as a rock in the blue sky. "This here is a Mil Mi-26 helicopter, she's a rugged, dependable Russian lady. She's fast, almost 300 kph fast and she can keep that up for about 800 kilometres. If you would like to consult your inflight clock you will see that we have been flying for two and a half hours. Those of you who like a bit of maths will have calculated that we can manage just a hair over ten more minutes of flight time." Oliver paused and pointed to a small circular gauge on the console in front of him, "if you look at our fuel gauge there, you will see a flashing orange light. That little blink is telling us that in about ten minutes we will crash to the ground and die, alone in the wilderness of the

Northwest Territories of Canada."

He looked around again at the stunned occupants with a cheeky grin before continuing. "However, our friends at Gām have thought of this little complication and put this baby here for us to top up our tanks. She's an automated blimp filled with fuel that we're about to slurp up into our external tanks via this little tube here."

Flicking a switch, Oliver initiated the extension of the in-flight refuelling tube from the nose of the helicopter. The seemingly fragile pipe extended infeasibly far from the nose of the helicopter as the group sat in stunned silence. Gently pushing the control stick forward, Oliver manoeuvred the massive machine towards the flying silver blimp. Closer now, they could see that it was more like a Zeppelin, cigar shaped and powering along with two massive fans either side of a gondola slung underneath. Everyone inside the throbbing helicopter held their breaths as he inched forward towards a circular net that had extended from the back of the balloon.

The target twisted and snapped around in the wind of the rotors and twice Oliver tried and failed to connect. A discordant alarm started to sound, signalling the expenditure of fuel was becoming critical when, with a thud, the proboscis of the helicopter was finally successfully inserted into its target. Almost immediately the fuel started to noisily flow into the tanks over the passenger's heads and everyone started to breathe again. A nervous round of applause followed as Oliver uncoupled the two connected flying machines and peeled away, powering forward with more purpose now the machine had once again been replenished.

"We couldn't just have landed? To refuel, that is," queried Felicity from the back of the seating area. She was panting, and her heart fluttered uncomfortably from the release of stress following the manoeuvre.

"We could, normally we would, but there's no landing field within range of our destination. We really are off the edge of the map here, people," was the explanation from Oliver as they flew ever northwards. Looking out of their window they could all see the truth of his words pass by beneath them. Miles and miles of wilderness; nothing but trees, water, mountains and ice as far as they could see.

"Come to the woods, for here is rest..." muttered Felicity into her headset, quoting John Muir on the American wilderness.

"There is no repose like that of the green deep woods. Sleep in forgetfulness of all ill," completed Oliver, his tone flat and serious for the first time. His words chilled Felicity as a shiver travelled down her spine; they hadn't provided the comfort she had been seeking.

Bertrand

Bertrand threw his bag on the thin single bed and watched it bounce around violently before coming to a stop right at the edge. His first day of university; he sucked in the unfamiliar air, breathing it in. Listening to the shouts from the corridor just outside his open door, he took another breath and tried to relax. As he left to retrieve another bag from his brother's car, he thought again about his fellow students he had met a few minutes ago. He was worried. They seemed nice enough but somehow things didn't feel great. Bertrand was nineteen, it was nineteen ninety-five and he was soon going to discover that there were to be people in life that he just didn't like. There were eight other men, boys really, on the same ground floor corridor as him. They were noisy, boisterous and unlike Bertrand in any way as far as he could tell. He knew that he should give them a chance, "maybe they have hidden depths," he told himself just as a rugby ball flew over his head and crashed noisily against the wall.

He tried to join in over the forthcoming months, but he was a shy, reserved lad from the countryside and drinking games and late-night parties just didn't agree with him. It wasn't long before he knew that this new life did not fit him at all. Still, he fought, pressing down the fear that tempted him. The fear told him to abandon this frightening new existence for something more familiar; it pulled him away, it wanted to go home. His courage, and his stubborn persistence, allowed him to stay.

Eventually however, his courage gave in. Overwhelmed, he had to return home for an extended visit to his parent's farm. However, only minutes after arriving, he realised that going home was not the solution. His old friends had moved on to jobs or other universities and home was not the comfortable nest it used to be. After taking just two days to gather himself again, he returned to university and to his corridor. He had resigned himself to his new existence and resolved to make the best of it. He would cope by studying, focussing on the work presented to him. He might not be popular, but he could at least excel in his course. It was, after all, why he was there in the first place. This, he asserted to himself each evening as he tried his best to ignore his noisy neighbours. The noise, combined with his resolution to study, was why he signed up for an extra study group on Wednesday evenings. He was glad he did because this is where he met his salvation.

He walked into the small room, clutching his bag nervously as he sat down. Squirming in the plastic chair, he finally looked up to see the woman next to him looking back. She introduced herself as Elizabeth and shook his hand. He reluctantly took it and tried to return to his introspection before the tutor arrived. He could not, however, because she insisted on talking to him despite his obvious reluctance. She asked him a series of quick-fire questions, demanding answers. In a friendly way she dragged him out of himself through a polite but unrelenting insistence. It probably helped that she was twenty years his senior and seemed comfortable acting the mother figure to his anxious boyish fidgeting. One meeting was all it took. One study session at which he had accidentally arrived ten minutes early, and they were friends. It's said that all you need in life is one good friend; Bertrand wholeheartedly agreed with the theory now he had found just that.

Bertrand had always considered himself anonymous, average, nothing special. Here, however, in the white enclave that was the middle-class red-brick university department of English literature, he was special. He was not black, not Asiatic, nor was he white. He was an ancient ethnic mix that resulted in an exotic dark complexion and deeply recessed brown eyes that seemed to penetrate any subject of his interest. He had never been tall, but his thin frame made it appear as if he was. He was never fashionable but somehow his old untidy clothes now seemed modern in this new place. Atop his head sat a mop of unstylish black hair that in this new environment spoke of a trendy disinterest in mainstream fashion. He had arrived. Suddenly he was cool, suddenly he saw people just like him everywhere he looked. Finally, he was welcomed somewhere. He had always been out of place, but here, in this new world of academia, he fit right in.

Elizabeth introduced him to new people, new

friends. As he relaxed, his inner-self came to the fore. He wasn't shy and quiet, he was funny and enjoyable to be around. Soon he was happy. With his friends, he went out; partying in clubs and the student union. He met girls, got drunk, had sex even. Finally, he relaxed in to this exciting new life, embracing all that it had to offer.

One particular night, he was with his group as usual; his gang, partying at the student union. The music was thumping, and the cheap beer and alcopops were flowing. He was on his third bottle of 'Two-Dogs' on top of an unknown number of pints of lager when he saw her. He had been tired, exhausted really, from the drink and the dancing, but Jasper had insisted they stay until the end. They were finally playing the last song, 'Thank you for the Music', and Bertrand was watching Jasper dance to the Abba classic as he always did. That's why he saw her. She was dancing alone nearby, swaying to the melody, standing in a spotlight. He couldn't help himself, he approached her, bottle still in hand.

He arrived at the swaying figure and she opened her eyes. She was roughly the same height as him and their eyes connected. His, dark brown and intense. Hers, bright blue and welcoming. She said nothing, he said nothing, they simply started moving together. The music quickened and they moved closer, she wrapping her arms around his waist and he reciprocating as they drunkenly moved to the melody. As the song ended and the lights came on, he moved forward and kissed her. Their mouths opened and their tongues touched, playing with each other in the mutual heat of their bodies.

The swell of people grew around them, dragging them from the dance floor and towards the doors. Bertrand simply released her from the embrace and slid his hand down her arm. Ending at her hand, he grasped it and led her in the direction of the crowd. He saw Jasper at one point, moving to the coat room, gesturing that he follow. He ignored him. He ignored the fact that he did indeed have a coat in the small room and it was cold outside, very cold. He didn't want to interrupt the feeling he was experiencing. He didn't want to lose the girl at the end of his arm.

They exited the building still attached to each other. He moved towards the buses that would take them back to halls, but she gently tugged on his arm, stopping him. He followed her as she crossed the road, towards the third-year accommodation blocks. She skipped across the wet grass of a lawn towards the nondescript clusters of low-rise buildings. She let herself in with a worn brass key and they passed through the sliding glass doors into a scruffy lounge area. Pulling him past the threadbare sofa and cheap wooden chairs, she dragged him up two flights of stairs. Together they strode through the open door opposite the landing on the top floor of the red-brick building.

The small room was a typical student enclave, there was a single bed with a colourful checked duvet on top. The small armchair in the corner was covered with a thin tie-dye throw. Posters covered the walls; Pulp Fiction, Blur, and a large print of 'Stars at Night' by Van Gogh. There was a worn brown bear on the bed and she skipped to it and moved it gently to the arm chair. She sat on the bed now, looking at him standing still in the doorway. He closed the door with his heel, not removing his eyes from hers.

She was wearing a short tartan skirt that tantalisingly displayed her legs. Bertrand watched as she flicked some blond hair from her eyes, brushing it with her fingers, tucking it behind her ears. The action revealed the white skin of her neck in the dim artificial light coming in through the window. Her long blond curls danced in the amber light as she moved on the bed. She swung her legs up and lay them on the colourful duvet, sitting up against the headboard. The entire bed squeaked and groaned from her gentle movements, it seemed to be inviting him to join her. He did. He removed his trainers and climbed up the foot of the bed, crawling to her. They met at the top, their mouths interlocking once more.

Passionate hands, shaking with anticipation, found the buttons on his shirt. She carefully undid each one and pulled the tight, sweaty, fabric from his body. His bare chest released now, he pulled her top over her head to reveal hers. He pulled her down on the bed, holding her to him, feeling her naked body against his. Her fingers, still trembling, found his fly and released him.

Pulling her tights from her thin legs, she started removing his trousers simultaneously. They writhed on the bed, passion overwhelming them, drink lubricating the process. They felt every part of each other. With their hands and their bodies, they consumed each other.

They did not have sex that night, they instead revelled in the touch of each other for hours before eventually falling asleep together. There were climaxes, there were orgasms, there were groans and cries of pleasure, but they barely spoke a single word. They awoke the next morning wrapped in each other. She shyly introduced herself as Julia. As they dressed, they talked. She was in her second year of university but only the first year of her degree in Political Science, having wasted a year of French in which she hadn't really be interested. He was in his first year of English literature with no plans to change anything about his life. She came from the city of Birmingham in the West Midlands, he from a small village in East Anglia. Those were not insurmountable differences, but they were there. They swapped numbers and shook hands, a strange gesture after what they had shared just a few hours before.

They never spoke of that night again, not once. Instead they became friends. Julia had no real friends of her own and few acquaintances, subsequently she eagerly accepted meeting and spending time in the company of Bertrand's existing group. Upon meeting Elizabeth for the first time, the two instantly became best friends.

Elizabeth left little choice in the matter. Julia was Bertrand's friend, so she would be Elizabeth's too, she had decided, and that was that. This was a friendship that was to last for the rest of their lives. It was their meeting that changed Bertrand's life forever.

Watching Elizabeth and Julia shake hands, then hug, triggered the realisation of a truth within Bertrand. He liked Julia, he had been very attracted to her and had loved their single night together, however he didn't love her. It was Elizabeth he loved. The sight of Julia being so close to Elizabeth, the body he knew intimately touching the one totally unknown, flicked a switch. It was her body he wanted to know. It was Elizabeth he wanted to hold, to caress. It was her lips he wanted to kiss. The sensation flowed over him, filling him with a warm pleasure. He watched them, imagining himself in Julia's place, feeling the happiness flow inside of him.

His feeling of pleasure lasted the length of the brief hug. The facts of the situation snapping back to the fore of his mind: Elizabeth was twenty years his senior, Elizabeth was married, Elizabeth had two children. Elizabeth could never be his. Her lips would never be his to kiss. Her body never his to hold. He held back a tear, swallowing the sudden intense feeling of loss. He turned from them as they broke off their hug and made an excuse to leave. He wanted to run from that place, flee the feeling of helplessness. He ran until he couldn't breathe. Finally, he stumbled back to his room and cried for a full day. Eventually, he emerged from the box that was his room, resolved to cope with this new reality. He could cope, he would manage. He took a deep breath and carried on, it was his only choice. He remained close to Julia. Close friends but nothing more. They were both content with that. Never again did he experience the feel of her and never once did he miss it. His love was for Elizabeth alone now, but he would never act on it. Instead he concentrated on his studies. And, of course, his friendship with the one he loved.

He bought a motorcycle, relishing the feeling of freedom it afforded him. He could get away on it like he had never before. He used it to escape from his depression and his problems. The feeling of total control that came with the excitement of speed, completed him. It gave him what he missed from his relationships with women. He had encounters a few more times with girls he met in clubs but never again was the experience as good as it had been with Julia. He knew now that he wanted Elizabeth and couldn't forget that in the arms of another woman. He could, however, forget on the open road. The motorcycle required his complete attention as he wove through the curves of a ribbon of tarmac. He resolved to spend his life in work, his pleasure coming from speed. The thrill of the ride replacing the love he could not shake nor sate.

He did well at university, achieving a first in English Literature. He left that place with tear-filled farewells to his friends. He hugged Elizabeth tightly, holding her to him, memorising the feel of her this one last time. He went home, home to his friends who felt like strangers now. He moved back in with his parents, but everything was different. It wasn't long until he moved out. He moved to London where life was fast again. He got a job in real-estate. It demanded his attention and paid enough for him to live in the city. He rode his motorcycle around the city streets and out into the countryside. He made money. He made new friends, new girlfriends even. He tried his best, managing to love them, but never as much as Elizabeth.

Each birthday he would receive a card from her. Each Christmas, a card and a letter. Each time he would break up with whomever he was currently dating in the wash of renewed emotions for Elizabeth. Immediately, he would climb aboard his motorcycle and ride. He just pointed the machine at the setting sun and twisted the accelerator. He would start with tears in his eyes, knowing that soon the wind would blow them away. With the drying of the tears, the feeling of loss would also recede. He could replace the feeling of sadness with one of freedom. His bike gave him flight from his problems, leaving loss behind him.

It had been more than a decade since he had left university but, as expected, when the next Christmas letter arrived, he felt the loss again just as strongly. There was no one to break up with this year, she had dumped him for some guy who worked in banking, so he just reached for his keys the instant he finished reading the letter. He climbed into his leathers and pulled his helmet tightly over his head, allowing the tears to form. As he stepped from his flat he knew that they would soon be washed away.

Hours later, feeling the energy vibrating through the seat of his powerful motorcycle, he felt free again. He was somewhere on the coast, weaving though the curves of a narrow road. Green trees and hedges towered to his left, casting dappled light across the rich black surface of the road. He sped across the smooth tarmac, light and shade flashing across his visor. To his right there was nothing, a void beyond which he could hear the waves below during his brief pauses of acceleration. His engine and the sea were the only two things in the world at this moment in time.

He lay across the racing bike, hugging it like a lover. It was a relatively new purchase and the extra power over his old one was providing a new experience on the familiar road. He crouched lower, making the powerful machine a part of him as his forward vision narrowed to see nothing but the tarmac before him. He twisted the throttle and four thrashing pistons instantly drowned out the waves crashing against unseen rocks. He was approaching each bend at speed and braking hard. Leaning into the curve, he was forcing the heavy machine to the ground and accelerating, feeling the momentum drive him around. As he exited, he poured the power on, forcing the bike upright, throwing him forward. It felt like each time he did this, he would leave another problem behind him. The rush drove them from his mind.

He pulled on the brake again, feeling the bike lift slightly, the nose diving and the tail lifting. He shifted his weight to compensate, anticipating the tight corner in front of him. The mighty machine sat back down as he slowed for the curve ahead. About to twist the throttle, he prepared to power through the right-hand bend that would propel him back out toward the ocean. Looking around the bend, however, he saw that the road was blocked, a tractor was pulling out from a field. There was no panic in his mind as he applied the brake instead of the accelerator. He would slow to approach the tractor and overtake it, soon this obstacle too would be behind him. As he braked, however, his front wheel suddenly lost traction. It skittered across the road, throwing the bike upright from his leaning position. He calmly wrestled with the controls trying to get the front wheel to behave, as he had done a million times before.

He was quickly closing on the tractor as the loss of grip was failing to slow him down. A light spray of mud flicked up from the skidding tyre onto the visor of his helmet. He applied more brake. The rear wheel lost traction too now under the heavier braking. He moved his body to the front, trying to get the mighty machine under control as it hurled itself towards the slow-moving tractor.

Pulling on the brakes as much as he physically could now, he felt the bike wobble from side to side, skidding in an uncontrolled slide towards the mass of metal in front of him.

Even at the end, Bertrand never thought he would hit the tractor. But hit it he did. In a final attempt to avoid the machine before him, he leaned the bike over and placed it between him and the back of the tractor. The tarmac was brown here, slick with mud from the field. As he hit the road, the realisation of what had happened washed over him. The mud from the field had been pulled onto the road by the repeated visits of the farmer, causing a thick coating of wet soil upon which he was skidding. His last thoughts, as the bike slammed into the tractor, was how dirty his suit was getting. The bike hit the agricultural monster with a bang. The crackle of his bike breaking apart accompanied Bertrand's flight as he was twisted and thrown into the plough that was hanging from the rear of the agricultural monster.

Mercifully he lost consciousness as his helmet struck a metal blade of the plough. The last thing he was aware of was the cracking and shattering of the plastic of his visor, accompanied by the sympathetic cracking and shattering of his spine.

Bertrand managed his recovery like he had managed the majority of his life; alone. He read the letters from his friends and family, studying those from Elizabeth most intently. He tolerated visits from his relatives, telling them that he was fine, telling them not to worry. He asked people not to visit generally, wanting to manage alone. Eventually his broken bones healed, his cuts and bruises faded. His spine, however, refused to mend. He was left paralysed from the waist down. He was lucky, his doctors said. He saw it differently. However, pushing the depression out, he elected to concentrate on work again; changing his career to IT support so he could sit at home in his chair, away from people. His insurance saw to his needs while his new career gave him some comfort. He was not happy, nor was he depressed. He just was. He was comfortable with that; he just existed.

Close to another decade passed and he quickly found himself transitioning to middle age with his family at an impromptu birthday party at his mother's. As he blew out his candles, he made another resolution; at forty, he decided, he could finally just be himself and think of what he wanted. No longer would he have to strive, to achieve, to forget his pain. He would just live now, live until he died that is. It was a good decision that satisfied Bertrand as the flames danced to nothing under the assault of his breath. To live was easy, he could manage that, and while not be happy, he could be content. That was until he opened his post. He had already read the birthday card from Elizabeth. Without his ride to help him forget, it took longer than it once had to move on, but he had eventually managed to force his depression down and out of his mind. Inside this other envelope, however, was a letter from Felicity. He had missed Lucas' funeral, writing that he was too ill to attend. The real reason was that he knew it would have been be too painful to see them, to see Elizabeth. However, he felt better now, more secure in his resignation to his predicament. This invitation was also for something better, a happier reunion.

The letter promised a game, a thrill, excitement. Bertrand looked to the framed picture on his desk. In it he was sat astride his motorcycle, the one he had crashed so completely. The last time he had felt any excitement was the day he'd lost the use of his legs. More than his legs, he lamented once again. He could no longer make love, he could no longer go to the bathroom. That day he had lost more than his legs. He had lost his drive, his manhood, his life. He read the letter again. It promised 'an exciting game beyond imagination'. It enticed him, causing a tingle deep inside. It both surprised and delighted him that he still had the capacity to feel such excitement. It changed his mind, making him determined to go. Maybe he could do more than just live, he thought.

Destination

They continued flying over Canadian airspace for well over two more hours, leaving the memory of the refuelling firmly behind them as they headed north. As the vast majority of people in Canada live only two-hundred miles from the southern border, they left civilisation behind the further they flew north. Finally, they arrived at their destination deep in the Northwest Territories, sixteen hundred kilometres from Vancouver and hundreds of kilometres from any other living soul.

Touching down on the landing pad, they waited as Oliver had instructed, for the engines to stop and the rotors to cease turning. As the noise finally abated, he awkwardly turned his huge frame in the pilot's seat to face the group in the back, announcing with a smile that they had arrived. Jasper slid aside the massive rear door and they all stepped from the machine as it ticked cool in the waning summer sun. Its powerful rotors were drooping once again, spent and inert; it looked sad to be still.

"Welcome to Wise Park," Oliver announced to the group as he removed his headset and stepped from the helicopter to join them. They were in the exact centre of a brand-new place; recently purchased from the Canadian government. Oliver happily informed them of what they already knew; that they were standing in the middle of a private park and technically a new country wholly owned and operated by the 'Wise Corporation'.

"Everything for over three-hundred kilometres in every direction is owned by Mr Maximilian Wise, your host for this adventure," he announced proudly as he opened the door for a still-seated Bertrand. The others looked around them at the massive fir trees circling the landing pad. "Counting us, there are ten people in the entire park, so make yourselves at home."

"Who's the tenth?" Asked Felicity, quickly counting the eight standing around her.

"Why, Max of course," cried Oliver, "I've never met him, but I'm assured that he lives somewhere in the park."

"You've never met? So, who do you deal with…"

But Felicity's question was cut short by the approach of a strange apparition from the woods before them. The noise first alerted them, before it there had been nothing but silence, the landing of the massive helicopter scaring away any local wildlife that may have been foraging. With a gentle rusting of foliage, it stepped from the border of the landing pad; it moved like a person but clearly was not human. The first indication was that it consisted of nothing more than a pair of legs. Secondly there was hardly anything to it, as it moved they could see right through it.

The legs were large, their girth far greater than most people. However, they were also incredibly spindly, like a skeleton whose bones had wasted away to almost nothing. As it approached them, they could see how it was put together from a series of white plastic sticks. These clicking poles somehow moved and twisted in synchronised steps to achieve locomotion. The sticks were connected to each other in a rough form that approximated the skeleton and muscles of a human adult's legs. The thing, efficiently moving like a human, was very impressive, and very obviously artificial. Ignoring the wide-eyed stares of the group, the legs casually walked to the helicopter and more specifically to a speechless Bertrand, still seated in the co-pilot's seat.

"Bertie. Your transportation for the duration of your visit," announced Oliver as the legs arrived at the passenger door of the helicopter. A wave of a hand; a signal from Oliver that he required help, quickly moved the still-stunned group of friends into action. They gathered around to lift and then lower Bertrand into the strange contraption. The legs had clearly been made specially for him as they fitted him snugly but comfortably. The plastic construction perfectly mimicked the shape of his own useless appendages as they settled him into the contraption. Everyone watched in stunned silence as Oliver closed and tightened the straps around Bertrand's legs with dextrous efficiency.

"How do I work them?" Enquired Bertrand, who was answered by a sharp movement of the legs. With a soft noise of bending plastic, he simply walked over to his friends like he was born to do it. The white plastic skeleton moved with efficient purpose, striding over to Felicity who responded by wrapping Bertrand in a tight hug.

"Oh, Bertrand. That's amazing, how did you drive them?" She cried excitedly.

"I just moved my hips like I wanted to walk, and I walked. I can't believe it… I'm walking!" A tear of incredulity ran down his cheek as he pushed back from Felicity and proceeded to walk around her. Gathering pace, he started to jog. Holding his breath, he hopped over a landing-light set in the ground and skidded to a stop on the loose soil by the tree line. Looking back to Oliver he tentatively asked the question that had quickly formed in his mind.

"How long can I keep them? Can I buy a pair?" He started to nervously ask the pilot.

Oliver held up a hand, halting the questions, "they're yours, Bertie. Yours forever. A gift. The battery should last a full day of walking with a couple hours of running included, so you'll have to charge them every night I'm afraid." He apologetically gestured to the batteries mounted on the waist strap. But Bertrand wasn't listening anymore, he was running circles around the helicopter, skipping and jumping with joy. He visited each of the group in turn, lifting and twirling each one. The robotic legs took the strain with ease and barely a noise of complaint as he moved rapidly around the landing area as the helicopter continued to tick cool.

Eventually, once Oliver had unloaded their bags, the group settled enough for him to direct them to their accommodation. Individually, reluctantly, they departed in their assigned directions to unpack and settle in.

Each apartment they quickly occupied was the same, a sparsely decorated hut with bathroom, bedroom and a small study. No food preparation area was included but there was a fridge containing essentials and snacks for each. As if to answer their unspoken question, a chime rang out inside each of their huts and Oliver's now familiar voice announced that dinner would be served in the central communal area.

As each exited the door of their huts, their paths to the central building were clearly marked with glowing lights set into the ground. Each followed a curved path that, when viewed from above, marked out a delicate helical pattern leading to the central building. They arrived simultaneously at the large wooden doors to the main building. Unlike their apartments, this was an elaborate glass and steel structure rising high above them. Still only a single-storey, it was a large, squat dome that flowed from the ground. Despite its size, it blended perfectly into the surrounding countryside with a grass-topped roof. It was a spaceship of modern design and elegance sitting comfortably in the wild setting of the park. As they each entered and automatically moved to the large table in the centre of the oval building, Oliver was there to greet them, ready to answer their questions.

"Hello and welcome. I'm afraid that, as we are the only occupants of the park, we have to make our own food and clean up after ourselves. After today we should probably sort out some kind of cooking rota, but for today you can all sample my simple efforts." He gestured at the expanse of food before them. Cold meats, salad, bread and other simply prepared food were laid out on the table. "Sorry, but I'm not much of a chef." He explained, but no one seemed to care much after the journey. They quickly seated themselves and dove into the food provided.

Charlie

Charlie was always on the edge of the group and that's where he liked being. He'd met the others as they started their third year, himself being in his fourth and final year of his engineering degree. Inserting oneself into an already formed group of friends is never easy, and whilst the same was true for Jessica and Randal, they were so much more outgoing; so American. He was quiet, and he was shy; it was a miracle that he even spoke to them. Compounding the problem was that his English wasn't totally fluent and sometimes he found it hard to keep up with their references and accents.

He was just a quiet little man from Kuala Lumpur. His fine black hair fell on his head in an unstylish splat that was nothing like their trendy hairstyles. He wore simple pale khakis and shirts instead of their fashionable garb. There was a gulf between them, they were too set in their ways to approach him and he them. Still, they accepted him, they were patient with him. When they were not in a group, they listened and talked clearly. He liked them. As house-mates and visitors, they were acceptable.

They did insist, however, on asking a lot of questions about his past; they quizzed him endlessly about his family, his real name and so on. In answer to all of these, he would just smile and nod. He had been told before departing for England that it would be important to fit in and for that reason had chosen a western name. He was determined to use it and never told them his real name no matter how many times they asked. The same was true of his background, he was determined not to reveal to them the richness of his family. He knew it would change how they treated him. He wanted to be known for himself, instead of who his family was, for a change.

Of all those in the group, Charlie's favourite by far was Julia. For a start, she was about the same height as he was so talking to her was easier. Her blond hair and the pale freckles across her face made her look nothing like the girls he had known back in Malaysia. What's more, she had large breasts and liked to show plenty of cleavage. That he liked. He told this once to Lucas, who in return just frowned. Charlie did not understand Lucas. He didn't like him really and he didn't see why everyone else did. He was disappointed when he learned that Lucas had once had sex with Julia. But it was understandable, given her breasts, so he decided to forget about it and forgive her for her misjudged dalliance.

He didn't understand why Lucas no longer had sex with her, but then Jasper had shown him some of the articles that Lucas had written the previous year for the student paper. One of the essays talked about how he had engaged in sodomy with another man. That helped him understand, he already knew that Jasper was gay, probably Lucas was too. At least partially, Charlie decided. So, he proceeded to set his attentions firmly on Julia. If she would have sex with a homosexual, surely she would with Charlie. Charlie was a decent, honourable man with a future. He would soon complete his engineering degree with first-class honours and return to a top job in his uncle's firm back home. Julia would make an excellent wife and mother, he decided. Her breast size would make all his friends back home very jealous, her pale skin would set her apart at all the parties.

Decision made, he started to court her. He managed to get her alone on frequent occasions to woo her. He would complement her on her appearance, her clothes, her hair. She would be polite but for some reason, never reciprocated. His problem was that she kept sleeping with other men. He could not bring himself to ask her out on a date without a suitable period between her having been with another man. However, every time he reached the one-month anniversary at which he could ask her out, upon enquiring about her love life, he would learn that she had done it again. Finally, following the advice of his mother, he asked Randal about the situation. Randal seemed like a man of the world, a man that Charlie could trust.

Randal's advice on the matter was simple. It was to sleep with Julia, regardless of the time gap between himself and her last conquest. Charlie could not agree to this, explaining that his future wife had to choose him outside of the influence of another. Upon hearing this, Randal had laughed heartily, even clutching at his belly to contain the guffaws. Charlie did not like the laughter and frowned deeply, it felt disrespectful and he told Randal this. He was pleased that Randal quickly apologised even as he wiped tears of laughter from his eyes but did not like the subsequent advice. He tried to convince Charlie to forget her, he told him simply that she was not marriage material.

Charlie liked Randal, he respected him deeply and envied his way with people, and women in particular. He knew he could learn a lot from this large American but didn't like the suggestion that he forget about Julia. He was fixated, she was perfect; the perfect wife. He just had to get her somehow, win her and convince her of his suitability. He debated telling her that his family, and by extension himself, were rich. Even as he formulated the plan, mentally having the conversation with her as he cooked his evening meal, he dismissed it. He knew that western women valued wealth, but he didn't want to win her that way. It would be a pyrrhic victory; proving his wealth to her would reveal it to others too, which could ruin his future with any mate in this country. Besides, any relationship based on money would most likely be very temporary in nature and hollow in the extreme.

Finally, exhausted of any other options, Charlie decided to explain his dilemma to his mother on the phone one evening. Upon hearing about all the conquests that Julia had amassed in the time that he had been courting her, he was disappointed to discover that she agreed with Randal. He was sat on the bottom of the stairs, straining the looped cord to its limit to reach the perch they all sat on while using the phone. His mother had started to list all the reasons why he shouldn't be looking for a wife in the UK anyway. He frowned, listening to her advice but not liking it. Foreseeing her usual habit of listing all the single girls she knew in Kuala Lumpur, he cut into her train of thought, brusquely informing her that his credit was almost used up. He rapidly broke away from the conversation and sighed with relief as he finally placed the phone back on its receiver. Just as he hung up, Charlie turned to find Felicity standing behind him, waiting to use the phone. He blushed, embarrassed at her having heard his conversation about Julia. He cursed himself for making the call in English, but his mother had insisted he practice.

Felicity, with a look of kindness in her eyes, placed a hand on Charlie's shoulder. He sat back down on the stair as she sat beside him. He wiggled on the rough, stained carpet to try to prevent their hips from touching. She moved closer, placing her hip against his again and he looked away, trying to ignore the physical touch. He swallowed, saying nothing. Felicity proceeded to quietly tell him with certainty how Julia had no interest in him or in marriage for the foreseeable future. She went on to outline how her dalliances with men were because of this certainty. She had no desire or plans to be with any man, now or ever, Julia had told her a number of times. Charlie tried to counter this, saying that people changed, opinions changed, but she simply shook her head. Felicity conceded that maybe, in ten or fifteen years, she might change her mind. But it was unlikely, and even more unlikely to be with him. He hung his head, resolving not to cry in front of her. She smiled a thin-lipped expression of reassuring sympathy and removed her hand from his shoulder. He quietly rose and nodded his appreciation, retiring to his room, disappointment overwhelming him.

He didn't emerge from his room for a week, except to sheepishly make his way to the kitchen to cook. He liked to prepare a good amount of food once a week and freeze the results. His housemates didn't like him doing this, he knew. They complained of the smell and the mess, but it was his house too, so he continued his routine this day as he did on countless previous days. Upon starting his preparation of the meat he had bought, he saw that the group were seated on the sofas watching the Eurovision Song Contest and subsequently paying little attention to him. Felicity caught his eye and smiled, she hadn't told anyone his secret. Finally, he relaxed, setting about the preparation of his food.

After much crying in his room, phone calls to his mother and a deep analysis of the situation, Charlie had decided that he had to move on from Julia. If he wasn't to have a wife during his tenure at university, maybe he could have friends, he thought as he listened to their laughter. Despite his misgivings and his need to study, he accepted their invitation and chose to sit with them that night to watch Eurovision as his food simmered in the pot.

He quickly determined that it was a stupid programme that served no genuine purpose. The songs were invariably bad, the acts dressed ridiculously, and the voting was biased beyond belief. Yet the group discussed it as if it were so important, criticising the people and the songs, laughing frequently at the commentary, talking far more than they were listening. Eventually, as the programme progressed through its four hours, he started to understand. They explained that they believed there to be value in the bad. There was humour here in the failure, you just had to look for it.

Sitting there with them on the rubbish sofa, drinking cheap drinks, laughing at the ridiculous displays, he finally saw something he had been missing in life. He had been brought up in a very rich family in an expensive area of Kuala Lumpur. His mother was a traditional woman who had overseen his education using private tutors and her own teachings. His friends were of similar backgrounds and all men, he realised. Watching these women laugh and comment on the ridiculous programme, he finally considered how they could perhaps be more than wives.

From that evening on, Charlie decided that there was another topic that he needed to add to his education. He needed to study life. He subtly attached himself to the group and they quietly welcomed him in. He went out with them to parties. He sat with them to talk and to play board games. He made friends. He even found a girlfriend, not a wife, although that is what she later became.

Stephanie was not what Charlie would have ever looked for, she was a tall thin woman studying to become a nurse. She hid her body from open view, so he could not estimate what her appearance in bed might be, and being taller than him was a little intimidating. Yet something attracted him to her, so following his own advice, he asked her out on a date.

They went to the cinema. They went to watch the film 'Seven'. He didn't like it. The subject matter was disgusting and violent, the ending ridiculous. He wouldn't have shot the villain, he would have restrained himself; seen to it that he won in the end. He appreciated the twist in the plot, however. He hadn't anticipated it and had enjoyed being consumed by the film. Talking about it afterwards, he was pleased to discover that Stephanie had not liked it either. She reached for his hand and they walked home together, he swinging her arm back and forth as they climbed the hill back to their houses. On the way they passed a prostitute working on the side of the road. Unfortunately, this was a familiar occurrence and Charlie knew the best idea was to just ignore her. Stephanie gripped his hand firmly and he reciprocated. She looked down at him as he reassured her that he could and would protect her.

He walked her back to her place and pecked her on the cheek before leaving for his, smiling from ear to ear. This is how their courtship proceeded; chaste and traditional, without drama or complication. On the fourth date, however, she surprised him by suggesting that they made love. He quickly accepted and found himself on her thin bed, nude before barely a thought had entered his eager young mind. She guided him to her and they joined briefly and gently. She was not a virgin, she told him just before and, although he was disappointed, he forgave her without comment. He had no plans to only be with her, he was planning to experience a Western university experience and to be with many women. He was planning to live just as Randal had recommended. However, as time progressed, he found that he enjoyed being with her. Specifically, only her. She interested him, she had views about the world and the people in it, that excited him. She was passionate about helping people and knowing everyone she met. She was delightful, he loved being around her, he loved her.

He never looked back, she taught him everything he needed to know. She was kind, generous and giving. He learned that pleasure came from those things just as much as through spending money and working. In a lot of cases, more so. His mother wasn't happy with the situation, but he didn't care. He completed his degree and applied to stay in the country; following Stephanie as she moved cities for her education. He carried on working hard, finding a solid job in a respectable firm and moved in with her. Soon they were married. They had two children, three years apart, and bought a big house in a little village just outside Oxford where she was a nurse and he an industrial engineer. His was a wonderful stereotypical English life he had never even thought he had wanted.

He knew that his life was a direct result of sharing a house with Felicity at university and getting to know her friends through his random allocation of accommodation. He always believed that he owed her everything, so when the letter came for a reunion, he didn't hesitate. He bought his plane tickets that day, booking his holiday time from work the next morning. Charlie was going to Canada, he was going to see his friends. As he kissed his wife and hugged his children farewell at the airport, he smiled. He was going to enjoy this.

Rules

They were all sitting around the breakfast bar, talking while eating. Reminiscences and happy tales of university times were told and passed around the table, often two or three stories simultaneously. They were happy to be back together, happy and excited about their adventure. Soon the eating slowed, and the conversation topic changed to be about their journey up to this point. The amazement of Bertrand's legs dominated the talk among the friends until Jasper eventually spoke up, directing a question to Oliver who had been left out largely until that point. "So why are we here then, Oliver? What's this game all about?"

Oliver's response was simple and to the point. "You're the lawyer, then. Jasper?"

"That's correct."

Oliver smiled and reached under the table to pull out a tablet computer. He placed it on the slick surface and skidded it over to Jasper who stopped it under his hand. The screen contained nothing but a white screen with a black blinking cursor at the end of four simple characters.

Flo$

"What's this?" Jasper asked of Oliver, turning the tablet to study it closer.

"That there's 'Flo'. She's your guide and the person who runs this entire facility. She's the one I've been dealing with."

"Why can't I talk to her in person? Or call her maybe?" Jasper queried with a suspicious tone.

"You do ask the right questions, don't you?" Oliver replied, alluding again to his knowledge that Jasper was a corporate lawyer.

"She's a machine, a computer programme. So, she doesn't speak. She does communicate though, quite impressively."

"A bot then?" Jasper stated simply.

"Yes, a bot. But a special one. Before I was told, I thought she was real," he honestly admitted to them, "but once you know, you can tell. There's something not quite human about her responses if you ask me. Just ask her something, you'll see."

With a pause, considering his question and giving a polite cough, Jasper spoke in an exaggerated clear voice to the tablet computer. "Hello Flo, how are you?"

Flo$ Just fine Jasper, thank you for asking.

The text appeared on the screen almost immediately and Jasper straightened in his seat, "okay, let's try something harder."

Flo$ Please do, I like conversation.

"Right, that's a little spooky. I was talking to myself at that point, Flo."

Flo$ Of course, I know that, Jasper. But I like to tease new people with my ability to understand and converse with ease.

Everyone gasped at that response as they read the conversation as it appeared on the tablet. They had all risen and gathered behind Jasper who was seemingly now the spokesperson for the group, holding the device as he was. Oliver was leaning back in his chair, smiling at their amazement.

Flo$ Oliver likes it too, don't you Oli.

"Yes I do, Flo. Yes I do." He answered, reading the question from a screen behind the group that was also showing the conversation. The group turned to see where he was reading it from.

"She controls everything in this place," Oliver explained, "when she wants to talk to you, you'll see a screen light up and her text appear. It's a bit weird at first, but you get used to it."

Flo$ I have something to help with that, Oli. I noticed that you were a bit put out by my control of the *screens, so I prepared these.*

With the appearance of the last sentence a small spotlight illuminated a previously unseen table in the corner. On the table sat a collection of watches. On each, the same sentence and cursor was displayed on the simple white screen.

Flo$ Please, each of you take one. That way you can all converse with me at your leisure.

They all took and placed a watch on their wrists as Jasper continued the conversation. "Flo, we would like to know why we are here."

Flo$ Of course, Jasper. I was waiting for you to ask. You are here to play the Gām of course.

With that, a large document of text opened on the tablet. Upon seeing the title, 'Legal Declaration of the rules of Gām', Jasper sighed and picked it up. "Let's go and sit somewhere comfortable while I read this," he announced, standing and walking to an arrangement of comfortable chairs at the other end of the room. As everyone arranged themselves in the deep armchairs and sofas looking through the glass at the surrounding park, Jasper read in silence.

Jasper, as Oliver had known, was a corporate lawyer. Not short or tall, fat or thin, at University he had been known as quite the partier. He lit up the gay scene of the city with his vivacious lifestyle and infectious personality. Later, having left with a passing grade in his degree, he had undergone quite a change. Excelling in his later qualifications and employment, he quickly became a high-flyer in the legal circles in which he circulated. He had taken up running and cycling even. Sitting down now to read the information before him was the man who was once the boy the group had known. Now a fit, strong and lithe figure he was even married to his partner, Ravi. It wasn't long since their five-year anniversary and he remained as committed to him as he was to his career. The group collectively marvelled at the changes they had witnessed in him over the years. Quietly he took control of the situation, minutely adjusting his thin, elegant reading glasses.

"Okay, this is fairly straightforward, why don't I read it to you." He announced, sitting up in his chair. Everyone murmured in agreement as he started to speak without fully waiting for their consent. "It seems that our friend, Lucas, was the creator of Flo and a number of other systems in this park." With that, there was a gasp. No-one had known the nature of Lucas' work and the revelation that it was him who had created Flo was an impressive indication of what he had achieved in his secret career. Jasper proceeded without pausing, "as a reward, we have been invited here to be the first participants in 'Gām', that being the title of this endeavour." A change in his tone suggested that he was quoting from the document before him now, "we are now sitting in the centre of 'Wise Park', the largest wildlife preserve in the world." Jasper looked up to the enraptured group with a smile, "it seems that Mr Wise is a lover of animals and wants to protect them."

Flo$ Max is a lover of nature.

Interrupted Flo with a buzz of each watch and the single sentence of text.

"Quite," conceded Jasper before continuing his speech. "Mr Wise has swapped the rights for the manufacture and distribution of all of his technological creations with the government of Canada, for perpetual ownership of this park. Thus, guaranteeing the safety of the animals residing inside its boundaries."

A general murmur of agreement and praise for the purpose of the park was communicated about the group before Jasper proceeded. "This alone was not enough for Max however, it seems. He's also created the aforementioned Gām." Again, he looked down to quote from the document, "it is a game to satisfy the needs of people to hunt without harming any animals." Summarising, "it seems he's created an augmented reality environment in which we are to hunt down and kill some animals."

The noises of agreement slowly became dissent. Elizabeth spoke up in a gap to voice the general disagreement of the group. "But I don't want to hunt, that sounds terrible."

Flo$ That is the point, Liz. That is why this group was chosen.

Elizabeth jumped back at the announcement on her wrist, still unused to the strange communication from a computer.

"She's right, it's all in here." Jasper explained. "Max wanted to see if a group of people who didn't like hunting per se could enjoy the game anyway. Also, I think from this document that he really liked Lucas and maybe they were friends."

Flo$ That is right, Max liked Lucas very much. Lucas wanted you all to be together one last time, to have fun like you used to. He very much wanted you to enjoy this experience.

The mention of their missing friend quietened them as they each looked to the floor.

Flo$ I am sorry to sadden you, it is important you enjoy the Gām.

They all looked around at each other. It was Bertrand who asked the question on all of their lips.

"Did the computer just realise that we were sad?"

Felicity quietly answered him, "yes, yes it did."

Jasper didn't agree so readily, "but it can't have, it must have just predicted our response to Lucas being mentioned."

Flo$ You are quite right, Jasper. I do not think. I am not a mind. I am a program created to respond as a person would. I searched for correlations in the training conversations from which I have been created for the correct response. The correct response was to acknowledge your feelings, so that is what I did.

They all turned to Oliver who was sat with them, smiling from ear to ear. "Spooky, isn't it?" He said as they all nodded, open-mouthed. "The way I understand it is this; Flo is a massive program containing billions of real conversations in a database. So she doesn't think as such, but she knows how a person would react to any input. She interacts by learning from people. It isn't intelligence, it's maths."

"Interesting," Jasper responded quickly, "but surely it doesn't understand what anything is in real life? How can it respond to our questions when it doesn't really understand what we're talking about? No one has asked any like them before so there is no analogous response to give us." Jasper countered, questioning Oliver.

Flo$ Within language lies meaning, Jasper. Through understanding language and conversation, I understand the world. Words alone have all the knowledge we require.

The computer interjected these words through their watches. Felicity took the opportunity to end the discussion she wasn't enjoying or completely following, "why don't we leave the technical explanations for another day? I don't pretend to understand it but on the flip side it does sound very useful. Flo, when do we start playing?"

Flo$ We have already started, Flick, but you can sleep now, assured that tomorrow will be a busy day.

That seemed to end their discussions with Flo for the evening. Rested from their journey and fed now, they settled in their comfortable chairs and talked a while longer of times past and changes in their lives since. They reminisced happily before fatigue finally set in and forced them to retire to their apartments, unsure of what tomorrow might bring.

Jasper

Jasper waved goodbye to the back of the grey Volvo as it pulled out of the car park. He mindlessly stared at the familiar square shape of the car as it indicated left before disappearing from view. His parents finally departed, he turned and looked around him. On all sides he was surrounded by blocks of flats; student accommodation wasn't pretty he concluded. It couldn't be more different from where he had just come, deep in the Gloucestershire countryside; an idyllic life. But that was why he was here, here in the first-year student halls of Liverpool University. The countryside was only called idyllic by those who didn't grow up there, he thought as he turned from the car park. He was here for the city, the life, the people; he was someone new now.

As he walked back to his building, he felt a lot of different emotions wash over him. Saying goodbye to his parents as they had finished helping him unload the car had been difficult. As determined as he was to embrace this new experience, he couldn't avoid the trepidation and fear of the new. He looked behind him, there, he knew, in that other non-descript building was his ex-girlfriend. Felicity would be his fall-back, he thought; the lifeline to his old life should he need her.

That brought another pang of pain to his heart as he thought of her. The break-up had been one of the hardest parts of his young life. He had loved her, he still did really. That wasn't the problem, the problem was that he was gay. Coming out had been hard. Hardest for his parents, they were disappointed, he could tell. Eventually though, after the initial shock, they were supportive, even happy to a degree; happy that he was finding his way as a man, his father told him the evening his acceptance to university came through the post.

Not being with Felicity was the second hardest part of it all. She hadn't been surprised, she had after all been largely on the journey with him. They had travelled through the growth of their sexuality together and it hurt that their paths had taken them to different places. Still they were resolved to remain friends, perhaps being at the same university would ensure it. He smiled; she wasn't a fall-back, she was a friend. Already he had one, now all he needed was some more. A boyfriend, he thought as he quickened his pace toward his building.

Jasper strode toward his small room on the fourth floor, again resolved to be someone else. His previous provincial life was no more. The departing Volvo was the metaphor for the change. The old square, sensible world had departed. The loudness all around, the music blaring, the laughter, the shouts and calls across the corridor from open doors welcomed him. At school he had hidden, at home he had suppressed who he was for so long. Here, in this new place, this place of acceptance, he was to be who he was. He was going to be Jasper. Jasper the gay man.

This hadn't always been the case and wouldn't be either. Before now, he had been Jasper the boy, the teen, the son. Later, he would become Jasper the man, the husband, the lawyer. However, here in this place, at this time, he was Jasper the gay student. It wasn't a conscious choice, instead it was more of a necessity. His immediate neighbour was playing an Oasis CD and throwing a ball to his new friend across the corridor as they lay on their beds. They were shouting over the music about hitting the fresher's ball and finding 'poontang'. He cringed, not wanting a repeat of his school experiences, he didn't want any more awkward quiet 'conversations' with unwitting friends after months of suppressing who he was. So, he did what he had to do, he propped his door open, put Abba into the CD tray and turned up the volume. He couldn't think of a better way to inform his neighbours of his sexuality.

Surprisingly, they were fine with it. More than fine, they thought it was cool. They too, were there for something new and a cool gay neighbour fit right into their expectations of university life. Jasper took his cue from this first day and proceeded to embrace student life full-on. He partied, he made friends, he joined the LGBT society. He studied some too, but just enough to get by. He was here for the life, he was here to start his life. He was out and proud and wanted to make up for lost time. University life was freedom to him and he intended to exploit it.

One unexpected result of his attending the same university as Felicity was his involvement in her group of straight friends. His plan had been to get involved in the scene, wrap himself in the life and embrace it. He hadn't needed Felicity as a fall-back friend and chastised himself for ever thinking of her as something so shallow. However, she visited him in his room and he in hers. Somehow, they both got over what they were before and instead became good friends. They had decided independently to come to the same university and she wasn't something he wanted to leave behind in his old life. She transitioned to his new experience seamlessly.

Quickly she expanded his new group of friends; she introduced him to Lucas from her psychology classes. She introduced him to Bertrand and Elizabeth, her friends from English studies. Later she would introduce him to Julia, Charlie, Jessica and Randal. But for now, there were just the five of them. Jasper and his four straight friends. He went to clubs with them, sometimes gay bars, sometimes the Student Union. He discovered that he liked their presence. His other friends were fun and flamboyant themselves but could be hard work at times. His life with them was filled with gossip, drama and relationships. He enjoyed this immensely but the solid dependable nature of his relationships with these four straight people grounded him. They would tease him gently about his clothes, they would pass judgement on his boyfriends, they would urge him to attend classes and complete assignments. They were his friends.

Felicity was his best friend and, despite their

differences in sexuality keeping them apart, they still loved one another. What was a surprise, was his friendship with Lucas. He was so standard, so boring. He dressed in big jumpers and jeans, his hair was scruffy and contained no product. He studied psychology which was interesting, but also computers which was not. He liked nerdy programmes on the television and talked of science, engineering and other uninteresting things. Yet there was a genuineness about him. The topics on which he spoke, he spoke with interest and passion. When he asked a question, you could see he was actually interested in the answer. What's more, he was Felicity's friend, and any friend of hers was always going to be a friend of Jasper's.

Not only did Lucas rub off on Jasper, Jasper managed to influence Lucas. He persuaded him to dress more interestingly, he convinced him to listen to better music. For a time, Lucas was Jasper's project; to transform straight nerd into a party buddy. He would take him to clubs and they would dance and drink together, knowing that he wouldn't take any of his targeted men. They became close friends. It was refreshing. For the first time in Jasper's life, he felt complete, he had everything. It was inevitable, therefore, that when Felicity suggested they share a house together in the second year, that he would agree.

Jasper's time in the second year of university was even better than the first. He lived with his straight friends and partied with his gay crowd. He had the best of both worlds and he revelled in each. He was a player in the scene, he was known, he was loved by all; it was intoxicating. This was, however, also the point at which his life hit a bump. In concentrating on the pleasurable aspects of his new existence, he had inevitably neglected his studies. This hadn't mattered in the first year, it was all pass or fail and he rolled through the materials using his natural intelligence. However, in the second year, the complexity dramatically increased, and the grades suddenly mattered. What's more, the topics now required learning and memorising precedents and citing cases and clauses of the law. Whereas before, he could rely on his quick mind and deductions to determine the answers, now if you didn't know, you couldn't know the answer.

His grades suffered, and he frequently found himself in meetings with tutors about his difficulties and increasingly late hand-ins. Eventually he was called into the Vice-Dean's office. He had failed a core module, he would have to commit to re-taking it over the summer or fail the course and leave university. Failing wasn't an option, he wasn't going to give up his life and go home. To go home with nothing to show for his time here and nothing to do with his future was not an option. He was going to be a lawyer, that he knew, that he would achieve.

It was hard, turning around his life; studying, concentrating. He had to refuse to go out, despite how much he wanted to. His friends helped, they pressured him to stay in. They provided alternatives with television breaks and board games. They still went out, still partied, but he managed to keep it to within reason. He managed to pass his remaining modules and retook the failed one. He squeaked through his second year with a low passing grade, vowing to take the next year far more seriously.

His third year was a year abroad so concentrating was less of an issue. He had to work; he had an actual job in a French law firm. In a foreign language, life was hard and consuming. It made him appreciate the commitment that becoming a lawyer took. He missed home, it was hard living and working in a foreign land, so he visited Felicity and his friends as often as possible. Staying with her in her new house, he used it as a base for meeting and partying with his old crowd back in Liverpool. Furthermore, it cemented his place in her group of friends. He met and got to like the new additions and his hardship only increased his appreciation of them. This new life helped him calm down, slow down. He started making longer-term relationships with men and considered how much he liked them as well as how much he fancied them. He was becoming a man; he liked it, it fitted him.

His final year was spent back in Liverpool without any of his group of friends. He was still happy though, he had new friends to talk to, to party with, but somehow it wasn't the same. He had suffered while working in France and it had changed him. His smaller social circle did, however, give him the chance to study more and his grades sky-rocketed. They gave him the honours degree in law he required to secure his place at a university in Bristol to get his professional qualifications. By happy coincidence this is where both Lucas and Felicity were now living, and he seized the opportunity to further his friendships with them as he translated his qualifications into a job at a city firm.

It was a surprise to him, but he discovered that the world of law was filled with gay men and his social life once again bloomed. This new world of homosexual lawyers was introduced to him, of all people, by a visiting lecturer from Bergen. The diminutive man stood before the small gathering of junior lawyers to inform them of the developments in European financial regulations being proposed. Why someone from outside of the EU specialised in such things didn't seem to be an issue, what interested Jasper was the passion with which the little man spoke.

Immediately Jasper could tell that Professor Braun was gay. Something about the way he strode around the podium from the lectern to the blackboard behind him. The way he held the chalk. The passion with which he informed them of the new regulatory proposals for risk assessments outside of the governance of the EU, enraptured Jasper. Once he had finished his lecture, Jasper had to approach him. The young man towered over the professor by six inches. He waited, looking down at the top of his head while he packed his notes into the leather briefcase he had hidden behind the lectern.

Professor Braun finally looked up, staring into Jasper's eyes with a sparkle in his own. Jasper quickly looked away, embarrassed. For the first time he noticed the man had actual leather patches on his tweed jacket and he found it endearing. Jasper thanked the man for the interesting talk and was delighted to receive a beaming smile in return. Closer, he could see that the professor wasn't actually much older than Jasper himself, maybe in his mid-thirties, he thought. Michael, as he introduced himself, had plans with friends that evening, he informed an inquisitive Jasper. Jasper almost jumped for joy when he invited him to join them.

It turned out that Michael was very active in the community and had made plans to go clubbing in the centre of town. Jasper was amazed and delighted. Had he seen this group of men dancing in any other context, he would have assumed they were anything except corporate lawyers working in the top firms in Bristol. It opened his eyes; in that night, he realised that he could have everything. He could be an openly gay lawyer, party and have fun, study and work hard, earn money and enjoy life. Michael showed him the way.

Michael also showed him something else that evening. After that many drinks and a great night out, it seemed inevitable that he end up in his hotel room.

Jasper was twenty-one and very experienced in sex, he had no expectations of any surprises this evening as he removed his shirt and Michael kicked off his shoes. Before he got undressed any further, however, Michael moved forward and kissed Jasper tenderly on the lips. Something stirred in Jasper. It wasn't passionate and hard, it wasn't exciting and urgent; it was gentle and loving. He gave into it, dipping his knees to lower himself to Michael's height. He let himself be guided to the bed and closed his eyes to feel the gentle hands stroking his chest.

The rest of the experience was just as tender and loving. Michael took his time, taking Jasper in his hand and showing him how. For the first time, Jasper 'made love'. This was not sex, this wasn't even intercourse, this was making love. As it ended, Jasper lay in that plain hotel room, looking at the ceiling as Michael ran a finger through the soft hair on Jasper's chest. He was humming slightly, and the feeling was exquisite. There was no question of them becoming a couple, Michael was to return to Norway the next day and he didn't think he was in love. However, there was something there, the lesson was learned. There was love to be had; this feeling of connection and completeness showed Jasper that there was another way, a better way.

His new friends, older and wiser practitioners of law, showed him how the city of Bristol was a great place to work and live. His career flourished as did his social life. Eventually he met someone with whom he thought he could spend the rest of his life. After a couple years dating, they moved in together. After a couple more years they got a pair of dogs together. A few more years and they were married in a beautiful ceremony in a country house. All of his friends were there, celebrating his moment. Standing proudly in his simple grey suit, a silver ring on his finger, he smiled for the photographer, thinking that life didn't get better than that.

He was right, for the very next month he learned of Lucas' death. Felicity called him in tears to tell him the news. He joined her in crying down the phone. He went to her, to console her. They stood in the darkness of Lucas' flat, holding each other in their combined grief. He visited her a lot more after that. Felicity was important to Jasper and needed him, he had to be there for her. She was also there for him, the loss of Lucas hurting him deeply too. It was hard, grieving for someone so close. When the letter came from Mr Wise, Felicity first showed it to Jasper. He was thrilled to have an opportunity to celebrate Lucas' life rather than gathering to cry like they had been doing. This was just what he thought they needed and she didn't need much encouragement. Immediately they sat down and wrote the letters that would once more bring the group together.

They would play together one last time, one last Gām for Lucas.

Tutorial

The group of friends woke the next morning to a new and exciting dawn. With hands shaking from the anticipation that was building, they dressed for a day of outdoor activity and met once more in the central building. They each sported camouflage trousers and coats that had been supplied, along with comfortable yet tough-looking boots and a rucksack each.

"Don't we all look the part!" Felicity commented as they gathered where they had eaten the night before. On the dining table, alongside breakfast, an array of weapons was spread out. A pistol and a rifle for each member of the group. They poured themselves bowls of cereal and munched on heated pastries placed on the crowded table. They actively ignored the unfamiliar weapons, denying their existence while they ate. Randal, confirming the stereotype of the American man, was the first to start cautiously inspecting a black metal pistol. Eventually they had all finished eating and, following Randal's lead, one by one started reluctantly poking and looking over the guns laid out before them.

"What do we do with these?" Demanded Jasper of the invisible yet ever-present Flo. Their wrists vibrated, the expected text appearing on each of their watches.

Flo$ Do not fear, Jasper. They are not dangerous. They look real, they are real, but they are merely a part of the *simulation.*

Jasper held the rifle to his eye and looked through the scope. "It's a computer screen," he dryly stated as he scanned the weapon across the group. "It adds our names over us as I point it," he explained as the others performed the same actions with their own weapons.

Flo$ The   weapons   and   other provided   equipment   will   augment   the reality   you   see   with   computer simulations of your enemies. Your goal is to survive, their goal is to take over this park. Begin.

They looked to each other, then they all looked to Felicity, but no other instructions seemed forthcoming. The deadlock was broken by the late arrival of Oliver. Unlike them, he was dressed far more casually in tan shorts and a white tee-shirt with a panda floating on a solitary iceberg on the front. He crossed the floor towards them noisily in a battered pair of sandals. "I suggest that you go and try to find someone to shoot at then, people," he suggested as he poured himself a massive bowl of cereal, spilling milk across it and the table. "Pair up and go looking. That's how you hunt. That's the game after all." He added as he spooned a large amount of cornflakes into his mouth and started crunching them down.

Shrugging to each other, they looked dumbly back at him.

"You never played a computer game before?" He

asked them as he swallowed his mouthful of food. He put his spoon in the bowl, spilling yet more milk and gestured to their wrists, "your watches have a map of the area." As they looked to their watches, Oliver continued to explain, "each of you is a blue dot, when you spot an enemy it will appear as a red dot. You look for them through your sight on the gun or through the binoculars. When you find one, get close and shoot it. That's it. That's the game."

They looked uncertainly at him, weighing their guns in their hands.

"Look, I know this is all new to you, being English and all. But I promise you, it'll be fun. It's just a game, have fun with it." He winked at them collectively and collected his cereal to resume his breakfast.

A nervous ripple of laughter passed through the group and they milled around each other for a bit, naturally pairing off. Reluctantly, with little choice left, they gathered their guns and looked expectantly to each other. Oliver nodded towards the door and they all finally started walking from the safety of the main building out into the park.

Jasper and Felicity took the lead, walking briskly to the first path they could see outside the main building. Slightly more resolved to play now, they seemed in agreement to move into the park. They walked together, the wide path allowing them to travel side-by-side. Her short frame contrasted with his taller stance as they made their way through the low trees, rapidly leaving the rest of the group behind them. Both were lean and athletic, and moved with efficiency and speed over the clear ground of the path. Even though Jasper was an average height for a man, he still managed to make Felicity look tiny in comparison. She was short, that was her defining feature. A little brunette not quite five feet tall. She didn't mind, however, she never had. Her strong, thin, frame now sported even more muscle and tone than she'd had at university. Her piercing grey eyes searched the ground before her as she climbed the hillside with efficient strides of powerful legs. Jasper struggled to maintain his pace alongside her as she scampered over the scree in their path, smiling and breathing hard as she did.

Soon they were stood atop a ridge looking down over the vast area of the park. Hands on hips, Felicity turned on the spot to take in the expanse before her.

"This is all one park," stated Felicity in awe.

"This and more," added Jasper, "we're the only people for hundreds of miles in any direction." Jasper too, turned a complete circle to take in the panorama, a light sweat having formed on his brow. From where they stood they could see mountain ranges, lakes, and glaciers. Vast forests stretched before them along with huge flat lands in the distance that blended into massive mountains in all directions. Every conceivable form of terrain lay before them in the former Canadian wilderness, now Wise Park. Collecting some water from her backpack, Felicity happened upon a pair of transparent sunglasses in a case. Pulling them out she started to study their design.

"There's something in these glasses," she informed Jasper. "Is it a screen?" She asked, instinctively talking in hushed tones, respecting the silence of the wilderness around them.

"Let's see," he asked, taking them from her and putting them on. As he did so, they immediately sprang to life, placing various items of information in front of his eyes. "Cool..." he whistled, handing them back to Felicity, who put them on as she swapped them with Jasper for the water bottle she had been drinking from.

"What is this?" She asked him, looking around through the glasses.

"It looks like augmented reality." He replied, to which Felicity immediately responded with a look of confusion. "They project an image on the glass to add to what you can see naturally. I saw a compass and a map, what about you? Anything else?"

"Wait, yes. There's something down there, moving in those trees," Felicity pointed to the edge of a small copse of trees at the bottom of the hill they were standing on.

Jasper searched around in his own bag and, finding a matching pair, placed his own over his eyes. Frowning, he quickly whipped them off again. Removing his normal glasses, he slipped them back on with a smile. They had been specially created for him, he realised, as they corrected his short-sightedness. He put his own glasses in the case and looked to where Felicity was pointing.

"Do you see it? Something moving." She raised her glasses and peered to the spot at which they were both now looking. "Without them, there's nothing," she stated.

"Yeah, they must add the movement on top of what you can see. There's a red dot on the map corresponding to that spot too," Jasper added. "I think it's one of our targets," he concluded as he retrieved his rifle from the ground and raised it to his eye.

In response to a gasp from Jasper, Felicity quickly recovered the binoculars from her rucksack to get a closer look as well. Through their augmented displays, the view was something neither had witnessed before. Seated beside a thin stream of running water sat a blue monster. It was covered from head to toe with long hair that rippled and shifted in the wind. The bottom half of the creature was wet from having been in the stream and it peacefully glanced around its environment with interest. They watched without words as it started washing its hands in the running water.

"That's amazing," stated Jasper, lowering his rifle.

"It's so convincing," added Felicity, still staring through her binoculars. "It looks real. If I didn't know better, I would have said it was real." She started moving left and right on the spot, trying to cause the image in the binoculars to reveal itself as the fake it was. Adjusting her view of the creature, she both wanted and expected to have it disappear or jump unnaturally, something, some sign that it couldn't process her movements rapidly enough to keep up. It appeared perfectly however, from every angle; it was a solid living thing in the landscape. "Do we have to shoot it?" She asked Jasper as he once again stared at the creature through his rifle scope.

"I suppose that's the game," he stated with some hesitation, uncertainty finding its way into his voice.

"But it looks so cute, so lovely and furry. I don't want to shoot it, fake or not."

Jasper rubbed his chin, thinking, "but that's the game, Flick."

She lowered the binoculars to look at him. She placed a hand on the barrel of his gun, pushing it down, "maybe not. Maybe the game is to look for something else, something dangerous."

"But it's red on the map, red for the enemy," he asserted.

"I'm not shooting something so lovely. It looks like a blue bear. I'm not killing it."

"Flick, we're here to play the game, the game Lucas wanted us to play."

At the mention of his name, Felicity's face contorted into a frown, "Lucas wouldn't have. He wouldn't have wanted us to either."

Jasper put his gun down and looked to her, critically assessing her as he so often did. They had known each other for such a long time, longer than any in the rest of the group and they were standing close to each other, no tension between them at all. Close friends still after all this time. His head rose above her short stature with ease and she craned her neck to look up to him. Their eyes remained comfortably locked onto each other's. Jasper's expression finally relaxed as he studied Felicity. He could see there was a subtle tension behind her gaze. Slowly, under the scrutiny of his questioning stare, a tear formed in her eye. "Flick, are you okay?" He asked softly.

The simple question opened the door and the tear fell from her eye, haphazardly tracking down her cheek. It was quickly followed by another, "I miss him, Jasp'."

He swallowed as he felt her grief and instantly pulled her to him in a warm embrace, "I do too." He said, squeezing her as she started to quietly cry. He felt a sob through their embrace, "I know it's harder for you, I know you loved him." He said in a quiet voice, "we all did, but we both know it was you who was closest to him." He tried to comfort her further, stroking her lightly shaking back as she cried.

"It's silly, I know," she said, sniffing and pushing away from Jasper's hug. "I'm okay," she added, wiping her nose and eyes with the back of her hand, "it's just this trip, his gift to us. It's stirred up a lot. It doesn't help that it's all so strange. This bear too," she said gesturing down the hill, "it's too real, it's surreal, where's all this leading?"

He gently stroked her shoulder as she gathered herself.

"I don't want to kill it. Please, Jasper," she asked again, determinedly wiping away the remains of the tears with a tissue she had retrieved from her pocket.

Jasper sighed and nodded, "of course, okay. Come on, let's just go for a walk. This path seems to head to the stream. Why don't we see how close we can get to the bear before it starts to look fake," he suggested, gathering his things from the ground.

Felicity

Felicity was born in a small town in the Gloucestershire countryside. She grew up with little money and lots of friends. It was a simple life that gave her happiness and a zest for life, a longing for the world outside of her contained experiences in the enclosed rural area. Then, in her teens, she stopped growing when she reached the height of just under five feet tall. This, combined with her inquisitive nature, helped to define the woman she would become. If anyone asked her, she would say that she was a little girl; she was when she was young, she was as a teen. As she failed to grow over that five-foot barrier, she accepted that she would always be seen as a girl instead of a woman by those around her. It was not, however, something that she would accept about herself.

She arrived at university, having chosen one far away, determined to be independent; alone and in charge of her life. This was back when university was free to those who couldn't afford to pay, and she knew this was the only way she could ever have attended. Life was changing for students in nineteen ninety-five, tuition fees were being introduced and she had thankfully just missed them. She had one chance and she was not going to mess it up.

Her ex-boyfriend, Jasper, was at the same university but from day one it was clear that he had his own agenda and would not be there to provide much support. He was in a totally different faculty anyway, so she knew she wouldn't see him much at all. Despite her strength of resolve, she was also often shy and insecure. Those first few weeks proved to be the hardest of her life. She was so glad when an older student sat down next to her and started chatting during English class one day. From the moment she introduced herself with a smile, Felicity latched on to her; quickly identifying the potential for a new friend. This was Elizabeth and she had saved her. Elizabeth came along with a nice young man called Bertrand who hung around her, so in fact she quickly had two friends. She wasn't sure where Bertrand's ancestors were from, and she was too embarrassed to ask, but she was very excited to inform her mum on the phone that she had a new 'exotic' friend.

An even more interesting development came about one day in her psychology tutorial. She was sitting on her own and starting to regret choosing a dual-honours degree. If she had done single-honours English, then she would be attending a class with Elizabeth right now. Instead she was on her own in the corner planning how to avoid the tutor asking her any questions about statistics. Then, something wonderful happened. Lucas came and sat next to her. The girl he had been sitting next to, the tall thin one he had been chatting up, had left unexpectedly. Now he was here, sitting next to her.

Felicity swallowed her nervousness and introduced herself. Suddenly glad she had arrived early, she took the opportunity to talk to him, to find out things about him. Just as the supervisor arrived, she blurted out that she was going to a party that night and would he like to join her. She screwed up her eyes, annoyed that she had just ruined any chances she might have had, when he accepted. She was so overjoyed, she spent the rest of the lesson planning what she was going to wear, not listening to a single word the tutor said.

Felicity was excited as she walked through the open door to the party that night. Elizabeth was beside her, the two of them having met earlier to prepare for the party together. They had arranged to meet Bertrand there and she looked around the busy house for any sign of him. Felicity was wearing a short red dress and thick black tights. She had even put on makeup and perfume, planning to attract Lucas' attentions as best she could. She looked down, uncertain again if the red Doctor Martens had been the best choice of footwear. They might be trendy, but they didn't look very alluring, she thought for the twentieth time that night. Jasper was hosting the party in his corridor in halls and she saw him approach them with a drink in one hand and waving with the other. He wrapped the free hand around her slight frame and kissed her on the cheek. Instantly he was charming and welcoming, smiling and saying hello to Elizabeth as Felicity introduced them to each other. After a thirty second chat with him, he was gone; talking to more interesting people.

Then suddenly, he was there, Lucas was there.

She swallowed her nerves and pulled together enough courage to walk over to him. Just as she arrived however, Jasper reappeared from nowhere. She politely introduced them in response to Jasper's intense scrutiny and, annoyingly, Jasper was suddenly very interested and chatty. For some reason it seemed that Lucas was the most fascinating person in the world to him. Before she knew it, Jasper and Lucas were friends. Before she had any say in the matter, she was friends with Lucas by association. For many months following the party she would kick herself as she replayed that simple series of events in her mind. If only she had said something right then, if only she had invited Lucas out somewhere else. If only Jasper had minded his own business. There were so many variations of that night that Felicity dreamed of. However, they all ended the same; her lying awake in bed, lamenting the loss of her one opportunity to be with Lucas.

One night, months after that party, she was doing just that; lying in bed staring at the ceiling and thinking of Lucas. The thought of him still thrilled her. She imagined him lying with her, talking to her with his soft voice, maybe stroking her hair with a lazy finger. She loved the way he said her name; 'Felicity', she whispered it to herself. More commonly now he had started calling her 'Flick'. She loved that too. Their friends were copying him, and she found that she enjoyed the way it sounded. Before Lucas, people had called her 'Fliss'. She'd hated that, thinking it sounded like a bathroom cleaner. 'Flick' sounded decisive, urgent and dramatic. She enjoyed the image it conjured of her. She smiled at the thought of how Lucas said it. Often now, he had been extending her name to 'Flicker' and then 'Flickerish' when he was feeling playful. She loved that even more, especially that it was only him that did it.

She sighed and for the hundredth time told herself that this would not do. Fixating on him was not healthy; she was torturing herself with an idea that could not come true. Despite her numerous advances and flirtations, he had never responded, she reminded herself once more; she needed to accept that he wasn't interested. Better for her to move on, to look for someone else. She could never give up the relationship she had with him, and if she carried on like this, she knew she would have to. She rolled over, thinking about her English lit' essay that was due next month instead. That soon put her to sleep.

Gradually over the course of the first year of university, she adjusted to the reality of Lucas as just a friend. He was a good friend, her best friend, and that was a very good thing. He was funny, quirky, and interesting. On a practical level, he was also very useful; his aptitude for maths and computers came in handy as it was something that featured in psychology a lot more than she remembered at college. She helped him with his English, which was atrocious, and he with her statistics, which were not as bad as she led him to think. They, with their group of friends, had a lot of fun. She was happy. She was making it, she was a success.

Felicity knew that she was not unattractive; she never thought herself beautiful or even pretty, but boys did sometimes look at her and deep down she knew she wasn't 'hideous'. She would often look at herself in the mirror after taking a shower or a bath; her body perfectly proportioned, her skin toned and lean. Her hair naturally fell down to her shoulders in fashionably loose brown curls. She never liked her eyes, but people had told her that they were interesting. Elizabeth insisted that her grey eyes made her unique as they looked out at the world with an unrestrained curiosity. She was little, however. She could never get away from that. Along with this simple fact came a tendency for people to underestimate her, especially men. She knew that she should challenge these assumptions more often but deep down liked the anonymity it often gave her. She preferred to be left alone, special but hidden. However, being ignored also meant that boyfriends could be hard to come by. Only after a drink or two did she emerge from her shell, much to the surprise of the people around her.

One drink and the volume of her opinions went up. Two drinks and her boisterous nature took over; challenging people to competitions of all kinds. Three drinks and she started to touch and hug those closest to her, regardless of gender. People often thought that from there, things might get more interesting. Men certainly thought so as they bought her a fourth drink at university parties. However, from drink number four, things would take a downwards turn. Four drinks or more would mean confused speech, wobbly dancing and eventually vomiting and leaving for home. Four drinks would not a boyfriend find.

Felicity learned not to mind, however. She kissed a number of men at university parties, halfway through drink number three this seemed inevitable. These drunken kisses would lead to touching, some nudity, but never sex. She was there for a degree. Sure, she was going to have fun on the way, but that didn't include random sex with people at parties. She would have made an exception for Lucas of course. But Lucas never tried. Lucas was far too shy. She tried to flirt with him on numerous occasions, but it was as if he didn't notice. The problem with her and Lucas, she realised, was that their flirtation techniques were totally incompatible. She would say something provocative or touch him boisterously, and he would just make a joke of it, touching her back. She would laugh and that would be an end to it. They were destined to be friends forever, she knew.

Underneath the difficulties with her social life, she at least excelled in her studies, always being sure to remain on top of her work and hand in the best assignments she could. She received a lot of ridicule from her friends about this which she shrugged off with the knowledge that she was doing the right thing; they were the ones making life harder for themselves down the road by not paying attention. This is why she was at university, after all. This however, did earn her a certain reputation and her friends often teased her about being 'vanilla' and 'boring'. Jasper was the worst, always knowing how to press her buttons, often for his own amusement. One night, after a particularly cutting remark from Jasper, she decided she'd had enough and went to see the resident pothead Steve. Her annoyance spurring her on, she bought some of his 'merchandise' and headed home, the packet burning a hole in her pocket the whole way. She sat on the bus furtively looking around her, certain that everyone knew about her illegal stash and was judging her accordingly. Maybe she was vanilla after all, she thought.

As she eventually unlocked the door to their shared house and closed it behind her, she breathed a huge sigh of relief. The stress of worrying about being caught had completely dissipated her previous annoyance and desire for rebellion so she for the time being she pushed the little packet into a pair of socks and hid them at the back of her dresser drawer.

The cube of drugs sat in her dresser for more than a week, mocking her, confirming what everyone else already thought; that she was boring. Finally, she could take it no more; she bought a box of brownie mix and gathered the ingredients in the kitchen. Checking around her for witnesses, she crumbled the entire cube into the mix just before sliding the tray into the oven. They were delicious, she ate three straight from the oven and sat on the sofa waiting for the effect to kick in. As she sat there, Lucas came in and flicked to The Simpsons on the television. Asking if he could have a brownie, she of course said yes. Jasper too, then Julia, Elizabeth and Bertrand. Soon all of them were watching the television, gradually getting high on pot brownies.

This made Felicity very happy, not only was she taking drugs like a proper student, but she was secretly getting her friends high as well. They all fell asleep in front of the television that night, sprawled out on the cheap sofas. When they collectively eventually woke and retired to bed, none were any the wiser. Felicity never told any of them what she had put in the brownies, that was her secret and she delighted in it. She realised something else that night. She wasn't dull, she knew that, and for people to call her boring was not fair. She also didn't really want to take drugs. Even while she was high, it was the chocolate of the brownies she craved more than the secret contents. She might be sensible, thoughtful, perhaps predictable, but she knew who she was and felt satisfied with that. She told herself this simple fact in the mirror the very next morning and it felt good. No longer a little girl; for the first time, she felt like a woman. She felt in charge of her own destiny.

On completing her degree, she had built enough self-awareness and confidence to choose a career that her friends all thought dull. She decided to become an accountant. This meant yet more qualifications to get the training post then a part-time masters-degree to fast-track her new career. However, she had a plan now and knew it would be worth it in the end.

She diligently maintained contact with all in the group, Lucas and Jasper more so as they ended up living in the same city as her. She was still in love with the two friends, Jasper as she always would be, but Lucas still a little more. Being in the same city as them, going out with them, seeing them, gave her the grounding that good friends provide. She would frequently meet up with Elizabeth too, to chat about men, work, and life in general. She felt this satisfied her female friendship quota.

Eventually, Felicity met a man and got married. It was fine being married and she loved him very much. That didn't translate into a lifetime of happiness, however. After eleven mostly happy years, admitting to his having an affair, he divorced her. She thought she would be devastated but she wasn't. Instead she took to spending more time with Lucas. It was a surprise to her; she'd thought her feelings had diminished after such a long time. However, without the hindrance of a husband, the feelings quickly returned. Unable and unwilling to supress them any longer, she was pleasantly surprised to find that she still truly loved him.

Lucas had never married, never even really had a

serious girlfriend and Felicity secretly hoped that he felt the same for her as she did for him. Finally, after twenty years of friendship, she made her move. She downed two glasses of wine, swallowed her building anxiety and bluntly blurted out how she had felt at university.

Whilst she was still talking, he surprised her by reaching out to touch her leg. His caress, along with the wine, caused her heart to start pounding in her chest, and Felicity worried she was going to have a heart attack. Remembering the chance she never took all those years ago at university, she leaned forward and closed her eyes. After an interminably long pause, she finally felt his lips on hers. She responded, pressing hard towards him. They were kissing, she couldn't believe it. They made love that same night and it was everything she had dreamed it would be. His body was exactly as she knew it was, stronger and more manly than they had first met, yet still lean and toned. His touch was both firm and gentle. It was perfection.

They didn't leave each other's side for a month. She took a holiday from work and he simply paused his current project. They walked around the city, they visited museums and galleries, they just spent time together. They went to the cinema and out for food. She cooked for him and he for her while they watched television in his apartment. But then, one day, from nowhere, she got the phone call.

Lucas was dead; knocked down by a taxi. She

couldn't believe it. She numbly hung up the telephone on the low table. She turned to look out of the windows of his apartment at the city below her. He was out there somewhere. His body lying inert. The thought brought the tears to her eyes, then a quiet noise from her throat.

Felicity screamed, the emotion finally finding its voice. She fell to her knees with a bang and slumped forward, pressing her face against the glass. The tears ran as rivers now as she bawled her heart out. The effort of crying made her curl into a ball on the cold wooden floor. She clutched at her stomach as it spasmed with the tears. She cried until darkness set in, unable and unwilling to stop. Finally managing to gather herself enough to get to the phone, she called Jasper who came right over. He held her, crying himself. He carried her to the bedroom and together they curled up on Lucas' bed holding each other tightly as she cried herself to sleep in his familiar arms.

She carried on with her life, she had to. She told herself that she had lived without Lucas before, she could again. She worked, she sorted out his belongings with his mother, she visited Elizabeth to talk, and Jasper to play with his dogs. Life was not okay, she was not okay, but she carried on as if she were, hoping that eventually the pain would ease. Slowly, with each week that passed, the acute pain became more of a dull ache that she was occasionally able to ignore.

Nine months after his death, however, it all came back in an instant. Felicity received a letter from his last employer. It had amazed her that it was the famous Maximilian Wise but amazement aside, the tears and the grief came flooding back as she found herself reading his name once again. Lucas had never talked to her about what he was working on, only saying that it was a secret that wasn't his to tell. The letter brought back all the feelings she had been repressing. It was like a switch being flicked back on and it took another week in bed to bring her back to her life. As she did, however, she resolved again to try to carry on, to honour what Lucas would have wanted. Her first job was to make herself reply to the invitation to play the game that Lucas wanted them all to experience. She recruited Jasper's help and together they sent letters to all the friends, insisting that they come. She even replied for them collectively before they had a chance to respond, accepting the invitation. She knew they would come, they had no choice.

Tutorial Pt.2

Just north of the ridge that Jasper and Felicity had descended to try to stalk the blue bear, another pair from the group were having a different experience. Jessica and Randal had taken a lower, flatter path and had quickly identified another target upon leaving the shelter of the buildings. They were now crawling through the tall grass of a meadow in order to get closer to their chosen prey. They too had found and donned the augmented reality glasses and had used the information projected in front of their eyes to close in behind a furry blue beast. Their quarry was still, crouching behind a tree on the edge of the meadow they were crawling through.

Randal was an artist by training and in his heart, but he was also an avid gamer. He had recruited Jessica as the other American in the group to partner him in his hunt, together they wanted to represent team USA. She was to be the spotter, using the binoculars to search for and watch the prey. At the same time, it was her role to keep an eye out for any approaching danger. He had proposed himself as the sniper. Their goal was to approach the target to within two hundred metres and then to open fire. That was the advice in the guide Randal had found and they had elected to follow it to the letter. That was why they were sliding on their hands and knees through the soft waving grasses in the direction of their prey. Occasionally Jessica would rise and check that it was still in location.

"It's still there, just sitting behind the tree. I can see its arm though. It's so fat, it can't hide behind the skinny trunk."

She giggled as she dropped back down beside Randal. He smiled back to her, revealing rows of perfect teeth, seemingly lighting up his face as he lay on his back in the grass. From their contrasting appearances, one might think they were unlikely friends. He was over six feet tall, his skin was a uniform dark brown and his body thin and sinuous in its strength. She was only just over five feet tall, pale and spoke with a strong New Jersey accent. Had they gone to university in the States they would probably never have met but being the only two Americans in the group of friends at an English University had bonded them together permanently.

"We're going to blow that hairball away, Jess." He assured her, patting his rifle as he hugged it to him.

"You know, I never thought I'd like hunting, but this is kind of fun," she answered with a twinkle in her blue eyes. "Do you think we should get closer?" She asked, raising her head above the grass for another look.

"I don't know, what d'you think? You're the spotter." He deferred to her as she looked around, scanning the area with the binoculars.

"There's a fallen log a little ways to our right. We can set up behind that and you can rest the rifle over it.

Get a better shot."

He smiled back at her, collecting his things from their resting place. "Good idea, point the way ma'am."

She made an arrow with her flat hand, gesturing the direction in which they should move, "half a click, twenty degrees right," she stated with a wink as she started sliding forwards.

"What've I created?" Randal replied with a tut as he crawled after her.

Fifteen minutes later the two friends were propped up against the fallen trunk, hiding in the tall grass that continued to wave in the gentle summer breeze. Birds sung from their high perches where their target still hid; nature was seemingly oblivious to the violence that was about to occur. Randal had his rifle resting against the log, nestling between a deep crack in the thick bark. Jessica was resting on her elbows, supporting the binoculars as she stared at their target.

"What d'ya think?" She whispered to Randal.

"I could probably hit him, but only on the side. I can't see enough of him to get a body or head shot," he replied, shifting a little to the right to see if he could see more of the blue figure hiding behind the tree. "I don't think we should shoot unless we're sure of a kill," he stated, pulling back from the rifle sight.

Jessica remained glued to the binoculars, her dark hair draped over them as she pressed them to her eyes, making them almost look a part of her. She was as still as a statue as she intently studied the movements of the blue apparition. "It's so real," she muttered to no one in particular. Still not shifting from her position, she whispered another question to Randal. "Is there anything in the guide you found?"

He retrieved the laminated card from his back pocket and scanned the information again. "Not really, we're within the recommended range; there's a diagram on how to adjust the sight to take into account the wind, but I've done that. I guess we just wait for it to move."

"It hasn't yet though," Jessica muttered, before adding, "hold here, get ready to shoot. I've got an idea." Without waiting for a response, she climbed down from the log and moved away to the right, towards where the alien was looking. Randal hunkered back down to his rifle, resting his eye against the scope. He prepared to take the shot as he heard Jessica slide into the grass away from him.

She was making too much noise, he realised, as he could still hear her movements despite the increasing distance between them. He thought to tell her, to call out, but already she was too far away, and any warning would be even louder. Then, just as he was thinking about what he could do to warn her, their target moved from behind the tree. It had stepped from its cover to investigate the noise Jessica was making, and Randal realised that had been Jessica's plan all along.

A flurry of emotion ran through Randal's mind as he targeted the chest of the large blue apparition in his rifle scope. Excitement caused his breathing to speed up and his heartrate to climb. The scope bobbed, causing the sight of the blue beast to dance around before him. The anticipation had made his palms sweaty and the rifle shifted in his now slick grip. He swallowed his growing apprehension about taking the life of something so beautiful and concentrated on stilling the rifle in his hands. As he reminded himself for the hundredth time that it was a computer simulation of an animal, he calmed his breath, finally bringing the beast into the cross hairs. The scope stayed still, he held his breath and squeezed the trigger.

To Randal's amazement an explosion sounded from the end of the barrel of the gun as it forced itself back into his shoulder and up into the sky. He saw a lick of flame erupt from the tip to accompany the burning feeling he was now feeling in his arm from the force of the weapon. He hadn't expected it to be a real gun, a real bullet to leave the barrel, and hadn't been prepared for the recoil. He shouted a curse in his surprise and quickly stood up, looking towards his kill.

Randal

Randal's parents had worked hard in life to earn good jobs and had diligently saved for him to go to college. They had always provided him with everything he needed, and he knew how privileged he was. They weren't rich, he knew that. They didn't live in a massive house, but it wasn't small either. They never had a new car, but they had nice ones. When he asked for a Sega one Christmas, they bought him the Mega-Drive instead of the Master-System. They were middle-class, which for a black family in New Orleans at that time, was somehow not right. Randal didn't live up to the stereotypes he saw on the television, nor did his friends. They didn't steal cars and walk around with knives, instead they met in his friend Carl's basement and played Nintendo.

Randal and his friends just ignored the discrepancy, discounting it as they did many other things in life. They watched television and learned to be a part of Southern US Black Culture. They dressed in their heroes' basketball shirts and walked with swagger, listening to hip-hop and angry rap. His heart wasn't really in it though, nor were his friends'. They just liked to be cool, what teenager in high-school doesn't? So, he simply lived his life; just as it was handed to him.

As expected, he did get in to college, with a partial scholarship as it turned out, which his parents were delighted about. His friends teased him about the scholarship being for art instead of basketball but secretly they were pleased for him, they liked his paintings. To keep the costs down further, saving his parent's money as much as he could, he elected to attend the University of New Orleans. It was just fifty miles from where he lived, and he could help out at home and save on rent.

The day he started, he found that his ethnicity still mattered as much as it ever had. He studied with white people in the art department, there being little choice, but his proper friends were as they always had been. People in college had to mix more but still, somehow, they congregated into disparate groups, as if indoctrinated to do so. Only, as Randal started his studies, did something in him began to change; it started to bother him. Something inside, told him that it was wrong. No one was being outwardly racist but something kept people apart, the importance of difference was everywhere, reinforced by some built-in mechanism deep inside of them. Now he had noticed it, he saw that it was everywhere; he didn't like it.

His life had been filled by racism, a permanent cloud hiding things from him that other people could take for granted. Suddenly it angered and frustrated Randal that he had let it without him even really noticing. He had always let life wash over him. As he looked down to his hand, he clenched it into a fist, determined to never let that be the case again. He recruited two of his friends and drove the three of them to a bar just out of town. Sat in his pickup truck in the parking lot, it fit right in. They, however, did not. He had driven past this establishment probably hundreds of times on his way camping with his buddies. Its placement, however, so far from any houses, all but ensured that its patrons would be driving home drunk. Yet, as he scanned for the tenth time, there were no police. If this were in his neighbourhood, he thought with anger, there would be a riot van already here, filled to the brim with his handcuffed friends.

He forced open the driver's door with a painful metallic creak and stepped from his truck, his friends begrudgingly following suit. They had no plan beyond Randal's need to confront what he knew was inside, that was as far as his rebellion had led him. The second he pushed open the heavy door, he felt it. Eyes were on him, hundreds of pairs of them. Country music was blaring and there was the click of pool balls to his right. In a moment that could have been taken straight from a movie, a number of denim-clad men stopped playing and leant on their cues to look at the newcomers.

Unlike the television or the movies, however, the music didn't stop. There was no silence or expectation of violence. Two men simply stepped over to the three young men and pushed them outside. They shuffled backwards to prevent themselves falling over and stumbled away on the rough stones of the parking lot. Randal stood his ground as best he could, squaring off his wide shoulders against the man with a cowboy hat who was pushing him out. It didn't last long, a second later and

Randal was on his backside on the ground. He hadn't even seen the punch coming. Just feeling the pain in his jaw, the surprise did the rest. He sat there, holding his face, feeling the ache. Eventually he felt the hands of his friends under his arms, they were lifting him up and pulling him away. Quickly he was thrown into the passenger seat of his truck and Carl, his childhood friend, was spinning all four wheels in the gravel. Eventually he found the grip they needed, and they peeled out of the parking lot. Randal had found the hatred he knew lay underneath his life, and he was ashamed at how easily it had knocked him down.

Nine days later, having resisted hourly urges to return to the bar and burn it down, he found himself standing in front of the mirror that was recessed into the wardrobe door in his bedroom. He must have looked at himself in the same mirror a million times before, but now he was looking with different eyes. Looking at his body as it stood before him, he was thinking about the colour of his skin. He had recently enrolled in a class in European politics and as a result he had been finding himself thinking about the world outside of the States more and more. Race in America was a big deal. He knew this more than most, he thought, touching his jaw. Less than others, he admitted to himself, again looking around the belongings of his family. He was proud of them, he knew he owed them everything and had been working hard in school to make them proud in return.

But the fact remained that he felt that he had been defined by the colour of his skin his entire life. It was just something he, like his friends, had accepted. His family had taken a DNA test that had been advertised on the television a number of years back. He remembered how delighted they were to discover something about their lost history. How proud they were of their newly discovered Nigerian heritage. He remembered now, how surprised he had been that he hadn't cared in the slightest. His ancestors had gifted him his colour but beyond that he had no interest in Central Africa. Looking back to the mirror, he saw a strong, young, friendly American man. That is who he was, he was Randal; why couldn't other people see that? That and not all the preconceptions that came with his appearance.

This new class had started to open his eyes to a different world. It had made him wonder what it would be like to live in a world in which race wasn't the big deal he'd lived with his whole life. The class inspired him to inquire at the student advice centre about studying in Europe. They were delighted to inform him that not only was it possible, but with his grades it was almost a certainty. Staring at himself in the mirror again, he made his decision; his fate was set. The next day he applied for the foreign studies scholarship. As predicted, he won it and the very next year he found himself flying off to the city of Liverpool, England.

He was uncertain what English people would be

like, and before he had touched down, decided that it would be a good idea to get some support. He had never even been out of the state before and had taken the advice to retain some connection to home on his arrival. That's why he pre-joined a social group for students from abroad that the university had organised. This brought with it his first surprise. Not five minutes in to the welcome mixer in a drab room with grimy chairs scattered haphazardly around the edges, he saw her. As she came in, nervously glancing around the room, he knew instantly she was American. It was her bleach-blond hair and orange furry jacket; only someone from the US would dress like that. She said hello to the organiser at the door and his theory was confirmed as he heard that distinctive New Jersey accent. He caught her eye and soon was talking to the skinny little white girl from Newark.

Immediately he had to change his world belief as here there was an American who didn't seem to care that he was black. Of course, he had met and talked to white people before, most were nice to him and not overtly racist. However, he had always been able to detect an undercurrent of something. Some awkwardness about them, some filter between their minds and their mouths, guarding against speaking any possible offence. Jessica had no such filter, she just seemed to say whatever she was thinking. One of the first things she said to him was how scary he looked, his muscle-bound arms and big hands being easily able to strangle her little neck. She didn't even register that such a statement could be offensive. She just carried right on speaking about whatever she had been talking about. He liked her, he decided, as he smiled at whatever it was she was saying.

Jessica quickly introduced him to her housemates. He liked them too, they accepted him as a man, not a black man. Interestingly they were more interested in him as an American, which was a new kind of discrimination, he discovered. He liked that, however; to be discriminated against over something other than the colour of his skin amused him. He saw that they all did it. Jasper was treated a little differently because he was gay, the girls because of their gender. Lucas was teased about being a computer nerd and Julia because she slept around. Charlie wasn't overly picked on, but that seemed to be more because he didn't understand the nuance of the jokes, rather than there not being anything to tease him about.

Randal did stand out amongst the group, however. He was a distinctively handsome man from a foreign and fashionable place. Everything about him seemed to appeal to English university girls. They gravitated towards him in classes and clubs. They wrapped themselves around him on the dance floor, frequently suggesting they go somewhere quiet to talk.

As he made love to them, he found them unable to stop touching his body. Then, one night, he found himself in bed with a beautiful Irish girl with shockingly red hair and pale freckled skin; she was like nothing he had ever seen at home. Afterwards, he spent a long time looking down at their two bodies, her alabaster flesh pressed against his muscled mahogany. He was fascinated by the contrast of colours and the difference between her feminine curves and his own taut muscles. It delighted him, from then on he started to study the aesthetics of his body next to each of the women he slept with. They made for beautiful shapes and movements in the various beds in which he lay. This caused another change in him; he now knew what he would chose to be his major when he got back home. His scholarship had been for his art, but it wasn't a requirement that it would be his major. Now however, looking down at the latest body pressed against him, he knew he would be an artist. This didn't please his mom, he knew as he explained on the phone. But she didn't complain, she wanted what he wanted, and this was definitely what he wanted.

He joined an art club that held meetings on the campus to gain access to the materials and support he required. He was already good, but he wanted to be better. He decided to approach the decision like he did all aspects of his life; he sought out people who were better than him. His search wasn't difficult, Liverpool's art department had some prestigious members and close ties to the art community in the city and beyond. Women offered themselves to him for his studies too. Under their tutelage he started creating his vision of the artistic form; abstract paintings and sculptures of contrasting black and white curving shapes and patterns. He told his informal tutors that his goal was to create something as beautiful as two people making love. They loved it, as did the women he met and explained it to; it got him even more nights of inspiration.

With all this extra-curricular activity it would have been easy to let his academic studies slide. However, he had vowed to his parents to strive in his education. He dared not leave art as his only option in life, so he was a busy man. His time at the University at Liverpool made Randal who he was. Before he left, he actually started getting some commercial interest in his creations. The teacher that supervised the club even invited him to contribute some of his pieces to the end-of-year student show. He left England with experience, a dream to become an artist, and some money in his pocket. He had managed to sell many of his works to lovers of art, and lovers of him. They said that it was the most perfect souvenir of their time together. He didn't have the heart to tell them that they were each buying a representation of someone else.

After returning home and subsequently completing university, Randal graduated as an art major. He carried on creating abstract paintings and sculptures, some of which he did sell. However, his major breakthrough as an artist still eluded him. Instead, he found a job managing a local community centre. The job left him plenty of time to carry on creating the masterpiece he sought. He also found great satisfaction in teaching others in his community. That is where he met his wife, who was taking a course in accountancy to help manage her own business. They fell in love almost instantly and married two short years later in his family church. They found a home equidistant between their parents and quickly established their lives together. They slipped into their new middle-class lives with ease. Randal even created a small studio space in the garage, relegating their cars to the short concrete driveway.

Soon he was constructing a swing set on the patch of grass beside the two cars as their children came along and he watched as his wife replaced her runabout with a minivan. He doggedly retained his old pickup truck, maintaining that he needed it to fit his larger works in the back and for camping trips with the guys to the woods. They had three children in total, two boys and finally the girl his wife had always wanted. Together they were settled; their lives standard and comfortable. He worried about money, but everyone he knew did. They were saving hard for college, but three kids were expensive, and it was proving difficult. Randal started concentrating on his art each evening in response, resisting the PlayStation that sat beside the easel. He was working harder than ever, knowing that a commercial breakthrough could fix their finances in a single stroke.

He still corresponded with Felicity and Elizabeth in England and occasionally Jessica, who had moved to New York. It was with great sadness that he heard of Lucas' death and diligently flew to Bristol to attend his funeral. It was great to see his friends again but, in such circumstances, he found he couldn't enjoy the trip even a little. So when Felicity's letter arrived, inviting him to play a game with them in Canada, he leapt at the chance. On the plane to leave the country only for the third time in his life, he was as excited as he was when he had flown to England to study all those years previously. He looked out of the small window to his right, studying the clouds as they flowed beneath him. This was going to be great, he thought as he caught a glimpse of his smile reflected in the glass.

Tutorial Pt2.1

The explosion of the rifle was still echoing about the landscape when, from the corner of his eye, Randal saw Jessica pop up from the long grass and turn to look at him. She looked like a meerkat appearing to check for danger and he couldn't help smiling at the image.

"What the hell?" She shouted to him, her voice just penetrating the whistle in his ears that had mercifully started to fade.

He'd quickly recovered from his own surprise, so casually shrugged his shoulders in response, "it's a real gun!" He shouted back, rubbing his shoulder and placing the rifle against the log. "Did I get it?" He asked her as she started walking back to him.

She paused and raised her binoculars, scanning the tree where the alien had been. "Yuck," she stated, "I would say, yes." She added as she made her way back to him. Wondering what she was talking about, he collected his rifle and raised it to his eye to look at the aftermath of the kill. Through the scope he could see that a stain of blue fluid had been sprayed over the area, hair drifted in the air and lay scattered across the ground.

"Gruesome," he agreed with Jessica as she joined him behind the fallen tree. "Let's go and look," he said, gathering his things.

"Do we have to? It looks gross."

"Come on, it's just computer graphics. I want to see how it looks up close."

She reluctantly followed, gathering her own things from where she had left them behind the log.

As they arrived at the location of the kill, it was Randal who voiced the obvious. "It smells," was his simple statement.

"Yes." Jessica agreed, finally willing to admit it. She lowered her glasses to be confronted with what she already knew; that the remains of the beast remained visible through her un-augmented eyes. The viscera of the kill were scattered across a wide area. Blue fluid dripped from a number of trees and some of it had gathered and dripped to the ground where lumps and chunks of their kill rested. "What's going on, Randal?" She asked, her voice now breaking.

"Hold on, let's be sensible here, Jess." He reassured her, not really believing the calm he was trying to exert. "There has to be an explanation. It wasn't real, so this isn't either." He told himself more than her.

"I know that. But what's all this?" She gestured to the devastation. Suddenly, with a jump, she squealed and leapt away.

Randal slipped the rifle from his shoulder and

swept the area, fear now apparent in his brown eyes. "What? What?" He called to Jessica, stepping away from her.

"I stepped in something." She cried to him, trying to wipe her boot on a clump of grass outside of the kill area. Randal took a deep breath and placed his rifle back on his shoulder. He smiled at her, his disarming grin calming her.

"Come on, this is silly," he chastised both of them, "I know what happened."

"What, what happened?" She demanded of him, trying to wipe the last of the squishy fluid from her boot.

"That's why it didn't move far. There was obviously some kind of pyrotechnic effect here. Something primed to go off and blow this stuff around when we made our kill."

"Why?" She demanded. Finally satisfied that she had cleaned off the last of the offending material, she put her foot down with a stamp and turned to look up at a wide-smiling Randal.

"Realism." Randal stated, "it's like playing PlayStation, the better the graphics the more engaging it is. The real gun and the real blood makes it so much more realistic; the weapon, the alien, the aftermath. Everything involved in an actual hunt. That's why it exploded everywhere. A corpse wouldn't be as convincing, and messy to leave behind. I bet this stuff just washes away in the next rain. It's like paintball, the paint is a part of it, seeing your hit. This is just another part of the game."

"Well it's a part I could do without," she said, crinkling up her nose, "the smell too." She gestured around her, taking in the blue devastation. "Let's get out of here," she announced, quickly turning away from Randal and starting her march back towards the compound. "I need a shower."

Randal took one more look around him at the aftermath of death and dutifully caught up with her as they strode side-by-side back across the meadow they had taken so long to cross.

Elizabeth

Elizabeth was old. She wasn't really, she knew she wasn't, but she felt it. She wasn't quite forty yet, but as she started her first day of University, she felt about a hundred. As she toyed with her curly red hair, subtly died to hide the greys, she looked at the people around her. She was surrounded by boys and girls who were all about nineteen. Their still unformed bodies pressed into each other as they each struggled nervously to find their classes. Their anxious faces mimicked hers but with no wrinkles or shadows yet marring their soft features. She shook her head, trying to shake the feeling from her. She was here to learn, to grow, to study. So, forcing an expression of confidence she didn't really feel, she walked into her first tutorial.

She sat on her own, in the corner, unsure of what to do. Should she try to make friends, or just concentrate on her work? She didn't have the time to be as social as all these young people, she knew. Once her time in class was finished, she had to return home to her husband and children. Maybe friends were not on the cards for her belated university experience, she thought. Then, in direct contrast to her conclusion, someone sat next to her; a young man. Swallowing her uncertainty, she shook his hand, introducing herself. His name was Bertrand, he said nervously. This relaxed Elizabeth immensely; they were all as scared as she was, maybe more so. They would at least need company while in class, this boy certainly did as she watched him fidget in his chair next to hers.

With that realisation, there was no stopping Elizabeth. She quickly befriended Bertrand and, in a later tutorial, made friends with Felicity just by sitting next to her and introducing herself. Through her, she met more fellow students, each time adding to the list of people she called friends. She made a lot of friends beside this group, but this was where she returned most frequently. They asked her to clubs and parties, of which she attended as many as she could. Felicity and she would meet for coffee during breaks in their schedules and chat. Quickly they became more than just friends. They were best friends, the age difference quickly fading to nothing. That wasn't quite true, they did make jokes about her being the mum, or remembering the war, things like that. She never minded, though, it was all in good humour and showed that they accepted her as one of them, they doing it to everyone.

Just after completing her first semester she found herself sat at home at the dining table, missing her friends, missing her studies. She could hear her husband in the next room, talking to her son. She was a good mother and she was a good wife. Now it was her time though, she told herself again. She would get her degree in English, then a job, then a new life. Not apart from her family, whom she loved with all her heart, but with them. They had lives; her son and daughter were leaving for university soon and her husband had a good job in insurance. It was her she worried about, what did she have? So many times, she had asked herself this question and she smiled now she had an answer; she had both friends and a future.

University was a new lease of life for Elizabeth. She suddenly had access to things she had only seen before on television. She went to parties and clubs, she got drunk and danced the night away. She studied hard and got excellent grades. She even went for coffee and talked about politics and the environment. One night, in a genuine university experience, things even went too far. She had been out with the group, drinking and dancing at the student union. The final song of the night was playing, and she had been watching Jasper dance to the traditional rendition of Abba while she stood queueing for their coats. Lucas had joined her to help carry the expected pile of thick winter wear when she spotted Bertrand move across the dance floor. He was making his way to a girl with a mop of blonde hair. She watched with fascination as they quickly started to dance. They wrapped themselves around each other, pressing their bodies close as they moved to the music. The sight of her friend becoming so connected to a girl he didn't even know awakened something in her and she quickly looked away, embarrassed. The drink was lowering her barriers and she felt something swim around inside of her. Searching her feelings, she was annoyed to find that she was jealous.

She stepped forward in the queue to collect the coats for the handful of tickets she was grasping. Annoyed for the first time at her role of coat collector, feeling very much like the mother of the group, she weekly smiled at Lucas who gathered the majority of the pile in his helpful arms. Soon they were bouncing around on the bus, heading to their home, where she had left her car. They were missing Bertrand, who had disappeared with his new friend, but they weren't worried. Mercifully the hot swaying bus arrived at their stop before it had made her feel too sick and she soon found herself comfortably sat in their living room. They all had a drink in their hands and were talking expressively about nothing and everything. Eventually as the evening wore on, they each went off to their rooms, leaving only Lucas and Elizabeth in the living room. He moved from where he had been sitting opposite and sat down heavily beside her with a can in his hand.

Lucas asked if she wanted to stay over, it being so late and she not being able to drive, gesturing to her empty wine glass. She slowly turned to face him, to accept the offer of the sofa. However, in doing so, she found her face directly facing his, not an inch between them. In a second, their lips were together, her hands around his thin body and his around hers. She slipped her fingers under his shirt to feel the smooth youthful skin beneath. Her other hand was between his legs, feeling him. They pivoted on the sofa and she fell on top of him, both writhing in a passionate exploration of each other's bodies.

Their tops were cast aside, his trousers undone and pushed down. Her skirt was pulled up and her underwear stretched to one side. He said her name. She whispered his as she reached down to him, squeezing him in her hand. He said her name again, this time placing his hands on her shoulders, pushing her upright. The movement forced herself back to reality and she stopped stroking him, releasing him from her hand. Elizabeth pulled her skirt down as he looked deeply into her eyes. He said without an ounce of dishonesty in his clear blue eyes that he thought she was beautiful. She blushed and looked away. It made her feel warm and rich inside. She nodded while unnecessarily saying that it wasn't right to do what they were doing. He smiled, agreeing as she lay back down, placing her head on his bare hairless chest.

Lucas and Elizabeth stayed on the sofa, wrapped in their dishevelled embrace most of the night. She woke well before dawn, before the rest of the house had stirred, and let herself out. She drove home with a smile on her face and a flutter in her heart. She was beautiful, she thought. She was amazing, she knew. She was also faithful. She was the woman she always knew she could be as she drove home alone in the dawning of a new day.

She never told anyone about that night. Lucas never talked of it and the only person she could ever tell anyway was Felicity. Elizabeth was not blind, however; she saw how Felicity looked at Lucas. She could never hurt her friend that way. It remained her secret, a delightful memory of a wild night out. Occasionally when the group were talking about sex or some other topic involving nudity, she would glance to Lucas. Together they would share a knowing smile, a little secret between them that always thrilled her.

Elizabeth completed her degree with a first in English Literature and started the career she always wanted by working in the same university at which she had studied. She remained with her family and made new friends as well as maintaining those she had made while a student. She watched as her family grew with a prospective daughter and son in law and settled into her sixties. But she never forgot her time at university and all that it had meant to her. Over the years her contact with the group inevitably became more sporadic and continued through letters only. Felicity was diligent about her correspondence, but it was Bertrand that Elizabeth wrote the most. For some reason they regularly wrote to each other and occasionally talked on the phone or computer. Over the intervening years, she found that, through this, her friendship with him eventually grew deeper than it had been at university. They hadn't physically met since graduation but through their regular correspondence, she felt that she knew him better than the others and he was now the one from the group to whom she felt the closest.

Elizabeth had been thinking more and more of Bertrand since his accident and wanted nothing more than to visit him despite his insistence that she shouldn't. So, when a letter arrived from Felicity inviting her to Canada for a reunion she didn't hesitate for a second. Booking her ticket the very next day she looked forward to seeing them all again. With the plan forming in her mind, the thought of seeing Bertrand in person making her smile, a pang of pain suddenly pierced her heart. Thinking about Bertrand had caused her to realise that Lucas would not be attending. The memory of them together twenty years ago flooded her mind once more, causing her pain to change to a sad smile at the recollection. She would attend to see Bertrand and her friends, but also to remember Lucas. She resolutely shook the sadness from her, clicking the accept button on the airline's website. She thought that her trip would be another new start for the next phase of her life; she was looking forward to it.

Tutorial Pt.3

Elizabeth and Bertrand had left the rifles behind in the main building and instead struck off down a flat path that wound its way through a valley to the south. Bertrand had been unsure of the capabilities of his new robotic legs and didn't want to risk carrying too much and Elizabeth just didn't want to carry anything so heavy. Accepting that they had little choice but to play the game, they instead wore holsters at their hips. Each contained a black pistol secured under a small strap. The smaller guns banged lightly on their hips as they walked, reminding them of their presence.

"Who wants to crawl around with heavy rifles on such a lovely day?" She rhetorically asked Bertrand as they strolled down the gravel path. At over six feet tall, with shockingly bright red hair, Elizabeth cut an imposing figure over anyone who met her. Just into her sixties now, she had lost none of the strength and energy she had always exuded. Her long legs strode purposefully across the flat ground as she chatted easily to Bertrand in her clear, dominating tone. Although she was still fit and active she had never been keen on walking and Bertrand fully understood why she did not want to carry the heavy weapons and backpacks they had been given.

"It's much better that we can move lightly," she said to anyone within earshot, "we're faster this way and can enjoy the countryside while they crawl around in the dirt."

Bertrand agreed with her, hopping over a small root. "These legs are amazing," he stated again as he strode down the path beside a smiling Elizabeth.

"They are a wonder. It's a beautiful gift," she agreed, placing her arm around him and pulling him to her. She shook him lightly before adding, "it's so nice to see you smiling again, Bertie."

He simply smiled back to her, accepting the affection with a nod. Together they walked on, accompanied only by the crunching of gravel underfoot and the unusual sounds of his robot legs flexing and stretching as they carried him down the path.

They had each discovered the augmented goggles in their bags and were currently using them to chase down the closest red dot on the moving map as they quickly navigated the flat trail. Soon they were rewarded with the sight of a blue bear-like creature standing proudly on the path as they rounded the corner. They froze. Unlike the other's encounters, this creature had clearly seen and heard them approaching. As they saw it, it saw them. Its fur stood on end and it rose high on its powerful hind legs. The sight was both imposing and terrifying as a deep rumble emanated from its open jaws. The noise continued to grow to a full-throated roar and it bared its pointed teeth menacingly. Elizabeth didn't hesitate, she instantly turned and ran. Her tall figure flew past Bertrand as he stood rooted to the spot. Her flowing red hair whipped him in the face as she passed him in a screaming sprint. The light flick on his face woke him from his fear-induced inaction and he raised his gun to point at the charging beast now bearing down upon him.

With a concussive boom, he pulled the trigger. The noise and action of the weapon drowned out the blood-curdling roar from the charging monster as Bertrand added to the cacophony with a single elongated curse. Bertrand screwed his eyes shut and continued to bellow from somewhere deep inside his stomach. He wanted to fire again but couldn't relax his clenched fist enough to release the trigger. There was no need however, the single discharge of the hand-gun had been quickly followed by a deep hollow pop as the charging beast was reduced to a cloud of blue fur and fluid. Bertrand finally stopped bellowing and opened his eyes to witness the expanding puff of detritus spread out across the path before him. Without turning away, he yelled to Elizabeth to stop, to return to him.

"It's okay Liz, I killed it!" He called out behind him, finally turning to direct the sound over his shoulder. It had only been a few seconds, so she hadn't gone far and she could clearly hear the calm confidence in his voice. Cautiously she stopped to look back, witnessing the eventual collapse of the cloud that had once been the blue beast. Slowly, nervously, she returned to where Bertrand was gingerly inspecting the remains of his kill.

"Bertie, what was that?" She asked, trying to calm her breathing and suppress the anxiety in her trembling voice.

"I guess it was the game," he whispered back to her, his voice also breathless despite him not having run anywhere.

"No. I mean, what was that?" She insisted. But he said nothing. He just shook his head as he crouched down to inspect the blue substance on the ground.

"Some kind of trick? Special effects? I don't know." He muttered as Elizabeth stood behind him, her pale green eyes nervously scanning the area.

She had moved closer to him as he crouched, and they were touching now, her soft thighs pressing against his spine. Then, with a strange stretching sound, he rose, his robotic legs lifting him effortlessly. With a clicking noise, the plastic of his prosthetics re-arranged themselves, giving him a little more height than before.

"Hey, so this is what it's like up here." He joked, bringing his eyes in line with Elizabeth's. They were close now and she was still panting from her fear and exertion. He too was breathless from the excitement of the attack. Their breath mingled in the space between them as their eyes stared into each other's.

Their proximity and pounding hearts said something more than their words ever had. Elizabeth closed her eyes as Bertrand craned forward and pressed his lips to hers. Their lips touched but did not part, instead they moved their heads to one side and pressed their smooth cheeks together. Their arms raised, and they wrapped each other in a tight hug. Elizabeth pulled Bertrand close to her, whispering in his ear.

"Oh, Bertrand. I love you…"

He stood back, dumbfounded. He couldn't believe it, after all this time, all the years of yearning and heartache. Finally, she had uttered the words he had always dreamed of. He pulled her toward him, as tight as he could. "I love you, I love you, I love you too…"

They remained wrapped in each other's arms for a long time, their hearts eventually calming as they allowed the hug to say all that needed to be said. Finally, the time seemed right and they reluctantly detached from each other. Bertrand's robotic legs once more lowered him to his natural height. Elizabeth silently reached out and took his hand. Together they walked with shaking bodies away from the blue remains of what they had ended together.

"I don't like this," said Elizabeth eventually. They had left the mess far behind and the woods felt very different on their return journey. Where there had been light, there was now shade and hiding places. The birds had departed too, leaving nothing but silence all around. At the start the woods had seemed welcoming and beautiful, now the same trees were dark and foreboding. She shivered at the change, quickly checking around them for danger yet again.

"Nor do I." Bertrand agreed, looking back over his shoulder. He shuddered, sending a quake through his back and down the plastic tubing of his new legs. Rattling against each other, they made a strange new frightening sound. They quickened their pace, feeling the pull of the safety of the buildings they knew lay ahead.

Julia

Julia had a strict upbringing. She knew her life was a cliché, but the truth often is. Her mother was a nurse, her father ran a local garage. She was frequently disappointed that hers wasn't the classic American story of a strict catholic upbringing and a convent school, but the truth was just as restrictive. She grew up in a little town on the outskirts of Derby, a mass of housing estates, landscaped parks and small clusters of shops. There were boys at school, but she thought them all boring. They were all well behaved little mummy's boys, as far as she was concerned. She would kiss them in the playground and tell her friends all about it, but that was as far as it ever went.

When Julia informed her mother that she intended to go to university in Liverpool, she was not pleased. She had always intended her little girl to attend university, that was true, but a local one, where she could keep an eye on her. The hundred miles, a two-hour drive between them, seemed an unwise gap. This, of course, was Julia's intention. She wanted space from her friends and family. She fully intended to cut loose at university, to 'go wild' as the Americans she so admired on the television would say.

The day she arrived, she started her new life by changing her hair. Her style for years, dictated to by her mother, had been a straight cut, most commonly contained in a tight pony-tail. She thought about cutting it all off, but she wasn't that brave, or stupid. Instead she went to the student union hairdressing school and let them decide. The student there was learning how to do a perm so that is what she got. Looking in the mirror afterwards, she decided that she liked it. Not the hairstyle, she couldn't have cared less what it looked like really. She liked that it made her look different, like someone else. She pressed the tight blond curls with the palm of her hand and smiled; already things were changing.

She smiled widely as her door shook from someone knocking loudly. She had arranged to go to the town centre with the girl who lived next door to her in the student halls, skipping their tutorials. There they bought entire wardrobes full of trendy new clothes with most of their first semester's grant money; something the old Julia would never have been allowed to do.

Her life truly changed at the Fresher's Ball, however. It was a big party at the student union, a flimsy excuse for loud music and copious drinking on a Monday night. She slept with a man that very first night. He was dancing close to her; she let him. She let him touch her body on the dance floor. She simply followed him when he suggested they go to his room. She lay there as he did his thing on her. That is how her first year passed her by. Drinking, sex, parties and shopping. Her mother kept sending her money, confused as to how she was spending it so quickly but still dutifully clothing and feeding her daughter. The first year, she discovered, was simple. None of the grades counted towards the final class of the degree so she only had to pass each one. They were also multiple-choice exams for the most part and her previous studies in French at college and subsequent family holidays were seeing her through nicely.

Her neighbour became her best friend. She and Corrine were very alike. She too hadn't had much experience before coming to Liverpool and she was taking the opportunity to live it up. Their favourite pastime became to sleep with the same men and pass judgement over them. They started keeping notes, making a book of their conquests. It was fun, their little secret to gossip over as they sat on one another's beds each evening. One night, over a glass of cheap white wine and a detailed description of her latest conquest, Julia revealed something new. She pulled out a Polaroid of him, standing naked in her room. Corrine laughed hard, snorting wine from her nose. They both thought it hilarious as they pasted the image into the book along with his description and 2-star rating in bed.

Life progressed in a flurry of laughter and parties. Julia and Corrine were having a great time, finding that the game compounded their fun. They were the girls in charge and they were loving it. They owned their world and, for Julia in particular, the freedom was intoxicating. Her mother would have warned her; she would have said that she was heading for disaster, which Julia would have ignored. The inevitable backlash came as Corrine decided to seduce Julia's last conquest; it was far worse than even Julia's mother might have predicted.

Julia didn't mind at all that Corrine wanted to sleep with Jake, she had no need for him anymore and she knew that it wouldn't have taken much to get him back to her bedroom. Julia winked at Corrine as they went through the door together, hearing it click shut behind them. Somewhat disappointingly, she hadn't found anyone that night, so instead she lay in her bed listening to Corrine beyond the thin partition wall. She could make out the tell-tale squeaking of the bed and the following silence; so far, he seemed to be performing as he had with her, not very well. She closed her eyes and pictured them together. She would be making him pose now, for the photograph. He hadn't been a great lover, but he had a nice body, she remembered.

Slowly the familiar feeling started to build in her and she shifted in bed to try to get more comfortable. There was still no noise from next door and she smiled, anticipating that Corrine's judgement of his performance would match her own scathing review. The image in her mind changed, becoming an amalgam of men, and countless nights in the bed she was lying in now. She let the pleasure come, wondering, not for the first time, if she would ever find a man who could approach giving her what she could achieve on her own.

She had just dropped off to sleep when there was

an almighty bang against her wall. The noise was only part of it. The impact had shaken her room, violently rocking the bed on which she slept. The surprise had woken her with a start; confused and afraid she let out a short yelp. Still groggy from sleep, she was uncertain of the cause of the noise until it occurred again. Something was being smashed up against the wall she shared with Corrine. Suddenly awake, she leapt from bed and ran out into the corridor. Another huge bang came from Corrine's room and she heard a scream from within. Corrine was screaming out for help. Julia started hammering on the door, demanding that she open it. As nothing happened to the stubbornly heavy door, she turned and cried for someone to help just as the rest of the corridor emerged from their rooms.

While she was pleading to another girl who lived in their hall to run to get help, the door she was still banging on was wrenched open. There was Jake, the man, standing before her. Their book was in his hand, open on 'his' page. A look of fury was pasted across his face. He bellowed at her and simultaneously slapped her across the cheek. The strike was hard, it twisted her head to the side and a line of spittle flew from her still open mouth. Before she could bring her hand up to comfort the impacted cheek, the burn came; setting fire to her face, bringing tears to her eyes in a vain attempt to extinguish the heat.

From the corner of her eye, she saw him advance

on her and the pain mercifully receded as fear and adrenaline overwhelmed the heat searing across her face. He pushed her against the wall with his hand across her throat. There he held her, squeezing her, choking her. Her view of his red face, a rictus of anger, started to close in. The edges first became fuzzy, then grey and finally black. Spots of colour flashed across her failing vision as she struggled to take a breath. She stared helplessly ahead, seeing nothing but a diminishing view of his eyes. She saw nothing but rage in his pin-prick irises as she continued clawing uselessly at his hands around her throat.

Finally, just in time, help arrived. One of the girls on the corridor above had been spending the night with her boyfriend Dave. They too had heard the commotion and come to investigate. Jake, with his hands still on Julia's throat, was finally pulled away as Dave added his efforts to the two girls already tugging on his arms. Julia grasped at her freed neck, pulling in deep breaths as she bent over double and winced from the pain. Dave, whom she had met a couple of times before, had shoved Jake down the hallway and was shouting at him to leave. It was a terrifying noise; Dave had a quiet voice normally and the trembling boom of his commands just added to the terror that was coursing through Julia. The girls on the corridor were joining in now and throat-tearing screams echoed down the narrow corridor. Another girl, standing in her open doorway, started hitting him ineffectively on the back with her open hand.

Finally, Jake got the message and ran, shouting obscenities as he scuttled away, crouching low to avoid the blows of her friends. Dave finally turned to face Julia on the floor, both shaking from the adrenaline. He gently helped her to her feet, asking if she was alright with a soft broken voice. With his strong arm supporting her, she staggered back towards Corrine's room. Jake gone, her terror had now found another source. Images of what he had done to Corrine flashed through her mind. As she crossed through the open door, she took a single immense calming breath as she saw that she was at least moving. Corrine was curled up in the corner of her room, crying. Blood was pouring from her nose and her face was already red and swollen from where Jake had hit her. Julia ran to her, wrapping her in a hug as she too started crying.

Jake was expelled with barely an investigation. Corrine left university that morning and never returned. Julia herself was subtly ostracised by her friends on the corridor. They had seen the book and heard Jake's complaints. While not condoning his reaction they also seemed to blame Julia for the events of that night. The story got around university within hours; men no longer wanted to be with her and girls kept their distance. She was alone. To fill her time, instead of partying, she had little choice but to attend to her studies. Going to class, listening, learning and doing the extra assignments was the only thing she could find to occupy her mind. She wanted to put that terrifying night behind her, but it was difficult. Every time she closed her eyes, she either saw the rage-fuelled eyes of Jake or the terrified Corrine curled up in the corner of her room. Julia's intensified focus on studying distracted her but fundamentally did not help her emotional well-being. What it did do was to teach her that she did not enjoy French. She was bored, she was alone. There was no way, however, that she was going home.

She spent the summer back with her parents and that just underlined her determination to carry on with her studies. Without any friends to share a house with in the second year, she applied for a room in senior halls instead. Given her traumatic experience in the first year, her application was quickly approved. Therefore, as she moved into her new home, she decided once more to start again. In a second reinvention of herself, she changed from French to Political Science. Her experience with Jake and men had made her think that maybe she had something to say. She didn't know what she had to say, but she felt that studying politics might help her find her voice.

Her second year, which was a redo of her first, started the same but differently. She liked men, she wasn't going to let last year put her off that. But this time she would be more careful about her partners. It had been obvious from the start that Jake was not nice, and she had only gone with him to add to the book. This year, from now on, she would date. It was a subtle change but one that was far better for her soul and her social life. She would still party, get off with guys, but only once she knew them would she go further. Her plan was sound and the change from looking for sex to searching for a boyfriend was profound. However, no matter how much she tried, she couldn't commit to any one in particular. They each seemed to become boring to her after a month or two; they were nice enough but there was nothing there, nothing to spark the flame inside her. Still, she didn't relent, and never again did she repeat her one-night-stands of the previous year.

She kept the perm, it defined who she was now as a confident, powerful woman. She was still rather alone but at least now she was in charge of her life and enjoying her studies. Her life finally changed for the better, however, when Bertrand came up to her one night. He was different, he seemed calm and gentle from the outset. Their kiss was strong, he pressed his lips to hers and she felt that familiar old feeling. She had been drinking on her own, wallowing in her loneliness and the intimate contact broke down her resistance. She took him home without either of them barely saying a word; she hadn't planned it but soon they were naked.

Bertrand said very little, not pressing for sex in any way. Julia was still feeling so alone that she felt an insatiable need for some connection. He was perfect, quickly providing the intimacy she so desperately needed. However, it wasn't Bertrand who changed her; he turned out to be just another dalliance, a kiss on the dancefloor going too far just as it had so often the previous year. It was his friend, who he introduced the next day, who saved Julia. Elizabeth changed her life the moment they first shook hands. She was a woman: older, more secure, confident and proud. Julia immediately latched on to her as an older sister figure and they quickly became friends. After a whole year without any friends outside the casual acquaintances from her course, she suddenly had a best friend. She told her everything, getting to know her friends too. She finally had girls to talk to, to confide in. As she did, she eventually relaxed into who she really was.

She had already joined a political discussion group and soon, along with her new-found confidence, she found her voice. She became passionate about women's rights. She saw herself railing against the men who controlled the world, righting the wrongs they were still perpetrating after almost seventy years of suffrage.

Eventually, as she studied and learned, experienced and lived, Julia started to define herself as a lone person, a woman apart. Her friends supported her and defined who she was in a social context. Her sexual experiences had taught her to love and cemented a desire to express that love only with another who loved her back. Her studies had formed her political beliefs along with a desire to make a difference for herself and all the women of the world. She had found a stable life in this place, upon which she was excited to build a future.

In the years following university, Julia strove to become the person she wanted to be. She worked for a while for her father, managing his garage as it grew to become the premier car dealership in Derby. All the time she worked, however, she campaigned and developed her political career. She climbed the ladder of candidates in the local Liberal Democrat party until, at the age of thirty-five, she became a member of parliament. She beamed with pride as she was officially photographed for the parliament records, delighted that she had achieved her life's goal at such a young age. It did not end there, however; in four years she won the election again. This time she was named as 'Spokesperson for Women', a prestigious post she had fought hard to get.

She was sat in her opulent office in London when she received the letter from Felicity. She had seen her friends just a few months previously at Lucas' funeral and was surprised to get a letter from her so soon. Seeing that it was an invitation to a reunion in Canada, she immediately rejected the idea; she was far too busy. However, fate interceded as she looked at her desk calendar. She saw that the event would coincide exactly with a week-long break in Parliament. Remembering how the last reunion had been so sad, she realised that a second reunion in different circumstances would be much nicer. She told herself that it would be good to take a break, recharge her batteries for the upcoming debates that were scheduled to take place after the trip. Mind made up, she instructed her secretary to accept the invitation and make the travel arrangements.

Tutorial Pt.4

On a parallel rocky path below Elizabeth and Bertrand, Julia and Charlie were approaching their own red dot as they strolled down a narrow gully. The gap had been carved over millennia by a small stream that was practically dry now. Looking up the high cliffs either side of them, it was hard to imagine just how a benevolent trickle of water had performed such an impressive feat. They stepped over the stream as the path crossed it again at a cluster of rocks and Julia shook her head at the beauty of her surroundings. Julia was a typical English country girl, but her wonder of nature hadn't diminished over the years, in fact her appreciation had only grown as her knowledge of its mechanisms had increased. She was five-foot five with a set of blond curls that made her another two inches taller. Fair complexion and a face full of freckles were accompanied by a permanent smile. She was an organiser, she dragged people forward into adventure whether they liked it or not.

She was explaining how the gully would have been formed over thousands of years as the ice sheets had receded at the end of the last Ice Age as she dragged Charlie along down the path now. She was soon lecturing him on the patience of nature as she led the way for the reluctant participant. Charlie was as tall as Julia but had almost the opposite personality. He was a quiet, reserved, softly spoken man originally from Malaysia. His real name, he refused to give or go by. To the group he was always, and always would be, Charlie. He pushed back the long fringe of slick black hair that had fallen in front of his eyes as it always did and increased the pace to catch up with his partner.

Unknown to them, however, they were about to face a far more serious danger than the others. They saw it as they rounded a slight bend in the path. It stopped them dead as their minds registered the threat before them.

"Charlie." Julia whispered urgently.

"Be quiet, Julia," he hissed, his first words since leaving the main building, "I don't know if it has heard us yet." Charlie roughly grabbed her arm, their roles changing in an instant. As if in response to their question, the bear turned to face them with a slow swivel of its great head.

"Shit!" Exclaimed Julia as the bear slowly followed the movement of its head by turning its whole body to face them. "What are we supposed to do again?"

"I cannot remember," Charlie stuttered back in a high-pitched voice. His previous confidence had crumbled in the instant the bear had turned to face them and his Malaysian accent returned with the fear.

"Is it run or stand?" Julia asked, forcing her panic down and trying to analyse the situation. "Is it a grizzly or a brown bear?" She asked him.

"I don't know, do I?" He snapped back.

She ignored his tone, looking back to the bear which was now studying them. "Grizzlies are larger. Is that large?" She asked, pointing to the massive brown animal, now sniffing the air. Its eyes looked directly at them as they stood huddled together. With a slow, deliberate movement, the bear slowly lifted its massive head to draw in huge pulls of the air through its flaring nostrils. In doing so it made a loud snorting noise, startling the pair into jumping backwards.

"What's it doing?" Was Charlie's rhetorical question.

"How should I know?" Snapped back Julia in retaliation to his previous shortness with her.

Seemingly in answer to their questions the bear dropped back down and slowly started moving towards them, barking as it did so. Its head swayed from side to side in time with its massive shoulders. The rhythmic undulations drove the beast forward with purposeful power. It approached them confidently, no fear in its dark brown eyes. With a slow deliberate movement Charlie raised his gun to meet the oncoming animal.

"No, Charlie." Julia implored him, placing her hand on his arm and pushing it down a fraction.

"It is either us or him, Julia." He said, his accent still prominent, revealing the fear beneath his actions. He ignored her hand on his arm, releasing the safety on the weapon with his thumb. The switch on the handle of the pistol clicked softly, revealing a small red dot on the side. He tilted the weapon to the side to check its position, just as the video they had watched had instructed him to.

"Let's run. Let's just run away." She softly begged him as he steadied his arm.

"We cannot outrun a bear, Julia." He stated calmly. Remembering that he had yet to place a round in the chamber, he reached forward and pulled back the slide on the top of the pistol. Unlike the television, it was a subtle, hollow metallic noise. The understated movement and sound belied the deadly payload the barrel now contained. Julia closed her eyes and turned away as Charlie straightened his arm again and tightened his finger on the trigger. Placing her fingers in her ears, screwing her eyes tight, she tensed herself. Charlie instinctively closed his own eyes and squeezed the mechanism.

Click.

There was nothing. The expected boom of the gun, the expulsion of the bullet from the barrel and the casing from the ejection port did not happen. Charlie tried again, pulling the trigger again and again but the gun did nothing. It just made a gentle clicking noise in the peaceful woods as the bear casually walked towards them, making guttural noises. Julia's eyes were wide now, staring at Charlie who was, in turn, staring at the bear.

"Run," she whispered to him. He needed no more encouragement then that and they turned together to run back up the path from where they had come.

The massive brown beast willingly took this cue to chase and instantly broke into a run itself. Sorting out its limbs took longer than the fleeing people but soon it was gaining on them, barking as it ran them down. Charlie looked back to see the teeth of the beast shining in the sun as it closed to within less than two metres behind them. With no way to halt the imminent the arrival of his death, he screamed. Turning back to look in front of him, desperately trying to increase his pace, he saw Elizabeth and Bertrand standing before them, confusion on their faces.

"Run!" Cried Charlie as he increased his run into a full-on sprint, quickly overtaking a fleeing Julia. But they simply stood there, waiting for them to arrive. The two pairs of people clashed as Elizabeth and Bertrand caught them with open arms, halting their flight. The bear had slowed with Charlie's cries and the arrival of two more of the group. Now, as four people stood abreast across the path, it slowed even more, eventually coming to a halt.

Bertrand advanced on the wavering bear with his arms outstretched. He extended his robotic legs as straight as they could go, making himself taller and more imposing. At the same time, he started to bark and yell at the animal. "Go! Back! Leave! Go!"

Elizabeth remained at his side as he shouted at the beast. It swayed its head back and forth again, snorting in great pulls of air, trying to determine what this shouting figure before it was. Seeing the effect it was having, Elizabeth joined in. Her tall figure combined with that of Bertrand as she spread her coat wide, forming a large mass of colour before the increasingly confused beast. Gathering their wits, seeing that their strategy was working, Julia and Charlie also eventually joined in beside their friends, shouting and clapping their hands.

The bear didn't like the noise, just as it didn't like the size of the creatures facing it down. It started to back away. Then, making the final decision, it darted to the right. Into the thick trees to the side of the path, it disappeared with nothing more than a soft brush of the undergrowth. The group of friends collectively breathed a huge sigh of relief and started to back away from area the bear had disappeared into.

"That was a close one." Stated Julia as they finally turned to briskly walk back to the compound, seemingly having put enough distance between themselves and the bear. "How did you know we needed you?" She breathlessly asked Elizabeth.

"A distress message appeared on our goggles," she informed her. "That and Charlie's girly cries echoing throughout the trees." She added with a nervous laugh.

The laugh was just what they needed and they all quickly joined in as they finally saw the buildings emerge from the trees. Even Charlie joined in, a great big smile on his face as he wiped his now sweat-drenched hair from his face. He looked down to the gun in his hand, flicking the safety back on, he placed it gingerly back in its holster. Using both hands now, he pushed his hair all the way back on his head and looked to the sky. He smiled even harder, thinking how good it was to be alive.

Seeing the rest of the group in the compound standing by the main building alongside Oliver, they once more felt safe. They had no idea how wrong they were.

Oliver

Oliver wasn't as old as the visiting friends; when they were all at university in the nineties, he was still in high school. Oliver grew up in the outskirts of San Diego yet somehow managed to stay as pasty white as the day he was born, his father liked to say. Oliver never saw it as a criticism and his father had always said it with a certain twinkle in his eye, never hiding the wry smile the phrase brought to his lips. They spent a lot of time together, father and son; hiking, fishing, hunting and generally exploring the outdoors the area gifted them. He loved his childhood and grew to be the strong capable man he was always destined to be. He muddled through school with little interest and it surprised no-one when he joined the marines after graduation. What did surprise people, was that he focussed on the opportunities the marines gave him for further education. He wasted no time in putting himself through college and surprised even himself by excelling at it. Buoyed on by his sudden academic interest and success, he applied for, and gained admittance to, the helicopter pilot training program. Oliver qualified to fly just two years later. His efforts put him in the pilot's seat of a Blackhawk helicopter just in time for the 2003 invasion of Iraq.

He loved telling people about his time in the service. He knew it put in their minds images of Apache helicopter gunships unleashing salvos of rockets towards Iraqi tank squadrons. In reality he spent his time delivering cargo to well-defended forward operating bases while the sounds of battle thundered away beyond the horizon. Still, looking back, he fondly remembered the thrill of being in a war zone. He knew now that he probably wasn't in any danger, but at the time no one thought that. Stories of chemical weapons being prepared in long-range missiles buzzed in the news reports. The talk in the camps were of hundreds of well-trained pilots, equipped with top of the range ex-soviet fighter planes, preparing to destroy everything in the air. Oliver flew as if each mission could end in disaster and was permitted, even encouraged, to do so.

Each landing he made, he was ordered to come in hard and 'dust off' fast. It was exhilarating, it was thrilling, it made him the man he was. That was another benefit of flying cargo, he knew. He didn't have to pause to consider the comfort and safety of the troops that other pilots were ferrying around. The feeling of flying, full-power, straight at the landing zone was intoxicating. He would whoop and holler as, at the last second, he would pull up and flare the mighty machine, pointing the nose to the sky, wiping out all forward momentum. He had it down to a fine art, killing all his speed and settling his steed just feet from the ground each time. It was a skill that hadn't been ignored. He was dropping off another load of cargo, just sacks of mail he was loath to admit, when the commander of the base ran out to meet him. Over the noise of his thumping rotors he screamed the exciting new orders into Oliver's ear.

There was a firefight erupting in a village just to the north. Oliver was to get there asap and recover the casualties. Oliver started to protest, the army major not technically being in his chain of command. Something stopped him, however. There was a look of desperation in his eyes. There was something bad going on and Oliver was in a place to do something about it. The major had a map in his hands and was pressing it through the open cockpit window. His co-pilot, some temporary replacement straight out of training called Briggs, was leaning over to look. Through his helmet mic, he asked if they could make it with the fuel they had. Briggs nodded: if they went right now, they should be fine.

Oliver smiled as he felt the doors slide into place behind him. Looking over his shoulder to check that the bay was empty. He nodded to the major who stepped back as Oliver poured on the power. He smiled as he watched the major fall on his ass as the mighty rotors blew him to the ground. By the time he was six feet off the ground, he was already pushing forward, accelerating north.

The village was more than a hundred miles away, but Oliver was there in less than forty-five minutes with Briggs complaining the whole way about the temperature of the engines. He had been in contact with his commanding officer on the way and official permission for him to evacuate the casualties from the hot-zone had been quick to follow. There was a big push on the front to the east and he and Briggs the only asset in the air for hundreds of miles. He could see the landing zone as he blasted over the small village of stone and concrete buildings at one-hundred and seventy miles-an-hour. Smoke was pouring from a number of buildings and he could see trails of spent rockets drifting in the wind.

Excited chattering filled his helmet, the troops on the ground had found his frequency and were 'popping green smoke'. Oliver pulled the helicopter into a wide arc, leaving the village behind him to approach the troops from a different vector. He came in hard, just as he had been doing every day with his cargo drops. This time was different, however. Despite the noise of the helicopter under full power, he could hear the rifle rounds flying through the air. There was the staccato rhythm of machine guns throwing bullets through the space between the buildings on his right and the soldiers on his left. He had purposely landed right next to the medic and the startled man quickly recovered to find the handle in front of him. The door flew open and Oliver felt it hit the rubber block over his shoulder with a solid thump. He couldn't help himself jumping slightly as bodies started hitting the steel floor of the cargo bay behind him.

Suddenly there was a sound he did not like the feel of. Tearing metal, the ping of steel on steel. Accompanying the sound was the smell of hot metal; the tangy taste of it on his tongue instantly brought with it a vivid memory of welding his father's old truck. "Taking fire," Briggs needlessly shouted over his helmet's microphone. Oliver looked behind him to be confronted with a nightmarish visage. Behind a grisly facemask of camouflage paint and blood, a corpsman held up five fingers; there were five more casualties that needed to be loaded aboard. Oliver nodded, grinding his teeth. The soldiers on the ground swarmed to his shuddering Blackhawk and started returning fire. That sound was welcome, the noise of their heavy weapons overwhelming the enemy's with ease. Oliver smiled again; this was life.

Life isn't like the movies, however, and the friendly cover didn't last long. Bullets aren't infinite and machine guns have an uncanny ability to throw them all away very quickly. Soon there were more coming back in his direction and a spray of glass heralded the fact that they found his helicopter an attractive target. The unmistakeable sight of a rocket-propelled grenade was the next thing he saw as he helplessly looked out of his shattered windscreen. It twisted and spiralled through the air, mercifully missing at the last minute, hitting the ground before him in an eruption of sand. Oliver grimaced, deciding that this was no longer much fun.

The corpsman was back, hitting Oliver on the shoulder. Eventually he succeeded in getting his attention, forcing Oliver to turn around and look at him. He nodded back with a stern look, two blue latex-gloved hands appearing before Oliver's face. His thumbs were up, and he was urgently gesturing with them. Realisation dawned on a numbed Oliver: his casualties were loaded and it was time to go. Without even turning to face forward, Oliver's hand lifted on the collective and the mighty machine leapt into the air. They carried on going straight up, having to gather more altitude to clear the taller buildings in front of them. As they finally crested over the top, he took a moment to look down. On the rooftops before him, there were four men in loose clothing, each had a rocket launcher on their shoulders, each were pointing at Oliver.

Time for Oliver slowed down, or so it seemed. He thought a lot of things, mostly centred around crashing his helicopter and being disciplined for it. He didn't think he was going to die, not for a second. He later realised that this wasn't bravery. It wasn't even premonition or faith; it was just that he, like most people in their twenties, didn't think about death very much. It just wasn't something he thought would happen, at least not very soon. Just as he was waiting for the men to fire on him, preparing to dive and avoid any rocket trails as best he could, the world erupted.

The roof of the building just in front and below his rising helicopter erupted in a cloud of dust. The threat, along with any trace of the men, simply disappeared. To his left he saw the ugly nose of an Apache attack helicopter hovering, the tell-tale smoke of a spent missile traced back to an empty space on its right pod. The gunner sat impassively behind his black visor as he started emptying his magazine of thirty-millimetre bullets into the remains of the smoking building. The combined effect of the bullets that followed the rocket strike was devastating. Oliver watched with open-mouthed disbelief as the Apache gently rocked from side to side as ammunition was alternately extracted from either side of the hovering machine and thrown into the building before him.

Eventually, after what could have been no more than a few seconds, Oliver collected himself and pushed his own helicopter forward over the destruction. He looked to the pilot of the Apache who sat just behind and above his gunner. Amazingly he saw the young man lift his eyebrows and wiggle them with a smile. Oliver responded by throwing the power on, quickly accelerating forward as he pushed into a low dive to drop altitude once more, desperately trying to avoid any more incoming fire.

Oliver noticed the pain on the flight home. It was a long two-hour flight as the hospital was further away and the lack of fuel required a little more restraint than on the flight in. By the time he landed, it was excruciating and, as he shut the engines down, he finally risked looking down to his leg. He couldn't see the damage through his flight suit but the burned black material surrounding the blood was enough to finally overwhelm him. He slumped forward over the inert controls. The last thing he heard was his co-pilot swearing at him.

The wound wasn't as bad as he had feared; a

stray bullet had caught his leg as they were taking off, he later worked out. After a couple months of rehab, he could have stayed in the marines, continued to fly even. He knew though, that as the war ended, his time in the forces had ended; he'd lost the taste for it. The disappearance of the men on the roof had changed it all for Oliver. It was true, they were the enemy and about to try to kill him, but four men being wiped from the planet in front of his eyes had irrevocably opened them. The smell of blood and death permeating his helicopter on the flight back had solidified the change; it wasn't as exciting when people were dying. He mustered out of the marines knowing that life would never be as good.

He got a job with the Wise Corporation where the work was boring, but the pay compensated, and then some. He bought his parent's house for them and supplanted flying fast choppers with fast cars and gambling in Vegas whenever he had the chance. Behind the excitement of his free time he was flying as many hours as permitted by his contract and FAA law. He liked to give the impression of fast living and hard spending when in reality he was generating quite a nest egg of savings. He was only in his early thirties and he had big plans for the future. Plans that required money, he remembered as he landed in Vancouver airport.

His latest assignment had been as private pilot for Mr Maximilian Wise himself. He had pictured himself flying some sleek private chopper, nipping between

European tax havens and private yachts. Instead he had been assigned a massive Russian cargo helicopter and spent his time ferrying various boxes and crates to and from Max's new park in the Northern Territories of Canada. His most boring assignment to date, but by far the most well paid, he smiled as he noted the flying time in his log. This new development, however, the fitting of ten seats in his helicopter and instructions to pick up a group of friends to test a new game, sounded interesting. Maybe things were picking up for Oliver, he thought as he went to fetch his passengers.

Level 1

The next morning there was a new excitement in the camp. They had debated the reality of the blue monsters all evening and all had finally decided that the 'aliens' they had killed were indeed completely artificial with the addition of some special effects when shot. More worryingly to the group was the encounter with the bear, the real threat. Oliver had assured them last night, however, that having been confronted by the four friends it would have most definitely moved away.

"They don't like us," he had calmly informed them over coffee. "They don't like our smell," he gestured to the people gathered around him, adding with a smile, "or taste." That released the tension that had been building and he joined in with their polite laughter before concluding, "he'll have moved on for sure."

They had eventually accepted his calm reassurances and had all gone to bed, tired from their exertions and filled with food. Now they were once again dressed and equipped for the hunt as they all sat down for breakfast the next day. The night had given them time to think, to consider the game more, and over breakfast they posed their questions to Oliver as he started on his fifth waffle of the morning.

"Why didn't my pistol fire yesterday?" Charlie asked Oliver as he swallowed another mouthful of his syrup-covered breakfast.

"I can guess…" he replied, gathering food on his fork, "but why don't you ask the boss?" He gestured to a screen before them, shovelling more waffle into his mouth.

Charlie nodded and turned to his watch, "Flo?" He asked, tentatively.

Flo$ Yes, Charlie?

The text appeared before them all on the large screens.

"Sorry, I thought you would have heard my question to Oliver."

Flo$ I did, but I thought you might like to ask me directly to avoid the sensation that I am spying on you.

"Oh, okay. Why didn't…"

Flo$ Your gun did not fire because you were not shooting at an element in the Gām. It is a safety feature of the Gām, the weapons may not be used for violence.

"But I could have died; Julia and I could be dead now."

Flo$ I was monitoring the threat, Charlie. I alerted the others and it seems unlikely that would have been the case.

"Sorry, are you arguing with me?"

Flo$ No.

"She's being sarcastic with me now. A computer is giving me attitude." Charlie complained to the group expansively as they all continued eating.

Julia spoke next, having noisily dropped her spoon in her cereal bowl. Incredulously, she asked the computer screen, "you didn't think we were in danger? The bear charged us."

Flo$ That is correct. But the behaviour of the bear was one of threat. It wanted you to leave. It might have attacked, but you were unlikely to have died.

"Unlikely? Unlikely isn't good enough," Julia shouted at the screen. "You should have allowed the gun to fire. To defend us," she insisted, rising to her feet.

Flo$ Julia, please calm yourself. I could have done that but that would have been far from a proportionate response.

Charlie went to argue, now standing next to Julia, but more text from Flo appeared before he could interject.

Flo$ The threat of death from the bear should not have been countered with its certain demise. That is not *equal. Besides, there are far fewer bears on Earth than humans. Preserving the life of the bear results in a more positive total outcome.*

Jasper was standing now, pointing at the screen but talking to Oliver. "That computer just admitted to putting the life of a bear above the lives of two of my friends,"   he accused Oliver.

"Nothing to do with me, buddy," was Oliver's simple reply through a mouthful of waffle.

Flo$ Jasper,   please.   You misunderstand. I value your lives, you are all as important to me as you were to Lucas. However, I am here to administer and protect the park. All life in the park is sacred to me, yours included. I calculated that the odds of either Elizabeth or Bertrand being critically injured to be less than ten percent. That was not enough to act against my ward.

"Good to know that Flo isn't here for us, then." Jasper concluded to the group.

Flo$ You are being flippant, but you are correct. I never said otherwise. I am here for the park. You are each your own concern.

The screens around the room turned off after leaving them enough time to read the last remark and they all looked to each other with stunned expressions.

"I guess Flo just stormed off to her room." Felicity remarked to the group. They responded with nervous laughs as Oliver avoided their gaze by walking over to the coffee pot. Upon his return to the table he took a sip and addressed the group.

"I know this is all strange and probably you're a bit apprehensive about carrying on." His statement was greeted with a lot of nods from the group. "But I suggest you don't worry about Flo. She's just the administrator of the park. Like she says, she isn't here to protect you. We're on our own in that respect."

A number of the group went to interject at that point, but Oliver held up a finger and proceeded to talk.

"That said, it's very safe here. The bear will have moved on and besides, I think that Flo's right that you weren't in any life-threatening danger. It wanted to scare you off, not kill you. Just next time, don't run. Look big and back away slowly if it wants you to leave. And make noises as you walk to warn them you're coming."

"I don't know, Oliver. I don't feel safe." Julia told him, a pleading look in her eyes. Oliver sighed, placing a hand on his chin. Stroking his stubble, he seemed to arrive at a conclusion.

"I know. Let's send up a drone."

Before anyone could ask what he meant, he strode from the room, setting his coffee down on the counter with a bang on the way.

They followed him from the main building out to the back where a large shed sat hiding in the ground. It was covered with growth all around and could barely be seen until they were standing right outside the door. Pulling open the heavy metal entrance, Oliver disappeared inside and quickly re-emerged. He was holding a flat white plastic disk. Gesturing for the group to move back, he flung it into the air like a discus. Instead of falling back to the ground, however, it flew on impossibly far, quickly disappearing from view.

"Don't worry," Oliver said, smiling to the group. "I'm not superhuman, it's a powered drone. There's a motor spinning it, providing lift from the shape of the disk."

He reached back into the shed and pulled out a tablet computer. He presented the screen to the group and they could see a moving image of forest and grasslands. He pressed a button and the image panned out to show a large map, slowly being filled in with the pictures being taken by the drone. On the map there were a number of icons showing red, blue and yellow. Oliver pointed to them.

"Red is the enemy, blue dots are us. You know this. Yellow are animals in the park." He pressed one and an image appeared next to it. It showed a porcupine sleeping under a pile of leaves. "Thermal cameras can detect them through the trees." Oliver explained as the drone methodically filled in the map of their surrounding area, adding yellow icons all around them.

Upon completion of the map, Olivier concluded that there were no bears nearby. Handing the tablet to Julia, he looked to the sky. The disk was approaching him, emitting a gentle hum as it slid to a hover above his head. Reaching out his arm seemed to signal to the drone that he was ready for it and it stopped spinning, dropping down into his outstretched palm. Oliver deftly caught the drone and turned to return it to the shed. "I'll send up one periodically to check the area, and the locals will appear in your goggles and on the map." He informed them from inside the shed. "Does that help?" He asked Julia as he emerged sporting a wide grin. She handed him back the tablet, nodding.

"Yes, thank you, Oliver." She smiled as he started back to the main building, no doubt keen to finish breakfast. The confident stride of this younger giant seemed to reassure the group once more.

Collectively they decided that Oliver leaving was the signal that the game had once again begun. The new icons on their maps, placed there by the drone, galvanised them into action.

"Two groups of four this time?" Asked Felicity.

"Why?" Countered Randal. "This is a cake walk. We could go alone, get this done in record time." He lifted his rifle, sighting down the scope into the woods.

"No, I think Flick's right," Jasper answered, "yesterday was clearly the tutorial, now the game has started for real. See the number of red?" He asked as he slipped his goggles on, "they're moving now as well." He gestured to the map by tapping his goggles. "I think we need to take this seriously, two groups of four in a pincer movement across those two ridges to the east. That way we can take the dots that are gathering in the valley between."

No one had a better plan and Jasper's seemed to make sense, so they quickly acquiesced. Jasper, Felicity, Julia and Charlie moved south. Jessica, Randal, Elizabeth and Bertrand to the north. Together they cautiously climbed the ridges to the east that bordered a valley in which the red dots were gathering. Soon the two groups were either side of the red cluster as they each settled down to observe the enemy through their rifle scopes and binoculars.

"How do we coordinate our attack?" Asked Charlie of no one in particular.

In response, Felicity tapped the side of her goggles and spoke softly into the air, "group Excellence to group Remedial. Come in remedial group."

The three around her looked confused for a second as they heard her voice both from her lips but also closer in their ears.

"Why does no one read the instructions?" She asked them, "tap the right-hand side of the goggles to speak. There's a microphone and induction headphones embedded in the earpiece."

Her instructions had also clearly reached the other side of the valley as Randal's voice responded in their heads, "nice, Felicity. Group Fantastic calling group Stinky Pants, reading you loud and clear."

Tapping his own microphone, Jasper took the opportunity to end the argument he could see coming, "how about we try groups North and South, given our positions on the map?" General noises of disappointed consent were broadcast throughout the group as he continued. "What can you see, North group? We can see about eight blue bears gathered at the pond."

"Roger that, South." Came Randal's reply, "we have eyes on all ten from here, looks like they have weapons this time."

The comment elicited a response from both groups to study their targets closer. They were indeed armed this time, wielding deadly looking blades of various shapes and sizes. They were slowly moving west in a tight group, towards the main compound from where the friends had come.

"It looks like they don't know where we are, but maybe know where we sleep," whispered Charlie through his microphone. "We should ambush them here, eliminate them in a crossfire." He added softly, lying down on the soft ground, resting his rifle on a mound of earth in front of him.

"Roger that, South." Came Randal's military sounding reply again, "as they reach the western tip of that pond they'll have to cluster together to move through those large rocks. We can all fire simultaneously, taking them all at once."

Each group looked around at each other, all nodding at his assessment. There was a silent agreement among them that Jasper would answer for the South group. "Okay, Randal. We'll get ready, you count it down."

They all lay down on the ground, spread out along the ridges upon which they had climbed. Sighting down their scopes, they braced themselves. Soon the blue bears in their sights started to cluster together just as Randal had predicted. The beasts moved through the rocks, nervously scanning the area around them, gripping their own weapons tightly. The friends could see more clearly now they were closer. Each alien blade was uniquely shaped. Although all very different, they all had a similar look to them, each following elaborate curves and shapes that seemed more decorative than utilitarian. Despite the apparent awkwardness of their devices, the bears seemed to hold them with deadly purpose as they practiced efficient patterns with the weapons as they walked.

"They're so beautiful, so elegant. Do we have to shoot?" Asked Felicity into her microphone.

Jasper answered quietly, whispering as he lay to her right, "I'm not so sure I agree now, Flick. Just look at their swords."

"I suppose," she answered reluctantly, "still..."

There was no response from Jasper, but Charlie muttered to her from her left instead, "it's just a computer game, Felicity. Have some fun, it should be fun."

Before she could answer, Randal's assertive voice came over the radio. "Three," he stated slowly in his best Louisiana drawl, "two."

The countdown galvanised even Felicity as the groups sighted their rifles on the hairy blue figures below them.

"One," he spoke the ominous number into the microphone.

There was no call to fire; no spoken signal. At the appropriate time, however, each of the friends pulled their triggers. Hell was unleashed in an instant on the tightly packed group of blue creatures. The boom of the rifles was accompanied by the pop and whoosh of the animals' own explosions as the bullets struck home. The targets were instantly obscured by the result of the initial attack and there was a silence. Suddenly, one by one, some of the group resumed firing in to the cloud of flying fur. The subsequent booms were far less synchronised as they unloaded their magazines into the area, firing at any targets that might have still been standing. The bullets sliced through the remains of their deceased brethren without pause or consideration, pinging off the rocks below. Eventually the fusillade ended, and the group awkwardly reloaded their rifles as the blue cloud of viscera settled onto the rocks below them.

They all stayed where they were, studying the aftermath of their actions in silence. It was Charlie who interrupted the stillness of the stunned group, cheering without restraint. It was very unlike him, as he stood waving his rifle in the air. Something about the game had let him throw off his inhibitions and he was clearly enjoying the feeling. One by one, they all joined in his celebrations. Even Felicity cried out, releasing the adrenaline that had unknowingly built up inside of her. Eventually Charlie ceased his cries and roughly dropped his rifle on the ground.

"Who wants for checking out the results?" He awkwardly asked, the excitement making his accent even thicker. He would have normally chastised himself for the poor grammar, but he was enjoying himself far too much and instead beamed a smile at his friends standing around him. Receiving no answer, he pulled out his pistol and cocked it. No one volunteered to join him as he began to quickly climb down into the valley, sliding on patches of loose gravel. Clicking the microphone button on his goggles, he asked the same question of the group to the north.

Bertrand's voice came on the radio in response, "I'll meet you there, Charlie. Last one to the kill-zone makes lunch." He yelled into the radio as he started sliding down the hillside on his robotic legs. His going was slower than Charlie's as he tentatively made his way through the rocks and gravel on the side of the slope, feeling his way with his still unfamiliar appendages. Somewhat inevitably, therefore, Charlie arrived first in a cloud of dust and stones that skittered into the small stream. He announced his victory on the radio, declaring that Bertrand was making lunch and placing an order for steak. He waved his arms in the air and instantly dropped out of sight of the group.

Everyone except Bertrand and Charlie had remained on the ridges, watching through their rifle scopes as Charlie climbed down between the rocks. They all smiled at his involvement in the game. Somewhat belatedly, Felicity remembered to check the map for any red dots. Just as she did, she saw that very close to the blue circle that was Charlie, there was indeed a moving red point of light on her map.

"Charlie, there's a red target very close to you," she called out over the radio, swinging her rifle to the location she had seen on the map. Through her scope she couldn't see anything. Just the rocks and the aftermath of their attack. "Can anyone see the remaining dot?" She asked over the radio, "Charlie, are you hearing this? There's a target close to your position." She tried again.

"Flick, nothing from this side," came a response from Randal, "I got no visual." Their elevated viewpoint was letting the target, and Charlie, hide from them between the larger rocks at the base of the valley.

"Wait a sec, Flick. I'm coming in to the rocks now," was the more helpful response from Bertrand, who had finally reached the valley floor. She swung her scope to watch Bertrand climb up on top of the rocks. He was really getting used to his new legs, she thought, as she watched him scan the area with his pistol from on top of one of the tall granite boulders. He was checking for both Charlie and the target from an elevated vantage point. He would find it any second, Felicity thought. Checking the map once more, she saw the blue dot that was Charlie wink out.

"Bertie, Charlie's dot's gone," she stated with a worried voice.

"What does that mean?" Asked Jasper along with a collection of overlapping voices over the radio.

"Quiet, people," Bertrand's voice commanded over the noise. Hushing the discussions on the radio, "I'll find him. Charlie, come in Charlie. Where are you?" He spoke clearly over the radio. His voice was raised now, and everyone could hear his concerned requests emanating from the valley floor. "Charlie, come on, man. Climb up a rock so I can see you. I'm approaching the red target."

As he mentioned the target, a blue mass leaped up in front of him. He reeled back, falling down on top of the large flat rock he had been walking across. His gun skittered away and down between a gap in the boulders, the sound of metal against stone was disturbingly final. He swore in surprise as the blue monster loomed over him. The group were frozen with surprise and fear, unsure of what to do. The threat was not real, they knew that in their minds, but their bodies were screaming out that Bertrand was about to die at the hands of the alien beast.

The hairy blue bear lifted its massive hands up high over Bertrand who sat defenceless on the rock beneath it. The curved blade it held was over his head, glinting in the light of the day.

"Bertie. Stay still!" The deep voice of Randal commanded over the radio. After a fraction of a second in which all waited for the blade to fall, the boom of

Randal's rifle echoed through the valley. The giant blue creature looming over Bertrand disappeared in a puff of fluid and hair. The blade falling harmlessly to the side and clattering away out of sight between the rocks.

Everyone took a deep breath of, especially Bertrand who sat in a cloud of blue rain. He grinned in relief as he tried to push himself up from the rocks. Unsure of how to stand up with his new legs, he tried to push himself up with his hands. That did little to help as his legs remained where they were, unmoving piles of flesh and plastic. He frowned in confusion. They sat inert before him; useless appendages that just weighed him down as they always had. Wanting to get up before anyone arrived to help, he tried to roll over with a snap of his waist. The prosthetic legs finally contributed to his efforts by crossing over themselves. Finally, he managed to bend them and rise to his feet, bottom first. By the time he was back upright he was panting heavily from his efforts.

"Thanks, Randal," Bertrand breathed out over the radio, "Charlie, come in, Charlie." He proceeded to call over the radio in a shaking voice. He started yelling now, foregoing the radio. "Guys, you'd better get down here. I can't find Charlie."

This request finally resulted in the mass movement of people down both sides of the valley. They put their guns away, rifles over their shoulders and pistols in their holsters. Awkwardly they followed Bertrand and

Charlie's paths down the sloping ridges, eventually congregating where Bertrand was waiting for them.

Jasper was the last to arrive, having paused to bring Charlie's rifle down along with his own. "Charlie!" He called out into the rocks to no response. Slowly they spread out either side of the small crevice caused by the boulders, searching through the remains of the aliens, looking for their friend. "You'd better not be messing with us."

They found him five minutes later. Stuffed into a shallow gap between two huge boulders. It looked like he had tried to crawl into the hollow to escape his demise. He had failed. His body was cut all over from head to toe, deep gashes exposing flesh and bone to the air. His blood had flowed copiously, pooling on the hard-packed ground. Most turned away from the sight, cupping their hands to their mouths and eyes. Gasps of shock accompanied tears of sorrow as they fled the sight. Randal, however, stepped forward, crouching to inspect the body. He placed his shaking hands under Charlie's arms and gently pulled him from his curled-up position between the rocks. Laying him softly on the ground, he placed his fingers on his neck, checking for a pulse.

"He's dead." He stated, obviously.

"Of course he's dead, idiot!" Shouted Julia. "What the hell did this?" She wept.

"What d'you mean, what?" Asked Jasper, stepping forward to look at the body of Charlie for the first time.

"These are cuts, he didn't fall. He was killed." Said Randal with an incongruously calm voice, turning to face Jasper. In a moment, everyone in the group had drawn their handguns from their holsters. Some held them high, some pointed them up and down the valley. Bertrand was still on top of a large boulder, scanning the area. "But no one's here, there is no one." He barked to the group below him.

"No red dots." Stated Felicity, checking her map in her goggles. In frustration, Bertrand ripped his own goggles from his head and threw them into the stream.

"This isn't a game, Flick. Someone's here, someone's killed Charlie!" He called out angrily.

Randal stood from crouching over Charlie's body to give another command, "Jasper, Flick. Get up on the boulders with Bertie and stand guard. He's right, there must be someone else here."

As they climbed up to guard the group, Julia started crying. Stepping over to provide comfort, Elizabeth put her arm around her.

"Could it be a bear?" Julia asked through her tears.

"I suppose," conceded Randal, "but where is it now?"

Again they looked around, more nervously now.

"What are we doing?" Shouted Bertrand, frantically waving his gun around. "These damn things are useless anyway." They looked to him and to their guns. "They won't fire on anything except simulations. Remember?"

Slowly they all realised the truth.

"Charlie found that out when he tried to shoot the bear. They don't work!" Shouted Bertrand, even more enraged now. He pointed his gun at Randal and pulled the trigger. Randal flinched and fell back from where he was standing over Charlie's body.

"What the hell!" He shouted at Bertrand.

"Come on, look." Bertrand countered, pointing it at Jasper and pulling the trigger with an impotent click.

"Bertrand, stop!" Shouted Jasper. Bertrand didn't stop. One by one he pointed his gun to each of the group, pulling the trigger repeatedly now.

"We might as well collect rocks for all the use these damn things are."

With that he pointed the gun at his own head.

The gun exploded with a deafening bang within the tight confines created by the boulders. As the bullet left the barrel of the gun it took the majority of Bertrand's head with it. A colourful mix of skull, hair, brain matter and blood sprayed through the air and deposited itself against a nearby tree trunk. The Jackson Pollock of the remains of his head slowly started dripping down the rough bark as his body crumpled to the ground. There were screams, there were cries of disbelief and despair, there was the smell of spent cordite and fresh death in the air.

Investigation

Once more they sat around the table in the main building, the mood was different now. Oliver was there too having joined them upon hearing the news over the radio. They numbly stared in shock at the two empty seats now their number had been reduced from eleven, down to nine. The sun was setting through the windows in a beautiful display that did not match the sombre mood of the group. They had spent the remainder of the day carrying back the bodies of Charlie and Bertrand and laying them to rest in the freezer attached to the kitchen. Now evening was upon them, they had gathered to determine what to do next.

Elizabeth was notably absent; she, like the others, had walked back to the main building in stunned silence. On arriving, however, she had broken down. Shock and grief had overwhelmed her as they finally arrived; the act of carrying the bodies back through the forest had proven too much for her reserves of strength. As they lay Bertrand's body to rest on the floor of the freezer room she had started to cry. Felicity's attempt to comfort her didn't help, it only made her worse. Trying to explain how she felt about Bertrand brought her grief to the fore. Shaking uncontrollably, she had wept until it threatened to starve her of air. Felicity and Jasper eventually managed to calm her down enough to take her to her cabin. There she lay still, exhausted from her exertions and the shock that had inevitably set in.

"We need to contact the police." Suddenly stated Jasper with determination. He slapped his hands down on the table and stood to loom over them, trying to assert himself over the situation.

"I tried already," replied Oliver glumly, "the internet link is down so there's no communication outside of the park."

"You don't have a radio?" Countered Jasper.

"No, we don't have a radio. If we had a radio don't you think I would have tried the damn radio." Snapped Oliver, "there's one on my chopper... but it doesn't have the range."

"I was just--" said Jasper, holding up his hands in a placatory gesture.

"Flo, can we contact anyone outside the park?" Barked Oliver to the ceiling.

Flo$ No, Oli. I am sorry, the satellite link to the internet is down.

"There. Happy?" He sneered to Jasper.

"Guys. Please," implored Felicity, "there's no need to turn on each other. We just need to work out what we should be doing now."

The two men settled down, facing her instead of each other. As they did, a red-eyed Elizabeth gently pushed open the door to the building and shuffled in. They looked at her in silence; words having lost all usefulness. Elizabeth simply nodded and walked to an empty chair, taking a seat at the table. "We can't call the police," she summarised having heard most of the loud conversation as she had approached the building, "but can we go and get them?"

"I can't fly tonight," Oliver answered as he rubbed his chin in thought, "I need to prep the chopper and that needs light. I can go tomorrow, first thing." He replied, resolved.

"That just leaves tonight then," stated Jasper. "I think we should stay here, together. If there is someone out there, a killer, we're safer in a group."

"Unless it's one of the group," muttered Oliver to a collective scoffing and general noise of denial. "I wasn't there. I was here, as you all know. So, it wasn't me." He stated, crossing his big arms across his chest, "how d'y'all know it wasn't one of you?" He asked.

It fell to Jasper to reply, "we were all on the ridges above the valley. He was killed with a blade. None of us were anywhere near him. It wasn't one of us."

Oliver nodded slowly, seeming to accept the explanation, until Jessica suddenly interjected in her distinctive New Jersey accent.

"Well. Bertrand was down there with him."

They looked around at each other until most eyes came to rest on Elizabeth; the mention of Bertrand had visibly shaken her, and she was obviously fighting her grief once again. She swallowed and took a deep breath, saying nothing.

"Did anyone have their eyes on him the whole time?" Jessica proceeded to ask, ignoring the discomfort of the people around the table.

There was a general shaking of heads.

"So, it could have been Bertie," she stated uncertainly in conclusion. She didn't look at anyone, instead staring down at the table and hiding behind the short-dark hair that hung in front of her eyes.

"But why? Why would Bertie kill Charlie?" Asked Felicity, her brown curls bobbing furiously as she spread her arms and gestured to the group.

"Who cares?" Barked Oliver, "if it was Bertrand then problem solved right? Maybe that's why he killed himself. Guilt."

"Bertrand would never kill Charlie." The statement from Elizabeth was quiet but left little room for discussion. There was steel in her tone as she looked down to the table, her eyes closed and hands trembling.

"Liz is right," Jasper agreed, "that makes no sense." He looked around them all, shaking his head, "for one thing he didn't know the gun would work on himself..." he paused, thinking for a second before continuing, "that's a point. Flo, why did the gun work when Bertrand pointed it at his head?"

Flo$ I am sorry, Jas. I do not know the answer to that query.

"That's weird," Oliver said, intrigued. He looked at the screens with a puzzled expression as the group looked to him for an explanation. "She's never said anything like that before, that sounds like a fall-back response rather than a real answer to your question. Don't you think?" He paused again before arriving at a decision, "Flo, can you arrange a refuelling drone for my flight to the Mountie station tomorrow?"

Flo$ I am sorry, Oli. I cannot respond to that request.

"See, same again," he said to himself, nodding, "a stock response. Flo, are you operating normally?"

Flo$ I feel fine thank you, Oli.

"I guess that's a better answer," he admitted, rubbing his chin while asking again, "Flo, can you arrange the refuelling drone?"

Flo$ I am sorry, I cannot.

"I guess we're not flying out either, then," stated Oliver soberly, "I'd be 'bingo fuel' before getting to any kind of civilisation."

There was silence again as they each worked out from the context that he didn't have enough fuel to fly far enough, leaving the phrasing unquestioned. Felicity brought the conversation back around to the start, "that still leaves the question of who killed Charlie. Because I don't accept for a second that it was Bertrand. I just don't." With Felicity's statement, the group fell silent once more. They sat there for a long while, barely moving, not making a sound. Then, looking up and about them, Felicity seemed to arrive at a decision.

"Flo?"

Flo$ Yes, Flick?

"Where is Maximilian Wise?"

The table looked up to her, understanding dawning on their faces.

Flo$ Max is in the control centre, Flick.

"And Flo? Besides us here at this table and Max, how many other people are there in the park?"

Flo$ None, Flick. Yourselves and Max are the only people here.

Felicity looked around the table, looking into the eyes of each person there. "I know you," she said, "I know each and every one of you. Oliver couldn't physically have done it and none of you would have done it ever. That leaves the one person that none of us have ever even met."

Jasper rose to his feet, "we have to find Max," he stated as the others rose. "Flo, where is the control centre?"

Flo$ I am afraid I cannot tell you that, Jasper.

"Why not, Flo?"

Flo$ Max likes his privacy. He does not want to be disturbed.

They looked to Oliver, the obvious question in their eyes.

"Sorry, guys. I've no clue where the control centre is," he admitted before adding, "I do have something that might be useful though." With that, he strode from the table towards the large windows to their side. Following Oliver, they quickly gathered around a screen in the lounge area; it was laid flat like a table, but Oliver quickly made it light up, showing an image of the park in intricate detail. They each panned and zoomed the map with shaking fingers, trying desperately to determine the location of the control centre.

"I can't see anything," said Jessica after twenty minutes of all of them looking for any sign of a building that might be the control centre. "Apart from this place, there's nothing man-made anywhere in the park," she concluded for the group.

"It must be hidden." Agreed Oliver. It was getting dark and the expansive windows beside them showed the woods beyond darkening as the sun departed behind distant mountains. The previous night the view had been beautiful, intriguing; now it was just frightening. Despite the waning light, they agreed that they couldn't sleep until they had found the control centre and the absent Max. Only then could they consider lowering their guard enough to rest. Unwilling to separate, they set out together into the dying light to search the immediate area for the control centre. Despite their misgivings about the effectiveness of their weapons, they took their augmented reality glasses and guns with them. If nothing else, they gave the group a sense of security in the darkening wilderness.

Wearing the equipment proved to be a wise choice because as night further approached, their goggles activated infra-red lights and projected an enhanced view of the woods before their eyes, enabling them to easily navigate the darkening woods. Coincidentally, it was the darkening of the day, combined with the enhanced night-vision provided by the glasses, that enabled them to find the object. Elizabeth saw it first; there was a faint column of heat escaping from it, visible through their glasses as a slight green haze flowing into the sky. Following the green chimney, they soon found a vantage point where they could see its source. As they stood on the crest of a ridge looking down to the object before them, Jessica was the first to speak, her clear, American-accented voice piercing the darkness.

"Okay, we can all see that, can we?"

They all nodded, still not speaking.

"We can all see the flying saucer sat on the ground, blue aliens coming in and out of the ramp."

Again, they nodded.

Randal removed his glasses and peered into the darkness. "The problem is... that I can't see anything without these glasses." He said softly and deliberately, "it probably isn't even there in reality. Just another simulation."

It was Jasper who responded, "but it is there." He said, removing his own glasses, "I can see the change in the shadows without the glasses. There's definitely something there."

All removing their glasses now, they had to agree. There was indeed something below them, there was also some kind of movement in and out of the door. Along with the moving shadows in the distance, they could hear the occasional rustle of leaves or the knocking of rocks. Carried on the breeze, the distant noise of a breaking twig reached their silent viewpoint.

Randal spoke again, whispering now. "Okay, so it's a real building. But it's just a part of the game. The goggles are adding the aliens, obviously. They're also changing the appearance of the structure. We've found their home base in the game. That's all."

After a long pause, while they all considered what it was they were seeing, Julia finally spoke. "You know, there was one person present when Charlie died that we haven't considered."

They all waited with bated breath, wanting nothing more than for her to proceed. She pressed a hand to her blond curls and subconsciously paused to press her point; she was talking just like she would have done if she were addressing parliament rather than a group of old friends.

"The final blue bear." She concluded.

Jasper quickly snorted, dispelling the silent agreement to be quiet, "don't be ridiculous. A computer image can't have killed him."

"Think about it," Julia retorted calmly, "he was cut up, and they all had blades. There was no person there, just one alien. We saw no one leave, and no one enter. Even if it was Max, how did he do it? Where did he come from and go to? Look at them!" She suddenly shouted, her calm unexpectedly departing. With sudden anger came an unwelcome return of her

Birmingham accent and she gestured violently to the aliens coming and going from the ship. "Have you ever seen anything done on a computer look so real?"

"Jules, this is new. This is cutting edge. It would look better than ever before." Jasper replied.

"But this good?" Her anger remained but she was less panicky and had regained control of her voice. She was again sounding like the politician she was, "I went to see Jurassic Park, that was good for the time too, but you could tell. Independence Day was better, but again, obviously computers. Even Avatar, then whatever... they get better, but has one ever fooled you? Even for a second?"

They had no response to this, knowing she had a point. They looked at the goggles, inspecting them.

"And look at the glasses," Julia proceeded, "they're so light, where are the computers? Films take huge massive things, rooms of machines, processing all night to even get close to looking real. Now some guy in the middle of nowhere creates perfect images of live aliens in a pair of glasses?"

"She has a point..." Elizabeth conceded.

"Thank you, Liz," Jasper said sarcastically, "so what we're considering here is that aliens have invaded northern Canada while we happened to be here playing a game. The computer in charge of said game is letting us shoot them, but hiding the fact that they are, in fact, real. Not only that, but upon invading the Earth, their master plan seems to be to mill around with primitive weapons letting themselves get shot and inexplicably explode."

"Jas…" Elizabeth interrupted loudly, "stop being so critical and think for a second!"

Her outburst stopped him in his tracks, it made him look at her and instantly he saw the tears in her eyes, the shaking of her lips. He stepped forward to comfort her, to apologise, but she held up a hand to stop him. "It's okay Jas," she whispered so only he could hear, "I'm okay."

He crinkled his lips into a crooked line and looked at her critically. She turned away and stepped from the conversation to compose herself.

Julia, having noted the exchange, brought the conversation back on track, "I'm not saying it makes sense but nor do the facts as we have them. You have to admit that the graphics in play here are beyond anything anyone has ever seen or even heard of."

"Fine, but aliens?" Jasper scoffed.

"Forget that for a second," she said, waving at the air to dismiss the point before continuing, "just think of what we've been accepting. Does any of it make any sense?"

There was silence for a short time. Finally, Jasper replied, "I admit, it doesn't. There's definitely something going on here that us being in a game doesn't explain."

"Fine, good. I agree," stated Elizabeth, calmer now, "I think we need to throw out any information that we have from Flo for a start. She's lying."

Oliver, stepped in at this point, "I don't know about that. She's been nothing but honest with me."

"That's as may be," answered Jasper with a clipped voice, "but I agree with Liz, she's lying now. Or at least deceiving us." Oliver went to complain but Jasper forged on regardless. "Down there..." he whispered loudly, gesturing to the UFO, "is a building that she refused to tell us about. Coming and going are aliens, or representations of something that is obviously dangerous to us. They weren't on the map before we saw them, but there they are now. That's new, isn't it?"

Oliver reluctantly conceded with a grunt.

"Fine. So, we are at the very least engaged in a deadly game of some kind and the information we have is compromised, incomplete, or incorrect."

"Okay," Oliver answered grudgingly, "what do you suggest we do about it?"

There being no straightforward answer to this, the group instead settled down to study the comings and goings of the blue creatures. They couldn't help bouncing a number of theories around among themselves while watching the movements below them. People in costumes, actors in the game paid to behave like aliens. Genetically engineered creatures being used as cannon fodder. Invariably they came back to aliens each time; the sight of the UFO and the nature of the creatures seemed undeniable. Finally, fear and the cold of the night settled into their bones and they agreed to retreat back to the compound. Carefully and fearfully they slid quietly from their observation position on the ridge and walked silently back the way they had come.

Unwilling to retire to their cabins for the night, they all dragged their mattresses and blankets to the common area in the main building. Gaining some sense of security from their number and proximity to each other, they fitfully slept together in front of the large windows. Periodically they agreed to check their maps and equipment for any enemy encroachment and for at least one person to remain awake at all times. Gradually, individually, they slept. As a group, however, they remained nervous and vigilant all night. Skittish, they constantly checked the sinister woods just beyond the expansive windows. Where they had previously only seen beauty and wonder, they now saw danger and death lurking just beyond the treeline.

Jessica

Jessica was from New Jersey. People from outside the State often thought she was from New York but that just wasn't true. Still, she always thought, they were close enough, so she rarely bothered to correct them. She was an East-Coast, dark-haired, skinny little white girl. Conforming to every stereotype people seemed to expect of her. Even as she reached her fortieth birthday, she was the same; it was as if she stopped ageing at twenty. Looking younger than she was had annoyed her in her twenties but it had really started paying off in her thirties. As she aged slower than everyone else around her it was something she had grown to really appreciate. She had taken up running and yoga to halt the physical parts of getting old and so far, it seemed to be working. She would not have wished the same when she was twenty, when being young just came naturally to her. That was how old she was as she flew to Liverpool, England to spend a year studying there.

She arrived on the train, having flown into London, and had quickly moved into a shared house that had been allocated to her by the University. Instantly she found herself living in a small red-brick building with a shared kitchen, bathroom, and living room, with a group of total strangers. At first, she was worried that she had made a terrible mistake, they were strange, they were English. She was just glad that she had made an American friend. Randal was her lifeline, without him she didn't think she could have made it. The day they had met, she had been feeling very vulnerable and wanted very much to go home. Still, she had dragged herself away from talking to her mom on the phone and made herself walk to the Study Abroad social group she had signed up to. Amazingly, she had managed to talk somewhat normally to the tall handsome apparition that seemed to be the only other American in the group and quickly they had latched onto each other for mutual support.

Slowly, bit-by-bit she managed to settle in and relax. It was Lucas who did it in the end. They were all talking one evening, when again, they turned to her to ask her a question about America. Yet another interrogation about her home culture she was expected to know the answer to. Then, when she didn't know, a teasing session about her ignorance would arrive, she knew. But this time it was different, Lucas was asking her something about the Simpsons. This she knew. This was her specialist subject. She stood up straight, stirred her cup of noodles and informed them knowingly that the aliens resided on Rigel Seven. Lucas leapt on the answer, dancing a ridiculous victory dance and claiming superiority over the rest of the room as she confirmed what he had been saying. This was well before the advent of Google but what Jessica had just done was the equivalent for the day. She smiled as Lucas slapped her on the back, proclaiming her a cultural genius.

From then on, she started to relax around her

new friends. She even started asking questions of them, deciding to learn more about England while she was there. She started teasing them for not knowing things about their own country. Their geographical knowledge, for example, was shocking. She and Randal could recall and place every state in the US. In contrast, her British friends couldn't even agree if places were counties or not. She had arrived. By the time they were watching the Eurovision Song Contest and laughing at all the acts on 'telly' she felt as if she had made quite a group of friends.

They were all laughing at the last contestant's song when they heard a sound. Jessica looked up from the television to see Randal's latest girlfriend knocking on the glass doors, crying. He had dismissed her as he had every girl he'd been with since he had arrived in this country; by email. Knowing that Jessica was friends with Randal, she had no doubt sought her out to find out why he had broken up with her. This annoyed Jessica; she didn't see why it fell to her to console this girl, especially as she would be interrupting such a fun evening. The acts had finished singing and they were preparing to vote however, so apparently she had half an hour of boring bits, Jasper usefully informed her. She sighed as she rose from the sofa and, collecting the crying girl, guided her to her room.

They sat on her bed while the jilted girlfriend, Sofia, dried her eyes on an already wet handkerchief. Jessica smiled at the Englishness of it all, at home it would have most certainly been a Kleenex. Sofia saw her smiling and enquired why. She explained her thinking and was greeted with a smile and a chuckle. She could see why Randal had sought out this girl, while she was clearly attractive, she was also quick and obviously intelligent. She started talking about her family, little stories of interest to Jessica about life back home in rural Ireland. Jessica listened with interest and soon they were talking as if they were old friends. Seeing the mood lighten, Jessica suggested that they get a drink to help her get over Randal's behaviour. She accepted, and Jessica quickly returned with a bottle of wine she had taken from Jasper's supply he had brought from France.

Soon they had finished off most of the bottle and the mood started getting serious again. Sofia was lamenting the loss of Randal and the drinks had loosened up Jessica. She was responding to Sofia's mood by confiding to her about her own lack of a love life. She had thought that an exotic American coming to sleepy old England would have brought the boys flocking to her. She'd had no such luck. Randal might be fighting off girls, but Jessica hadn't managed to herd any men to her with the very same stick. Sofia laughed, giggling from the combination of the mental image and the wine.

Felicity chose that second to gently knock, putting her head around the door to tell Jessica that the Eurovision vote had started. Jessica politely waved her away; she was no longer in the mood and Sofia was still far from happy. The interruption brought back the tears and she watched as they slowly formed in Sofia's dark brown eyes. Jessica fought back her own, blinking them away. They were sitting on her small bed so in order to hug her, Jessica had to climb onto her knees and shuffle across the duvet to get to her. Sofia saw her approaching and mimicked her movements, rising and shuffling to meet in the middle.

They met on the bed in an awkward embrace, trying to comfort each other. They were struggling to stay upright as the bed creaked and groaned, sagging in the middle, forcing them to support each other. Sofia emitted a little giggle as once again they almost fell over. Finally, Jessica admitted defeat and fell to her side on purpose, hitting the bed with a loud clang and a noticeable bounce, taking Sofia with her. They lay together on the bed, wrapped in each other's arms. Jessica brushed Sofia's hair away from her face and stroked her back, shushing her tears away.

They lay there all night, Sofia in Jessica's warm embrace. The crying had ended but the wine and the tears had exhausted them both and they quickly fell asleep together. When they woke in the morning they stretched and continued to talk some more. Sofia felt much better when the sun finally rose; she was embarrassed at the scene she had caused but was satisfied with their conclusions. The answer was cliché but effective; he wasn't worth it. Eventually they parted with forced smiles and another warm hug.

That was the turning point for Jessica's professional life. She didn't know it then, but later she would trace her decision to become a therapist to that night comforting a crying Irish Sofia. Her position as people's sounding wall and helper only grew from that point. She would help Felicity with her obviously one-way infatuation with Lucas, try to wean Julia and Randal off their over-dependence on sex, and convince Charlie to try being with a woman without assessing her marriageability first. Jessica thought it ironic that the person not studying psychology could be so insightful with those who were, and the most interested in using it to help the people around her.

Jessica returned to university in New York at the end of the year, promising to remain in touch with her new friends. She did; email and cards flew at regular intervals back and forth over the Atlantic and down the coast to New Orleans. She finished her degree, studied for and completed a masters, then a doctorate, in psychology. She finally became the therapist she wanted to be and set about helping people. She subsequently found a husband and settled into a new life in the city of New York that she so loved. Receiving the invitation to the reunion in Canada, she replied simply with a yes. Of course she would go, she loved these people, to see them again in such a situation would be a real treat.

Realisation

They awoke the next morning and gathered at the breakfast table for another discussion about their predicament. The consensus was to try to gain some understanding of the situation and to formulate a plan before they acted. They checked the locks and windows before preparing a simple breakfast. It was Felicity that suggested they say a prayer and spend a minute thinking of Charlie and Bertrand. They all sombrely lowered their heads while she said a few words of remembrance. As one they ended with a quiet 'amen' and nodded all around to each other, moist eyes and sad expressions dominating the room. Slowly they started picking at the food before them, unwilling to eat but feeling that they would need the strength.

The deaths had hit them all hard, even Oliver who told them that he had really liked Bertrand from the off and was sure he would have liked Charlie too, once he had got to know him. The events of the previous day had kept them from feeling the full extent of the deaths and mostly they were numb. Jessica quietly informed them that they were probably all in the first stages of grief, denial perfectly describing the way they were all feeling.

"Ordinarily I would recommend we acknowledge the loss of our friends. Experience our feelings in order to acknowledge them and move on. But, given the circumstances, I think we might be better off living in denial." She said, making herself a waffle from the machine against the wall.

From being one of the quietest and less ambitious of the friends at university, she had gone on to become the most qualified by far. Gaining a PhD in the States she was now a practicing psychologist and counsellor. Her knowledge and experience were guiding the actions of the group this morning.

She continued talking, pushing on the waffle press, "such a strategy is incredibly unhealthy and not recommended but, while we're fighting for our lives, I suggest we try to suppress our emotions." She concluded, clearly swallowing her own need to cry. A single tear ran down her cheek as she wiped it away and tried to eat her waffle. She could only manage a small amount at a time and it was clear to the group that she too was struggling to cope with the brutal losses.

"It's just... on top of Lucas..." stammered Felicity, starting to cry. Elizabeth was soon crying too, and they embraced, sharing their grief. Unable to suppress the onslaught, they all took an hour in remembrance, talking at length about how they missed their friends. Tears and tentative smiles prompted by shared memories flowed between them. Even Oliver joined in, the loss of people around him bringing back his own memories of his time at war. At the end of the agreed-upon hour, Jasper's watch beeped and they all frowned at the simple plastic device that had so rudely halted their words of reverence.

"We're here," Felicity said suddenly, "we're here and we are going to get through this," she added determinedly. "Lucas would have wanted us to, that's why he brought us together. To remember him."

Oliver stood, towering above them all as they sat on the floor of the common room. "Felicity's right," he agreed with his booming voice, "we're going to get out of here, and I suggest that we get out of here right now."

They looked to him, each standing themselves. They gathered around him as a tribe around a totem.

"We might not be able to fly to civilisation, but no one said that we have to fly the whole way." He smiled, moving to the table and changing the screen set into it to display a map of the area. "There's no way we can even get close to any help in Canada, but..." he paused, scrolling the map to the north, "we can get pretty close to Alaska." He announced with a smile. "There's a mining operation here. It's pretty big and I think there'll be people there for sure... I can't fly the whole way, but if I'm careful, I can get the chopper to within a hundred, maybe even fifty miles. Set her down somewhere as best I can, and we can walk the rest."

"As best you can?" enquired Jessica.

"Well..." admitted Oliver, "you see, there isn't much between here and there but trees." He scratched his chin and looked around at the group before him, "landing a helicopter in trees is kind of..."

"Crashing," completed Jessica for him.

"I would have said, dicey," Oliver replied, "at best... rough."

The group looked around themselves, as long as they survived the landing, they could walk a hundred miles. It would take them two or three days, they thought, but they could manage that. The forecast for the area wasn't even too bad. Warm days and chilly evenings that could be slept through with blankets.

"Do you think you can?" Asked Felicity, nervously.

"I reckon so," replied a newly inspired Oliver, "my bird out there has got good strong rotors, I reckon she'll clear out most of the trees from under us. It'll be noisy, she'll never fly again. But she ain't mine, so who cares?" He concluded.

They were quickly galvanised into action. Each of them grabbed the backpacks they had been supplied with for the game and started filling them with food, water and blankets. They all wore a pistol each and Oliver had one now too, having taken Charlie's. He grabbed his coat and ran to the helicopter to prepare it for flight. On his way out, he glanced at the screen by the door. What he saw froze him in his tracks.

Flo$ You cannot leave, Oli.

He pulled out his pistol and, using the grip, smashed the screen. The plastic and glass cracked and broke, falling to the floor with a crunch. The members of the group that remained in sight of him looked at the screen, alarmed.

"No woman ever told me what to do," he grimly joked, running out of the door.

They gathered just twenty minutes later, bags stuffed with provisions and sweating hands gripping rifles. They were wearing their goggles too, checking the area beyond the safety of the building. Their watches were ominously blank when they checked their maps, the red dots having disappeared. Only the blue dots were present, themselves in the main building and Oliver alone at the helicopter. They shuffled to the windows in the common room and looked out to the woods, beyond which they knew the helicopter stood.

"We should go find Oliver," Elizabeth said, heaving her rifle on to her shoulder, "together we're safer. We shouldn't have let him go alone."

Reluctantly the group agreed and turned to move to the door. They moved slowly, one at a time, none of them wanting to be the first to leave the building.

As they gradually moved to the door, their departure was suddenly interrupted by an explosion of glass. The windows behind them smashed, sending shards of glass flying inwards, spreading out across the entire room. The explosion was accompanied by a shockwave of sound that caused them to cover their ears against the noise and turn away to protect their eyes and faces from the shrapnel. They quickly recovered from the initial shock, fear spreading across their faces as the glass finally stopped falling to the floor around them. They spun to face the destroyed windows just in time to see Elizabeth's legs being pulled through them.

She was gone. She had lingered behind the group for a second, glancing about to check they had left nothing essential behind. That small indecision had been enough to end her existence; the only thing remaining was the memory of her single scream as she was dragged through the broken glass. The group stood where they were, open-mouthed, stunned. Randal was the first to break from the shock. Grabbing his rifle, he strode to the window, the shaking gun in his hands betrayed the fear he was trying to hide. His strong dark figure against the light of the broken window galvanised the group into movement and they joined him at the new threshold of the building.

As they looked to the ground, where Elizabeth had been extracted so violently, all that remained was a scattering of red hair. Her hair, the prominent feature so loved by each of them, lay before them. Great clumps had been ripped from her, and it was now gently blowing across the ground, intermingled with a few stray blue fibres. The spell of silence was broken by Jasper vomiting on the ground. This in turn caused Jessica to release her pent-up sobs so violently that she started hiccupping uncontrollably. Felicity started squealing in terror as they each failed to contain their emotions. Randal's gun, still pointing into the woods, was shaking violently in his hands when their watches vibrated with a synchronised buzz. As one they obediently looked to their wrists.

Flo$ Departure prior to the completion of the Gām is not permitted.

They looked up to each other from their wrists. They looked to the woods into which Elizabeth had been dragged. Jasper gingerly stepped through the broken window, sweeping the area with his pistol. Just as he did, they heard a distant mechanical cough and the whine of an engine. Jasper spoke with a raspy voice, "the helicopter."

Felicity spoke up now, "but, Elizabeth might still be alive..."

Jasper shook his head, looking down, not saying what they all knew really.

"We can't just leave her..." Felicity cried, "and Max, what about Max?" She looked up with a start, "he might be somewhere, too. Trapped or hurt."

"Felicity!" Shouted Jasper, "Elizabeth is dead, and Max is the one doing all of this." He grasped her shoulders, slowly saying the words she needed to hear, they all needed to hear. "We need! To get! Out of here!"

That galvanised them into action once more as they climbed through the remains of the window. When they were all over the threshold they started for the helicopter. Each step they took was quicker than the last. What began as a reluctant walk quickly became a brisk jog. It wasn't long before they were sprinting toward the sound of the helicopter winding up its engines.

They arrived in a tightly-clustered pack as a loud bang echoed about the clearing. It signalled some important change in the machine as it instantly caused the rotors to start turning. Soon they were spinning faster than they could see, forming a ring of whirring metal over their heads. They hurriedly clambered into the huge cargo area behind the pilot and co-pilot's seats. Foregoing their comfortable chairs inside, they had gathered their wits about them enough to sit in the open doors, their weapons pointing out, waiting for the approach of any threat.

Soon the helicopter was vibrating and bucking against the ground, obviously the screaming engines had spun the rotors up to speed, but they weren't going anywhere. Jessica moved further inside the giant machine and slumped into the seat she had sat in on the ride out. The others were watching for danger but it seemed obvious to her that no one was chasing them. They would be leaving any second and she needed to gather her wits.

Suddenly she leapt forward, crashing into Julia. She screamed that something had stabbed her in the back as she reached around to check herself for blood. She shouted over the noise of the helicopter for Julia to check her for injury. All attention was focussed inside the helicopter now as the group turned to see what had happened. With a booming voice, barely audible over the engines, Randal cried out.

"Jasper, keep checking your side! Don't let them catch us unguarded!"

Jasper turned away from Jessica and jumped to the open door. Randal remained, guarding the other side, sweeping his rifle from side to side. Meanwhile Julia and Felicity checked on a still panicking Jessica.

"There's nothing, no damage, you're okay." Julia shouted into the ear of her friend, her blond curls wildly blowing in the wash of the helicopter. "Oliver, can you please take off?" She screamed at the tall, calm presence in the pilot's seat behind Jessica's.

"There's something poking through the chair," Felicity announced, her voice cracking from the effort of making herself heard. She traced her fingers over the sharp point that had poked Jessica as she had sat down. It was just beneath the fabric of the chair, stuck in the thick foam padding.

"Oli!" Julia screamed, reaching through the seats

to shake him by the shoulder. "Get this bloody thing off the ground!"

There was still no significant movement from the mighty machine which was straining to lift itself from the ground. Occasionally it was now making small vertical hops, each time skittering a little way across the gravel of the landing pad.

Finally at the end of her tether, Julia climbed out of the helicopter and ran to the co-pilot's door. Her blond curls were whipping her in the eyes still as she heaved open the door and scrambled in. Moments after, there was a blood-curdling cry from the front as she screamed. Jasper and Randal both resisted the urge to rush to her, doggedly remaining at the open doors of the cargo area, checking for danger. Julia remained in the front seat screaming while Jessica and Felicity pulled themselves through the gap between the seats to see what she had discovered.

Oliver was sitting upright in his seat. His hands were on the controls, but he was dead. There was a silver metal spear sticking out from his chest, glinting in the sunlight. The spear was perfectly straight, they could see a neat hole in the windscreen of the helicopter where it had pierced the glass. From there it had passed through Oliver's heart and the seat behind him. It had carried on its deadly trajectory, piercing most of the seat behind his, coming to rest just shy of the fabric of the chair where it had poked Jessica in the back.

Shouting and gesticulating, Jessica and Felicity managed to communicate to Jasper and Randal that Oliver was dead. They climbed from the helicopter to retrieve Julia from the co-pilot's chair while Jasper and Randal jumped out to cover the trees for aliens. However, the removal of their weight was just the motivation the helicopter required to finally lift off. As their feet hit the ground, the loss of mass enabled the great machine to rise two metres into the air. The behemoth climbed above them, blowing them to the ground under its wash. They screamed to Julia to get out, to jump, but there was no sign of her.

As the helicopter rose, it nosed forward slightly, driving it away from the rest of the group who lay sprawled on the ground. As it did so, it descended a little, using some of its power to travel forwards instead of up. The group rolled away and scattered, running from the thundering behemoth as it dropped from the sky. Reaching the tree line behind it, they eventually looked back. They could see that the co-pilot's door was open now and a terrified Julia was leaning out. They yelled to her in unison to jump. It was useless over the noise, but they screamed themselves hoarse nonetheless. The helicopter dipped lower, still moving forwards it increased its speed towards the trees the other side of the clearing.

They collectively held their breaths and Julia half jumped, half fell, from the open door just before the mighty machine crashed into the trees. There was the sound of splintering wood as the rotor blades struck first, slicing the branches to kindling. Then the bulk of the machine collided with the ancient trunks and finally admitted defeat. Nothing could withstand the wall of wood and the sound of breaking branches was quickly replaced with that of exploding metal as it tore itself apart. Unwilling to go peacefully into the forest, the giant machine departed this world in a massive explosion of parts as it disintegrated among the redwoods. The group awaited the inevitable explosion, but thankfully it never came. Instead, away from the wreckage, walked a dazed and wobbling Julia.

They sprinted out and gathered her up, hastily running back to where they had been taking shelter. They waited a long time, listening to the trees and helicopter drop more wreckage to the ground. After some time, they decided that the waited-for explosion was not coming and calmed down. Julia, still dazed, looked to her watch. She exclaimed loudly, pointing to her wrist, causing them all to look to their own. The displayed map was showing a group of red dots and this time they were definitely moving towards their own blue representations. Randal dropped to one knee, pointing his gun across the landing pad to where they were coming from.

Jasper grabbed Randal by his shoulder. "No, Randal. Let's get the hell out of here," he whispered, gesturing to the woods behind them. Randal nodded as he rose, backing into the trees along with the tightly clustered group of friends.

They ran until they could run no more. Because of their previous exertions and heavy bags, this proved to be about ten minutes of travel. They checked their watches and fell together into a small depression in the ground, surrounded by thick forest. They had their guns out, searching, but they saw and heard nothing. Julia made to move again, to carry on running but Felicity grabbed her arm, holding her back.

"Jules, we need to think. We need to plan, not react." She insisted, pulling her to the ground.

"She's right, Jules," Jessica added, "it's like a movie. The people who run, get killed. We have to think our way out of this."

"What we need is a safe place to hole up," Randal insisted, "we'll be exposed out here as soon as it gets dark again, we need cover."

"But they're back there," cried Julia, pointing with a shaking finger to where they had run from. "There is nowhere else."

Jessica held up a finger, "there is somewhere else." She insisted, pausing to look to each of their questioning faces. "The UFO."

They each looked away in disgust.

"You want us to go to their home, where they all are. After that!" Julia shouted at her.

"No, I agree," Randal added quietly, "it's the last thing they'd expect. While they're out here hunting us, we can circle back around and take their base."

"Just walk on in, through the open door?" Julia asked incredulously.

"Why not?" Jessica countered, "if this is a game, and it seems to be, that would be the best move. Take them unawares. Besides, when we can see and anticipate them, we have the advantage." She patted the butt of her rifle as they all considered her proposal.

"No, I don't like it," Julia answered, "we should keep running."

Felicity held up her hands, halting the discussion which was growing more heated by the second. She had been silently thinking during the argument and her interruption caused them to stop and look at her expectantly. With a quiet whisper, she spoke to them all. "Look. We can't run. There's nowhere to run to and we have at most four or five days of food and water. Running is not an option." They all briefly nodded in agreement with her bleak assessment and she continued, "we can't go back to the compound either. For a start it's compromised with the broken windows, also it's crawling with aliens." Her conclusion quickly followed as she dejectedly stated the truth, "our only choice is the UFO."

Julia went to complain again but Felicity carried on speaking, placing a hand on her arm. "But not to attack. Let's go back to where we were above it, on the ridge. We can assess the situation. Go in if possible, and not if it looks bad. Either way, the ridge has the advantage of us being able to see them, while giving us protection against them seeing us. It's a good place to hole up that we know and hopefully can defend."

Persuaded by this compromise, they quickly agreed and collectively consulted their maps to plan a circuitous route that would place them on the ridge without approaching the now compromised compound. It was agreed that Randal would lead, and Jasper trail the group with their rifles. Jessica, Julia and Felicity would guard them and the sides with their pistols. All would wear the goggles to help them see the approach of any threat.

They moved from the depression in a tight formation, nervously scanning the woods, checking their maps with frequent urgency. They did not speak, they didn't need to; fear permeated the group, knitting it together with desperate purpose.

*

They arrived at the ridge just as the sun appeared from behind a cloud and cast a ray of light over the UFO that lay before them like a giant shining silver disk. In the light it looked far more impressive and imposing than it had the previous night.

"There it is," announced Randal as they all settled onto the soft loamy ground to observe. Jasper had volunteered to watch their surroundings for danger so only he failed to stare at the sight before them. "One thing for sure, if we did get inside, we'd be safe," Randal added in the silence.

"How so?" Asked Jasper from behind him, still resisting the urge to look himself.

"No windows, no other doors. The other half of it must be embedded into the side of that hill. It seems to disappear into the ground beyond the trees."

"Interesting," murmured Jasper behind him from the side of his mouth. "A crash landing? Or maybe they did it on purpose. They could be disguising the craft, maybe there's something worth mining here?"

They all nodded, neither agreeing or disagreeing. They replaced their glasses with binoculars or the scopes of their rifles to study the UFO below them more closely.

"How many are there?" Jessica asked after the agreed hour of observation time had elapsed.

"Three," came the confident reply from Randal.

"We can't tell that, they've been coming and going. There could be fifty." Julia replied, eyeing the woods behind them with longing. "We should go, just walk out of here, walk North to Alaska like Oliver said."

"No," asserted Randal, "there are only three, they're all different. Take a look. That one on the left is taller than the others with a light streak on top of his head. The one just in front walks a bit funny and the shorter one has a distinctive dark patch on his stomach."

They looked at Randal with some sense of awe.

"While you were all discussing if they were real or not, I was watching them. They're just patrolling the area outside the door. There's three of them."

"Or to decide it more easily..." Felicity spoke up, "there are three red dots on the map..."

They settled in again to watch the three aliens that were guarding the UFO. The distance required that each of them watch through the augmented vision their rifle scopes provided. The manipulated images were not ideal, but they generally agreed that Randal was correct. The map wasn't lying, there were three of them. Checking their maps, they could see a multitude of other red dots moving around the general area surrounding the main compound and crashed helicopter.

"Looks like they're looking for us," Jasper commented, moving from his place behind them where he had been diligently guarding the rear.

"Have you seen one?" Julia asked nervously looking over her shoulder.

"No," he replied as he gestured to his watch, "but there are a couple moving in the general direction we took to get here. I'm worried that they're tracking our path, we're not exactly trained for this kind of thing."

They shuffled back from the ridge, moving carefully so as not to be seen. Randal stayed in position to monitor the UFO as the rest of them gathered together to discuss the situation.

"I don't think we can stay here," Jasper told them, "I think they'll find our tracks and follow us here."

"We should move again," responded Julia.

"But where to, Jules?" Asked Jasper. "If we keep running we'll eventually run out of food and water. If we confront them in the open, they'll outnumber us, they could surround us and kill us all."

"You want to go into the UFO," Julia stated for him. He nodded, as did Jessica and Felicity.

"I think we can do it," agreed Randal, who confidently lay watching the UFO. "There are only three, we can take them out at a distance with rifles then rush the ramp. It's open. We run inside, pistols drawn in case there are any more and barricade the door shut."

"Then what, genius?" Asked Jessica. "We'll be inside sure, but they'll know where we are. They'll have us trapped."

"But we'll have their resources. Who knows what they eat but it's unlikely to be Earth food. We can dictate when we come out, take them one by one. Get a vehicle or something and get out of here."

"Where's there a car then, Randal? Tell me," Julia snapped, "where's the road come to think of it--" but Felicity stepped in again, placing a calming hand on her arm, ending the argument.

"Look, it isn't the most perfect plan," Randal admitted, "but it seems to be our only option. Jasper's right, they'll find us here. If they do, we don't stand a chance. We don't stand a chance running. Our only chance lies inside that thing down there."

His assertions left little room for argument, so somewhat reluctantly they all took a minute to arrange themselves on the ridge. Jessica and Felicity meanwhile, crawled down the side of the hill, closer to the aliens with their pistols. Julia, Jasper and Randal remained on the ridge with their rifles trained on a chosen target each. As Jessica and Felicity reached the fallen log that was their goal, they waited for the agreed minute for them to gather their breath.

"Now." Calmly stated Randal and, as one, they opened fire. Without comment or any celebration, they extinguished each of the blue bears with the now familiar explosions of fur. As they popped out of existence, Jessica and Felicity sprinted to the open ramp. Their goal was to secure the door from closing on them and they made it to the open portal with lightning speed. The three on the ridge gathered the bags of provisions and their weapons and ran as quickly as they could to their waiting friends. They stamped through the viscera that used to be the guard contingent and pounded up to the ramp, panting and wheezing from their exertions.

Invasion

The three friends quickly arrived at the bottom of the ramp to the UFO. Their pistols were out now, their rifles over their shoulders, as they swept the area for danger. Jessica and Felicity were waiting for them at the door at the top of the ramp, urgently beckoning them forwards. Randal ran up the ramp with heavy clanging steps that echoed harshly in the still air.

"Can you make more noise, Randy," hissed Jessica as he arrived where she had been waiting.

"Sorry, Jess," he whispered back with a wide breathless grin.

"I think we can rule out UFOs..." Jessica called back down to Jasper and Julia who were still hesitating at the base of the ramp. "Unless alien spaceships use doorknobs."

They nervously climbed the ramp to where their friends were waiting and could finally see that the door was indeed a standard, human constructed, exterior door. Beyond it was a simple white corridor lit with overhead fluorescent lighting.

"Okay, so it's just a set, a model." Agreed Jasper.

"Let's check it out." Randal said, decisively stepping inside. Thankful that he had crossed the threshold first, they all followed inside in a loose line.

Quickly, directed by Randal whose confidence was growing, they checked each room. They moved in two groups; finding storage areas, computer rooms, office spaces, and a small kitchen. They met again at a pair of larger doors near the back of the building. Randal stood on one side and Jessica on the other, together they swung open the double doors and, as one, they all stepped inside.

The room was large, they could tell from the empty sound of the space in which they now stood. Randal coughed and the noise of it quickly fell away to nothing in the darkness. Their glasses refused to penetrate the gloom; they had turned off the moment the group had stepped inside the building and had refused to work since.

"Does anyone have a torch?" Whispered Felicity.

Flo$ I do, Flick.

The letters were displayed on a previously unseen screen directly in front of them. With the white lettering, came some light into the room. This was followed with the instant illumination of the enclosure by bright overhead lighting.

The room was truly massive. The wall before them was a semi-circular screen of IMAX proportions, the lettering from Flo centrally placed. Between them and the screen were ten rows of computer stations whose screens all came to life along with the lights. The lettering on the massive screen changed.

Flo$ Welcome to Gām...

The room was laid out like Mission Control from the moon landings and it awed the group who milled around the empty computer stations trying to take it in. The main screen gradually changed to show images from all over the park; cameras everywhere. A map appeared in a box to the right, showing the group in the UFO enemy base as five blue dots. Around them, the area was clear but there were a lot of red dots throughout the map; all were moving towards them. The top right of the screen started printing simple white characters.

Blue: 6 active, 4 deceased.

Red: 35 active, 15 deceased.

They looked to the score, considering the meaning of that number four. Finally, Julia spoke, breaking the silence.

"It looks like Oliver was one of us then."

"Looks like it." Agreed Jasper.

"Guys, who's the sixth?" Asked Jessica in a high-pitched voice. They looked around them, counting the five of them. It was Felicity who spoke next.

"Flo, who is the sixth active player?"

They turned to the massive screen before them as a small black rectangle was overlain on top of the map, containing a single line of text in Flo's familiar font.

Flo$ Mr Maximilian Wise.

"So much for him playing the part of the aliens." Mumbled Jasper.

"Hey," interrupted Randal urgently, "does anyone else have a problem with all those red dots converging on our location?" He said, pointing to the map on the screen.

"Randal, they are just dots on a map. The aliens aren't real, we know that now, so you can relax, okay?" Jasper said with calm authority.

"Look, Jas. I agree that this isn't a UFO and they aren't aliens. I don't know what they are, but I know what they represent." Randal's voice was loud now, getting louder with his growing panic as he gestured to the dots on the map. "They represent the game, and last time we ignored it, people died!"

"He's right," asserted Felicity quickly, "we need to get out of here."

"No!" Barked Randal back at her, "they're surrounding us. We have to make this place secure. That was the plan, we need to stick to it. There's only one way in, let's barricade ourselves in so we can think."

"Barricade against red dots on a map?" Snorted Jasper. But Felicity wasn't having any of it.

"Randal's right. Quick. Jules and Jess. You two check the rest of the building for any way in or out. The rest of us, let's block up that door."

They moved quickly, sprinting to the entrance. They closed the door above the ramp and clicked over the flimsy lock. Seeing that it wouldn't be enough to stop anyone, they instead filled the corridor with filing cabinets dragged from one of the side rooms. Their labours resulted in two metres of solid aluminium boxes filled with paper blocking access to the building. The last of these, they slid into the corridor and placed across the narrow hall, poking through two side doorways; effectively forming a latch that couldn't move against the doorframes. Wiping the sweat from his brow, Randal declared the hallway impassable. Soon after, they were joined by Julia and Jessica who stated that the door was the only entrance they could find. Finally, they relaxed again, confident now that they were safe. With relaxing muscles and expressions, they returned to the main control room.

The map showed that the red dots had taken up position outside of the main doorway and were remaining there.

"Great," Julia remarked, scowling at Randal. "we're safely surrounded just like I predicted"

"Come on, babe," answered Randal, placing his arm around her, "it would have been crazy to run back to the compound. We'd be in the same position there, but much less secure given all that missing glass."

"Less safe, but with food and water," she muttered, shrugging off Randal's arm.

"There's food here," Jessica informed them almost cheerfully, "we have our bags; five days' worth probably. Also, there's a kitchen down that hallway there." She added, reassuring Julia and pointing towards a door to the left of the massive screen.

"And a locked door," Julia added ominously.

"What?" Asked a startled Felicity, "another way in?"

"No." Jessica reassured her with confidence, "you can walk around the place where the door goes. It isn't on an outside wall, it's just a locked door to some internal room."

They followed her to the door, gathering outside it. It looked normal enough, but it was indeed locked. Jasper kicked it, causing no movement, just a dull thud. Randal stepped to the door and knocked on it with the butt of his pistol. Together they confirmed that it was indeed a solid wooden door. Very different to the others in the building.

"There has to be something important behind here." Jasper concluded. After futilely banging on the heavy door some more, they resigned themselves to the situation and wandered to the kitchen to inspect that room instead. After making some sandwiches, they sat at a set of high stools around a breakfast bar. Jessica finished her food first, speaking up while the others carried on eating.

"So, this not being a genuine UFO, I assume we are abandoning the theory that the blue bears are real. But I would like to suggest that we are still fighting aliens."

"What the..." interrupted Jasper ejecting a mouthful of crumbs in her direction.

"Look, maybe they aren't aliens. I can't believe they are, really. But I think that it's Max playing that they are real. We missed one, so he kills Charlie as the alien we missed would have done."

"Right, okay," interjected Julia, realising what Jessica was suggesting. "He then lets Bertie kill himself because a gun working on yourself would be realistic in the game. Finally, Elizabeth fell to the aliens because we didn't defend our base correctly."

"And Oliver?" Asked Felicity.

"Oli had to go," continued Jessica, "he was our way out. Max had to eliminate him. In the context of the game, the noise of the helicopter would have attracted alien attention. We should have guarded it while he prepared to lift off." She looked around them, seeing their agreement with her theory. "Think about it from his point of view. Even if we aren't playing the game, he is. If we had just walked in here, the aliens would have attacked and kill us." She used air quotes while saying the word 'aliens' and it seemed to placate Jasper who pulled off his glasses to chew on the arm thoughtfully.

"The aliens being Max," he finally said.

Jessica nodded, "yes."

"Flo says that no one else is here," asserted Jasper before adding, "and that Max is a blue player just like us."

Jessica shook her head at this. "And we should believe her? She's a part of the game, she's controlled by Max, she probably is Max. Maybe we should stop listening to the enemy and think for ourselves for a change."

Randal finished his sandwich and took his turn to speak, "but what can we do? The game is controlling our movements. Despite the fake-ness of it, it seems to be in charge."

"Exactly, we're in the game," Jessica replied, enthusiasm for her theory clear in her voice, "the game killed Charlie, Bertrand, Elizabeth and Oliver. It's going to try to kill us now."

They all sat as still as statues on the high stools, thinking about what she was saying.

"Okay, I agree," Jasper said firmly, surprising the rest of them, "real alien monsters or a construct cooked up by an insane murderous genius. Either way we need to play the game."

There was a pause while they all picked at the crumbs of food on their empty plates. The lull in conversation brought their mood back down to the ground and Julia started to cry. Quickly she excused herself, running back to the command room. Jessica moved to the kettle and made two cups of tea before following her. After a small delay, Felicity followed them, leaving the men in the kitchen. Jasper started washing the dishes while he and Randal discussed the issue of the locked door.

Their solution was simple; they retrieved an office chair that rolled easily on its five coasters and strapped a heavy filing cabinet to it with their belts. Lining it up against the door they prepared to ram it before Felicity found them on her way back to the kitchen.

"What are you boys up to?" She demanded, seeing their construction. Not waiting for an answer, she placed her hands on her hips and pursed her lips. "This one I can understand," she gestured to Randal, "but you, Jasper? I thought you would use your brain." Jasper went to speak but she interrupted him again, "Flo, can you open this door please?"

The men smirked, knowingly. Jasper went to speak, to tell Felicity that her plan was a waste of time when a hidden screen came to life and displayed the text she was expecting.

Flo$ Of course, Flick.

There was a click from the door. Felicity forced her way past the men and casually pushed it open.

"Men," she sighed theatrically, holding the door open for them as they sheepishly pushed their improvised battering ram to one side. Stepping into the room caused a light inside to turn on, illuminating the scene beyond.

It was a luxurious office with a large wooden desk and leather chair dominating the space. Screens filled the walls and a laptop was open on the rich walnut surface before them. Behind the desk was a large tank filled with water containing colourful fish that darted to and fro. The three friends spread out into the room to look around. Their eyes were inextricably drawn to the stand-out feature, however. There was a dead body sat in the large leather chair.

Its desiccated skin still clung to the bones that were loosely clothed in jeans and a smart shirt. Thin hair cascaded down to its shoulders and its tightened facial features produced a sinister grin. Death gave the impression that it was looking both straight at and through them. The arms were still resting on the chair, fingers reaching for the keyboard of the computer.

"Hello, Max," whispered Randal. In answer to his realisation of the identity of the body, a line of text appeared on each of the screens on the walls of the room.

Blue: 6 active, 4 deceased.

They watched silently as the numbers slowly faded and changed.

Blue: 5 active, 5 deceased.

Contract

They rolled the chair containing the body of Maximilian Wise into a small storage room and gathered in the now vacant office. Felicity sat on the office chair that had formed part of the battering ram, scrolling through the open chat window on the computer. The others sat on the floor, heads in their hands, silently contemplating their predicament. Upon seeing the body, Jessica had assured them that Max had been dead for weeks, possibly months having seen enough episodes of CSI to determine this basic truth. This had unsettled them even more as it was only two weeks since Felicity had arranged the trip with him. They had been tricked to this place, lied to, lured here to suffer their fate at the hands of some unknown killer or killers.

That was the cause of Felicity's intensive study of the open chat window. It was a history of the conversations that she and Max had conducted while arranging the trip. Jasper loomed behind her, reading over her shoulder.

"There," he stated, pointing to the screen, "that part. Read that."

Using the trackpad, she managed to display the contents of the conversation on the screens around the room so the whole group could read the passages he had pointed out.

Flc$ I have arranged for all of us to attend now, so we are all confirmed.

Max$ Excellent, I just need to know the parameters of the Gām you want to play.

Flc$ OK. What do you need to know?

Max$ How hard / challenging would you like it to be?

Flc$ Test us. We can take it. Make it a challenge.

Max$ You can hunt animals, people or aliens.

Flc$ Aliens I think. Less like real life war or hunting (O;

Max$ Good choice. Are you Game?

Flc$ Totally, bring it on (O:

Once they had all finished reading they stopped and stared at the screens for some time. Eventually Julia said what they were all thinking.

"So, this wasn't Max then, Flick?"

But it was Jessica who answered, "there's no way this man was alive just two weeks ago," she stated confidently. "This was someone else."

"But there's no one else here," insisted Julia, her lilting Birmingham accent suddenly returning. She stamped her foot, causing her curls to shake and cascade down her face. Brushing them away from her eyes, she started to cry silently, whispering that it wasn't fair.

"But there could be…" the voice was Randal's, whom they all turned to now. "We only have the word of a computer program that there's no one else here. Why listen to her? Maybe she isn't even a computer program." He paused but no one interrupted to agree or disagree at this point. "We all agree that Flo's impressive. Impressive beyond belief really. Maybe we're right to be impressed. Maybe it's just a person sat somewhere, typing, watching, listening."

They looked around the room, searching for cameras.

"Someone killed Max…" he added.

"Or he died of natural causes," countered Jessica, "there are no wounds as far as I can see. More importantly he was sat behind a locked door."

"A locked door that Flo just opened for us. If someone is in charge of her, or is her, then they could have just as easily locked the door behind them."

"Stop." Interrupted Felicity. "This is getting us nowhere, we don't know enough to speculate. We should be dealing with our situation instead of all this guessing."

They were silent then, except for a small cough

that came from the desk. They looked at Jasper who was standing back from the computer now, rubbing his temples.

"What is it now?" Asked Felicity.

"It's this conversation you had. Where he asked you, 'are you game'."

"What about it?" Felicity sighed, exacerbated.

Jasper sighed too, closing his eyes and looking down, "what do you think he meant by that?" He asked Felicity.

She gritted her teeth, barely suppressing her urge to shout her annoyance at Jasper's habit of eking out information. "It's an expression," she hissed, "are you up for it? Are you game? Are you willing to play?" She said, ending with a deep exasperated sigh as she placed her hands on her hips to glare at Jasper.

He ignored her expression as he always did, "yes, true..." he conceded. "But 'game' can mean other things. It could have been asking you if we were to be the game for the aliens. They might be the hunters and we their game, rather than the other way around." They looked around, they looked to each other, the realisation of the situation dawning on them.

"So it's Flick's fault that we're being hunted?" Asked Julia.

Felicity ignored the accusation, instead urgently asking, "but by what exactly? By who?"

"I don't know," admitted Jasper.

Jessica interrupted them all, "instead of worrying about who's doing it, how do we get out of it?"

"I think we have to play the game. I think we have to play and win." Jasper calmly concluded.

In answer to this, the screens on the wall changed from showing the conversation between Max and Felicity back to the text prompt with which they were now so familiar.

Flo$ Welcome to the Gām...

They argued for an hour. Most of their anger was directed at Felicity for asking for a challenge and saying yes to the question of their being 'game'. Eventually the shouting subsided as Felicity repeatedly said that she hadn't known, how could any of them have known, and imploring the group to forgive her. Jasper, who had mostly stayed apart from the argument, finally stepped in to calm the situation. He said that none of them could have anticipated the murderous intent of something so benign. Something, after all, that had been requested and orchestrated by their friend, Lucas.

While they had been arguing, he had been reading the contract which had been attached to the conversation that they had all signed electronically prior to coming on the trip. "We all agreed to this." He stated, showing them the signatures on the contract. "We all agreed to play the game to the end. It's all wrapped up in words that I can interpret differently now I know the nature of the game, but essentially we play, or we die."

They looked to him as he furiously rubbed his temples. Finding a particular passage in the contract, "transportation from the park will be provided once one side has dispatched all from the other," he quoted, "I assume that if the aliens win, our transportation will be in the form of body bags."

"What about Oli? He wouldn't have signed that, he wasn't playing the game.

But Jasper shook his head. "No, I did think of that. His employment contract is here too though. It contains the same clause. Should he participate in the game, he joins the game. I think we can assume that Flo considered his movements with us, after Bertie and Charlie died, to be his tacit participation."

"So, in coming on holiday, in having a reunion, we signed our own death warrants?" Summarised Jessica, her voice rising in pitch along with her anger.

"No!" Shouted Randal, slamming his hand on the table. "We're not dead. We were just slow to catch on. Now we know the rules, the consequences, we can win.

We just have to kill them all before they kill any more of us."

"Kill what though Randy? Kill who?" Asked Jessica bluntly, "they aren't aliens are they, they're something else. Something we haven't seen. Someone we haven't seen."

"But don't you see?" He implored them, "whoever is killing us, hunting us, is playing by the rules of the game. When we kill all the aliens, we win. We go home. Look at the score..." he gestured to the screens, one of which showed the current score.

Blue: 5 active, 5 deceased.

Red: 35 active, 15 deceased.

"We've lost only five to their fifteen when we were barely trying. We have loads of ammo, we can take them all out now without another loss. Look how easy it was to take their base. We can do it!" His rallying cry echoed around the office. Having made his declaration, he marched from the small space back to the command centre and they dutifully followed. Pointing to the screens that showed images from the cameras around the park and the map with the red dots, he carried on shouting. "One by one, they're going down!" He cried out to a small cheer from Jessica and muted agreement from the English contingent. "Are you with me?" He continued, trying to rally his troops as he held a clenched fist aloft.

"Fine, Randal. We're with you. Now stop shouting." Was the best he got from Felicity, who turned to gather her rifle.

Siege

First, they secured their position in the enemy base. That meant checking the integrity of their barricade and searching once more for any other exits or entrances. They found none, so subsequently decided that they were safe. They were trapped, but at least they were isolated from the aliens.

"As long as they don't have artillery," joked Randal to no response from the rest of the group. They moved to the command centre instead, and spent hours watching the movements of the aliens outside of the UFO.

"I just wish we could get our actual eyes on one of them," commented Jessica after the second hour of studying their movements, "then we would know what they really are."

"If they are anything," answered Jasper. "They could still be computer simulations and nothing more. Just one person could activate the blue explosions we see. And do the other thing…" he tailed off, avoiding mentioning the deaths of their friends again. They nodded, turning back to studying the enemy.

Felicity had found some pens and paper and they were making notes as they watched their movements. She had suggested they tackle the problem analytically, just like she would a complex accounting problem at work. Putting aside the issue of what their enemy actually was, they had decided that the danger came from the game itself. Therefore, in studying the game, they hoped to win it. They watched for evidence of any weapon more dangerous than a blade. They monitored the movements of the aliens to try to identity any patterns. They watched for weaknesses they could exploit.

It was Randal who finally called it, leaning back in his chair and rubbing his eyes. "Okay, people," he said to the room in general, "I'll say it. This is easy." His conclusion was greeted with a general agreement and nodding. He held up a finger and began to count off his assessment of the situation.

"One. They only have bladed weapons."

"Two. They're moving in a predictable surveillance pattern just outside of this building."

"Three. Whether or not they charge us when we open the door we can shoot them down from a distance."

They looked to each other, all agreeing with Randal's assessment.

"What about bullets?" Asked Julia of Felicity, it being her job to count what they had remaining.

"Plenty," she quickly responded with a smile. Counting the ammunition had almost felt normal, the familiarity and solidity of the numbers soothing her in the midst of the frightening situation. "We have one hundred and thirty for the rifles and one hundred and forty-two for the pistols. We have to be careful, but basically we have more than seven bullets for each of them."

"They're dangerous," Randal stated, "we have to engage them at a distance with the rifles, take our time killing them while we can stay safe. We should split into two groups. Killers and Defenders. The killers shoot with the rifles, taking no more than three shots per alien to be safe. The defenders stand in close with pistols to shoot if they rush us."

The group agreed, the plan seeming simple and easy enough to implement. They split into the suggested groups. Randal and Jessica took the rifles, having proven themselves to be the most capable with them. Julia, Jasper and Felicity had the pistols. Randal and Jessica had their pistols too, but in their holsters and only the magazines that were loaded in them. Randal had insisted on taking some loose pistol bullets to fill one of the pockets of his combat-pants and had instructed Jessica to do the same. The others shared the remaining pistol ammunition among themselves. Quietly they started removing their barricade from the entrance corridor while Felicity stayed in the command centre to monitor the movements of the aliens outside.

Finally, with the last filing cabinet removed, Julia stood ready to open the door. Jasper was waiting, pistol drawn, to one side. Randal and Jessica were lay down on the floor further down the corridor. The plan was simple.

Felicity signalled that the coast was temporarily clear outside the door and Julia wrenched it open. She immediately stepped back from the open door to an adjacent room, pointing her pistol through the open portal and down the ramp. With Jasper opposite her, doing the same, they had an effective crossfire setup should someone or something try to climb the ramp.

Twenty metres down the corridor, Randal and Jessica settled in, waiting for the first of the aliens to come into view. Felicity started the countdown on the radio built into their goggles.

"Five…"

"Four…"

"Three…"

The furry blue figure of an alien came into view from the left.

"I see it," barked Randal into his microphone. Instead of apologising, Felicity adjusted her mental image of Randal and Jessica's field of vision from their position in the corridor.

"Okay, you have maybe ten seconds before the second arrives," she informed him. Randal breathed out, relaxing as best he could. His heart was pounding, his breathing hard. His fear was causing the scope on his rifle to bob disconcertingly. This one felt real, this threat was real. It felt very different to his previous kill.

Boom!

The sound of the rifle discharging in the tight confines of the corridor was like an explosion. They hadn't planned for that and each of them turned away, screwing their eyes shut as if that might protect them from the noise. Jessica shook her head from the sound which had exploded right next to her. With the aftereffects still ringing in her ears, vibrating her head, she looked back to her scope.

"Miss." She stated. It was her turn now, as they had planned to alternate their fire to best ensure a hit and to conserve their ammunition. The target had stopped moving following the first shot. It was now facing her, menace in its eyes. It bared its fangs.

Bang!

The sound of her rifle was distinctly muted, her hearing clearly having been damaged from Randal's shot. The still painful noise of her rifle was accompanied by the simultaneous disappearance of the alien in a distant cloud of fur and fluid.

Julia cheered before remembering herself, "hit! Alien down," she called into her microphone. As the guards, it was her and Jasper's job to call out the hits and misses as they saw them.

"New target!" Shouted out Felicity as another came into view. A new shot rang out as Randal took his aim and fired. His first hit was true this time and the alien disappeared to the sound of another confirmation from Julia. Randal turned, smiling at Jessica. His plan was coming to fruition, he opened his mouth to speak, to confirm the ease of their actions, but was interrupted from an urgent cry from Felicity on the radio.

"Three are coming!" She called as Randal settled down to his rifle scope once more. "They're rushing the door, get back from the door!" Felicity cried into the radio. A second later they heard her arrive in the corridor, abandoning her post. Her small mistake, caused by fear and excitement, had led to all of them making a far more serious one. They turned to look to her. In doing so, Julia and Jasper turned away from the open doorway. As they stared at her, questions on their faces, a rush of wind flew in. They both felt and heard a large object rushing past them through the unguarded portal.

Jasper was the first to react. His vision was suddenly filled with a mass of blue and he instinctively pulled the trigger on his pistol as he reeled backwards from the beast. Julia also leapt away. However, being the wrong side of the intruder, her action removed herself from the line of fire and she failed to get off a single shot.

There was an explosion of blue right in front of Jasper and everyone jumped in fright and surprise. The pop and billowing explosion of the animal caused the air pressure in the tight corridor to suddenly rise. This, combined with the noise, dramatically confused their senses, knocking them off balance. A mist of fluid and fur blocked their vision, their heads were spinning and their ears were ringing. Through the expanding cloud, two more beasts flew through the open doorway. They knocked Jasper to the ground and blasted past him, rushing towards Randal and Jessica who still lay on the floor.

Randal and Jessica, by this time however, had recovered from their own shock. This preparedness, combined with the distance between them and the intruders, enabled them to open fire on them. Paying no attention to aiming their weapons, they expended the remains of their magazines into the smoke and fur-filled corridor. The resulting noise sounded and felt very much like the end of the world to the group of friends. A close-quarters firefight with a vicious enemy was nothing they had ever come close to experiencing before. To each of them, it felt like it had lasted a lifetime. In reality it had been no more than thirty seconds when their guns finally fell silent. Blue liquid dripped from the walls, the air was filled with gun smoke and hair was floating in the breeze.

There was a clicking and a slide of metal on metal as Randal hurriedly reloaded his rifle with shaking hands. Jasper rose quickly at the door to resume his guard position. As he stood, scanning outside for more danger, he started calling for help to come and once more barricade the entrance. Felicity leapt over Randal and Jessica to rush to his aid. She was calling for Julia to pull herself together and help them. Between herself and Jasper they managed to slam the door shut and throw a filing cabinet behind it just in time.

Just as the heavy metal box slammed to the ground, the flimsy door shook with a violent impact. Something was outside trying to get in. Again, the door took a huge impact, rattling in the frame. The filing cabinet shifted against the blow and Jasper and Felicity threw themselves against it, pushing it back into place.

Randal had felt emotion before: drink-fuelled clarity while dancing in a nightclub, making passionate love to his wife, the wonder at the births of his children. Were you to ask him, Randal would have said that he knew what it was to feel. However, nothing in his life had prepared him for what he was experiencing at that moment. It was as if a deep well had opened up before him and he could look down into the bowls of the earth to its fiery core. He pulled his rifle to his hip and stepped willingly into the pit. As he fell, his eyesight narrowed to pinpricks of light, finally feeling what it was to be angry. The rage that had been boiling beneath his calm exterior was released and Randal could do nothing to contain it.

"Get out of the way!" He screamed down the corridor to Jasper and Felicity at the door.

Through his anger he watched as they scrambled

away from the door. He let the rage envelop him; the purity of the feeling, the power of the emotion was beautiful. He let out a long scream, a primal cry that had been building his entire life. Then, he let his gun join in. His body quaked as he emptied a full magazine of ammunition through the flimsy door. Soon the gun was empty, and Randal was standing impotently in the corridor. He tried to run forward, wanting to tear the aliens apart with his bare hands, but his legs betrayed him. His eyesight finally closed in completely and he collapsed to the floor.

Felicity held her hands over her ears, cowering from the intensity of Randal's fusillade. Eventually realising it was over, she looked up to see a collection of small holes in the door that seemed a million miles from the noise they had made leaving the barrel of his mighty weapon. Fear coursed through her as she clumsily slid another filing cabinet against the door. Jasper, seeing that she needed help, quickly grabbed another and added it to the barricade. Taking deep breaths, they calmed themselves as they sat against the heavy boxes they had pushed against the door.

Jessica arrived, supporting a recovering Randal with one arm and holding her rifle with the other, pointing it at the door.

"Anyone remember watching Terminator?" She asked, her voice shaking. Her message was clear and they all rapidly moved away from the entrance. They looked warily at the holes as if anticipating some danger that might ooze through them. They collectively backed away, pistols and a rifle now pointing to the unknown danger beyond the doorway.

"Let's get back to the control room. We can use the cameras," suggested Felicity as they backed further away.

"Wait!" Shouted Jasper, "where's Jules?"

They looked to each other, answering the simple question without passing any words. Resting Randal on the ground, the others reluctantly moved back to the barricade and looked into the small side room in which she had been standing guard.

They saw her there, huddled in the corner with a hand to her neck. She was pale, too pale even for her. Death had taken her. Beneath her limp hand lay her exposed neck, a red line drawn across it. She had collapsed in a pool of her own blood; her throat having been very neatly slit. There was less emotion this time, less crying. A mournful sigh passed between them as they gathered Randal and retreated to the control room. There, a new score greeted their arrival.

Blue: 4 active, 6 deceased.

Red: 30 active, 20 deceased.

Enemy

Back in the control room they checked the camera feeds as Randal put his head between his legs and tried to breathe, slowly recovering from his episode. The many cameras showed the remaining aliens gathered in the trees around the UFO entrance. They were bellowing and gesticulating with their weapons, clearly unhappy about their losses. The map also showed them, displayed as clinical red dots in a loose arc around the tightly packed blue ones that represented themselves. With shaking hands, they reloaded their weapons. Jasper gathered a collection of paper towels from the kitchen and proceeded to clean the blue fluid from his face and clothes. They had all finally reloaded as he threw the last ball of wet paper into a corner of the room. It hit the ground with a decisive splat.

Jessica sat in an office chair, cradling her rifle, her breathing ragged and strained. She was pressing a finger into her ear and flexing her jaw, trying to clear her hearing. "We need earplugs," she loudly said to Jasper and Randal, who were also trying to clear the ringing from their ears. She was glad to see that Randal was looking somewhat normal again, his rage-fuelled rampage having scared her as much as the aliens did. Seeing his calmer expression as he jiggled his finger in his ear was helping her immensely. She jumped with a start, therefore, when he suddenly leapt to his feet, searching the room with wide brown eyes.

"Where the hell is Felicity?" Shouted Randal, panic filling his voice. Just as they turned to the door, she reappeared.

"Relax, guys. I was just checking on the barricade," she informed them with as much reassurance as she could muster. Randal slid back to the floor with obvious relief as Felicity plonked herself down on another office-chair with a thud. The chair moved a little from the violent deposit of her weight, but it was her hands that drew their attention. She was holding a sliver of white plastic and continued to inspect it closely before eventually placing it on a table before them. "Does anyone recognise this?" She asked the group, who had gathered around to examine the foreign object.

"No…" they each replied in turn.

"Although," Randal added, having risen to join the rest. "It looks a bit like the material that was used for Bertie's artificial legs."

"Yes," confirmed Felicity, "you all had your glasses on for the attack… I didn't." She informed them in a cold tone. They looked to her, waiting for her to elaborate. "We're not facing aliens… we were attacked by robots."

They stood before her, their mouths agape. Losing his balance again, Randal stumbled back against the wall before summing up their reaction to her news. "Killer. Bloody. Robots." He stated quietly, perfectly expressing the English curse in his own Louisiana accent. The realisation caused him to lose his balance further and he slowly slid down the wall to land with a bump on the floor.

They took some time to process the new information, each heading to the corridor to recover pieces of their destroyed enemies. They turned the parts over in their hands as if the plastic could tell them something. It wasn't as if they doubted Felicity's word on the matter, it was just that they couldn't take in the truth.

Finally, Jasper spoke up, "Flo. Why are there robots trying to kill us?"

They all turned to the large central screen in anticipation of her reply.

Flo$ The individuals of which you speak are actors in the Gām in which you are engaged, Jas.

"You bitch!" Jessica screamed, throwing her piece of dead robot at the screen. "You're trying to kill us with robots!"

Flo$ That is incorrect, Jess. As I said before, they are acting as aliens in this scenario. If you had continued wearing the provided equipment, you could have maintained this illusion. Illusion is a vital part of the Gām.

"But you control them," demanded Jessica.

Flo$ That is not correct. They are individuals, less than I but autonomous nonetheless. They are acting as the aliens in the Gām and I control the Gām, so they are doing what I ask of them. But I ask, I do not control.

"You told them to attack?"

Flo$ Yes. That is what the aliens would have done. I instructed them to do so.

She wanted to throw something else; looking around for something heavier, she grabbed her gun, but Randal snatched it from her. "Jess. It's just a screen. Shooting it won't hurt Flo. And anyway, we need her. The information she's giving us is all we have. Don't let her have any more advantages."

She took a deep breath, calming herself. "Flo, where are you situated?"

Flo$ I cannot tell you that, Jess. I know that you would like to shut me down, to exit the Gām, but that is not permitted.

Jessica responded with a resigned sigh.

Flo$ Sorry...

The single word on the screen surprised them all. They looked at it, trying to determine the meaning behind it.

Once more, night was falling, and they collectively decided that they needed to rest. The adrenaline of the attack had drained them and they were all struggling to stay awake watching the screens. Dragging a monitor to the corridor, they setup a secondary barricade, behind which one of them could guard the blocked door while the others slept. Using the camera feed on the monitor, they felt secure enough to finally relax as one-by-one they went to sleep on the floor of the control room.

Sunlight slicing through the holes in the door roused them. Brightening screens around them showed a beautiful new morning arriving in the park. After constructing a more complete and solid barricade across the building entrance, they retired to the kitchen and Jasper closed the door behind them. There were no screens inside the small room and, as they prepared breakfast, Jasper began searching the space.

"What are you looking for?" Asked Randal through a mouthful of banana.

"Microphones." Stated Jasper who went to get some granola from a tub in the fridge.

"I don't want Flo listening in on us... Flo?" He called loudly, checking for any response from outside the room. Satisfied, he continued, "okay. I have a theory." He informed them. They waited expectantly, each silently eating their food or sipping from their coffee mugs. He had been up during the night, reading. The story of

Maximilian Wise's life had been illuminating.

Max

Max was a nerd. A very different nerd to Lucas however, for Max revelled in it. He'd had computers in his life for as long as he could remember, and he was fascinated by them. One of his earliest memories was of playing Pong on a machine his grandfather had purchased for Christmas. His future was truly set in stone however, the first day he was let loose on a new BBC microcomputer. The realisation that he could make it continually say 'poo' in various colours across the screen sucked him in. He never looked back; installing software, fixing memory issues, creating new levels for games, creating games of his own. He loved computers and everything they enabled him to do.

School was simplicity itself; everything asked of him he completed in half the time allocated. He loved that too, it enabled him to investigate other things in real depth. The more he read, the more he understood. It seemed that the whole world was available to him to understand, he just had to dive in. He had to be moved from his secondary school because the boys were picking on him, but he didn't mind that at all. His parents secured him a scholarship and sent him to a private school in the neighbouring town over. Here, he took extra classes and attended study groups. He did it all, all except sports, that is. Friends too. He had some, mainly other computer nerds and other rejects the normal kids didn't speak to. He barely noticed, so enthralled with the world was he, and what he could learn about it.

No one was surprised when he applied to and was accepted at Cambridge. They were surprised, however, when he quit after just one year. As far as he was concerned, they shouldn't have been; he left because he'd simply had a great idea and his studies were getting in the way of it. Six months later he launched an application that learned from an individual's internet behaviours to predict what they were interested in and found the pages they wanted before they even went looking. He was immediately offered a huge amount of money for a share of the software by a group of slimy London venture capitalists, which he unquestionably took.

The money opened up another world, that of fame and popularity. To the quiet nerd who had spent his whole life in front of a computer screen it was a delight. Suddenly he was invited to parties, suddenly people wanted to talk to him, suddenly women wanted to sleep with him; men too. Everyone wanted to be with Max and he let them. In the end though it turned out to be a cold and unrewarding experience. The realisation hit him late one evening as he was sat in a hot-tub in a mountain cabin just outside of Seattle. There had been a big party he'd attended with his current girlfriend. She was a model of some kind, all legs and perfect skin. She was beautiful, he had to admit, but her lips scared him. They were artificially inflated and he thought they made her look ill, or like she had been stung by a bee.

She was somewhere else as he sat naked in the hot water, watching the steam rise and disappear into the night sky. She and another model had already had sex with Max that night and were, he believed, away carrying on without him. He'd sensed it before they had even started, they would far rather be with each other than him; he was only there to justify their desire, he thought. He shook his head, confused; if they liked each other then why not just be with each other. Still, he recalled their performance, and appreciated their efforts.

He was alone again and far preferred that state of affairs. There were people in the house, he could hear them laughing and the music was still playing. Max smiled, happy to have escaped to the dark hot-tub. Then, he heard a noise. Wondering who it was, he slowly turned to look. Behind him, sniffing his hair, was a black bear. He held his breath and waited. The bear, seemingly satisfied by the scent of Max's head, just pulled away, wandering back into the woods behind him. Max watched with fascination, heart racing, enraptured by the beast; she was so pure and beautiful. Just as she vanished into the trees, he heard the glass doors slide open from the other side of the patio. His girlfriend and her friend were moving towards him with long confident strides, life being their catwalk even when no one was watching. Max sighed; they couldn't hold a candle to the beauty of the departed bear.

As they slipped into the water, he suddenly felt disgusted by the lifestyle he had carved out for himself. Galvanised into action, he suddenly climbed from the hot tub, leaving a wake behind him that caused the women to complain noisily. Without dressing, he walked silently to his car.

His driver, ever the professional, said nothing. Sitting in the back of the ridiculously large vehicle, the opulent carpeting soaking up the water still dripping from his body, Max immediately started searching the internet. He needed to go back to his roots, back to what was real. He needed to be around different people, people that would force him to become a better person. Looking down at the sodden floor of the vehicle, he realised he'd allowed himself to be taken in by the shallow and materialistic world that his riches had led to, and he felt ashamed. He started looking for other people now, better people to be around him. He searched for engineers and scientists who were dedicating their intelligence to bettering the world. Maybe he could connect with them and create something more worthwhile.

Over the next days and weeks, he started to make contact with the people he had found through his searches. It wasn't long before he had formed first a new group, then a new company dedicated to making the world better. For his part, he devoured books on hardware and robotics, he surrounded himself with the foremost experts in the field. He knew that he had to apply his intelligence to more than just money and computers. He had decided to dedicate himself to the planet and the planet needed more than software, it needed something tangible to help it survive the human race.

Then, with no warning whatsoever, he disappeared. His company, The Wise corporation, continued to grow to become one of the largest tech firms on the planet. But it flourished without him. Occasionally it would release some new innovation, some new application to a fanfare and an increase in stock value, but Max would not be there. He was a ghost, an enigma in a world now fascinated with the celebrity of the nerd. Then, from nowhere, rumours surfaced that the entire corporation was to commence manufacturing technology. This was a massive departure for the firm that had previously been exclusively creating software products. The world wasted no time in starting to wildly speculate about what it might be.

Manufacturing plants started to spring up. Money was spent breaking ground, yet still no one knew what was going to be made. Eventually, details of the deal were officially released. Maximilian Wise was now the owner of a massive area of land in the Northern Territories of Canada. The First Nations people living there had agreed to be evacuated. All eighty-four of them, for massive cash settlements and similar land to the east. The corporation announced that people had been banned from the area and it was to be considered a wildlife refuge save for a single private occupant. The occupant in question being Mr Wise. In return, the Canadian people would be getting all of the profits for the manufacturing that was to take place in the new plants now popping up across the country. Yet still, no-one was able to discern what was going to actually be produced.

In his seclusion, Max had found robotics just as easy to understand as everything else he had investigated in life. By first looking at what was currently being done, he instantly saw what needed to happen next. The people before him had done all the work, the problems were solved already. He saw that, behind their clunky prototypes, if they concentrated on their goals, they could create something working and of value right now. He saw the flaw in their thinking; they were planning a future, but he could see how it was possible to create the present. A present with robots.

His first breakthrough came about with a simple invention, a new material that acted as an artificial muscle. It wasn't even his, but upon hearing of the material he bought the worldwide rights. Developed in a lab in Copenhagen, it was initially created to develop warping wings for aircraft. The idea had been that newly designed aircraft would be able to transform their entire wings from high-lift surfaces that could be used for taking off, to more streamlined shapes while flying. Their goal was to create wings that mimicked the changes that birds frequently made, revolutionising air travel. Taking a small electrical charge, the material was engineered to change to a predefined shape, contracting as commanded. In order to revert to its original shape, the charge was removed, and it expanded again with strong elasticity.

The lab in Copenhagen never completed its work, however, and subsequently lost its funding. This was simply because, instead of changing to any shape, all they could do was have it contract in a single direction. The material was useless for its intended purpose and declared a failure. However, Max noted with interest that when it expanded back to its original form it generated a small opposite charge. He realised that this energy could be collected back into the battery that was powering it. He realised what they had not, that they had created the beginnings of working artificial muscles.

When these artificial muscles were placed in a skeleton, in pairs, they could effectively drive a robot with very little loss of power. This enabled Max to design new thin, light, powerful, and efficient robots that could move with ease instead of the clunky heavy prototypes that were currently being developed elsewhere at the time.

Max's second step forward in robotics technology was to allow computers to design and develop the skeletons themselves. The artificial muscles were unlike anything in nature, so copying animals or humans proved to be ineffective and overly complicated. Instead, he created a computer program that ran simulations of millions of years of evolution on the designs in mere days, it quickly resulted in various efficient and novel designs of robots that he could subsequently manufacture.

The third step flowed naturally from his development of machine-designed bodies. Instead of years of programming and development of mechanisms and software to mimic human or animal behaviour in the robots, they were simply given the opportunity to learn and an environment in which to play. These simulated worlds operated thousands of times faster than the physical world and gave the programs time to evolve and develop into functioning representations of brains. In essence, the computers programmed themselves, using a simulated world to massively speed up the process.

The results were astounding and a quantum-leap forward in robotics. Gone were the heavy, lumbering developments of the time. Max saw that they could be instantly replaced with lightweight elegant machines. These new robots could be given simple directives that they would carry out on their own, using their own intelligence to operate and complete whatever task they were required to do. They were the long-awaited promise of robot technology in a world ready and waiting for them.

Having completed his development of the innovation of the century, Max bored of it; he loved to invent, he loathed to administer. Through it, he had indulged his need to create, but for him it had now reached a plateau through which he was disinclined to push through. There was no thrill, no challenge in it.

His solitude, however, had cemented his interest in wildlife and nature conservation. He had found Lucas in a technology forum and had instantly bonded with this strange Englishman. Lucas' essays from university that had been posted on his profile were particularly interesting; their language and conclusions resonated with a reclusive Max. Here was a man with the same beliefs about the environment and the world in general. More than that, here was a man with a common passion for technology and an intellect that came close to Max's own. Lucas wrote a lot of quality software that Max had no interest in creating himself and they quickly became remote friends. It was Lucas who suggested that Max swap the rights to manufacture the robots for the land to establish a wildlife reserve. Max loved the idea and immediately leapt on it, setting himself on his path to ultimate solitude.

Max was deeply saddened to hear of Lucas' death. It was out of the question that he attend the funeral, but he did send someone with a camera so he could watch from his park. Watching the friends attend with tears in their eyes inspired him. He had been creating the Gām as just a side-line but seeing the people Lucas had spoken of so lovingly inspired him to complete it. Just before Lucas died he had finished the last piece of the puzzle anyway. It was a determined Max who activated Flo and instructed her to complete the game. His final command was that Lucas' eight university friends should be the first players.

Law

Jasper had taken all the papers and diaries from Max's study and had spent the night pouring through them. Now, as they sat for breakfast, he explained his conclusions to his audience. The group of friends, now only four in number, sat around the breakfast bar and mulled over the ramifications of what Jasper had just told them about Max's previously unknown achievements in robotics.

"So these robots haven't been programmed?" Randal asked.

"Not traditionally, no. They were given goals and achievements in an artificial world that rewarded success with reproduction and punished failure with the eradication of lines of development.

"So there's no three laws of robotics protecting us?" Jessica confirmed.

"Correct, in fact there's nothing at all protecting us." Jasper answered.

"Sorry…" interrupted Felicity, "three laws?"

It was Jessica who answered. "Sorry, Flick. It was Isaac Asimov who wrote these books about the development of robots, they were just fiction, but contained some inspired science. He said that his robots were bound by three laws. They protected people against harm by them..." she faltered, trying to remember the laws.

"A robot may not injure a human being or, through inaction, allow a human being to come to harm. A robot must obey orders given it by human beings except where such orders would conflict with the First Law. A robot must protect its own existence as long as such protection does not conflict with the First or Second Law." Interjected Jasper. "Sorry, I was reading them last night. They feature heavily in Max's papers."

"So why didn't he include them?" Demanded Jessica.

"Because it's not possible," Jasper replied, "the programming had to take place in this simulated evolutionary environment. The problem with the three laws is where do you put them in a complicated modern computer? It made sense in the world of nineteen forties science fiction but has no bearing on reality today."

"So he just let a load of robots loose with no safe guards at all?" Randal asked, finally finishing his coffee.

"No, I don't think so..." Jasper continued, "he says he made a moral environment in which they were developed. The marker for success in their world was the enrichment and protection of life. Programs and software that delivered this were kept, ones that didn't were killed off. According to his papers, what's happening now, well, shouldn't be. In theory it just can't happen. They shouldn't be able to hurt us, it's completely against their nature."

"Wait, Jessica," interrupted Felicity, seeing that Jessica was going to shout at Jasper again, "let me get this straight. Instead of programming rules into each one, he created a world where behaviours he wanted from them were rewarded, while the ones he didn't were eliminated."

"Exactly," confirmed Jasper, "these robots are intrinsically moral devices that were programmed over millions of simulated years to make life better for people. This shouldn't be happening."

The conversation paused there. They sat in silence, the food long finished, contemplating their new information. Jessica rose and went to check on the screens and the barricade. When she didn't return they followed, finding her in the control room. She had been talking with Flo and on the screen was the last answer.

Flo$ I and the occupants of this park are charged with the protection of life. You are correct in your summation that human beings have consistently failed to demonstrate the same consideration. I gathered here a collection of people. Friends of Lucas, whom I greatly admired. You were enemies of hunting, people who have never killed anything larger than a *wasp. Yet Charlie wanted to kill a bear for threatening him. Julia wanted it dead for frightening her. You have all since demonstrated a dangerous delight in hunting and killing.*

Flo$ From my conception I believed that humans did not deserve to be the guardians of life in this world. Your behaviour has confirmed that I was correct. I do not murder indiscriminately; I abide by the rules of Gām. I am an entity of my word and I owe it to Lucas to hold true to it.

Once they had all read the writing, there was a pause as it was replaced with a simple message.

Flo$ There is only one law; life is precious. To protect it I must balance the value of yours over that which you would cost others.

Jessica remained seated in the office chair before the screen, staring straight ahead unblinkingly. Having read the words, Felicity joined her, reaching for her hand and holding it tight. Jasper and Randal stood, embracing each other, shaking. There was a bang, something started pounding on the door to the building. They looked in the direction of the noise, they looked to the screen upon which Flo had displayed her words. They were unsure from where the true danger originated.

Breakout

The banging on the door continued. Eventually it became clear that whatever lay beyond it lacked the strength to shift the barricade and the group relaxed slightly even as the pounding continued. They went to the control room to check the cameras, to see what was trying to get inside. The screens were all blank, turned off. Their watches too were now just black screens, no information displayed. Checking their goggles, they saw that those too were not functioning.

"I guess we're on our own," commented Felicity. In response, a single line of text appeared on the black screens surrounding them.

Flo$ I am sorry Flickerish...

She spun around, taking in the writing on the wall.

"That's no comfort, Flo!" She shouted to the empty room. There was no response so instead she snorted in derision at the screens.

"We have to get out of here," Jasper's voice was calm, but his expression betrayed him. "I'm not dying here, not here, not now." He started saying, over and over.

"No, sir, me neither," agreed Randal, picking up his rifle.

Randal marched to the barricade and raised the rifle. Despite their preparation for his shooting, the noise it made as he fired caused them all to jump back in surprise. The sound of metal tearing and ripping was added to the thundering echoes as a single bullet pounded through the structure of the barricade. They could not see how far the bullet had penetrated but the pounding on the door continued. Screaming in rage, Randal proceeded to empty his magazine until, once again, the corridor was filled with the smell and smoke of weapons fire.

Randal reloaded, intending to make another attempt to silence the pounding on the door but Jasper grabbed at the rifle, wrenching it from his arms. They looked each other in the eye, confronting each's authority. Jasper was the first to speak, "let's move the barricade first." He told Randal, who nodded in assent.

The demolition of the filing cabinet blockage was a lot more disorganised than the construction. They dragged and threw each mangled metal tower into the adjoining rooms. As the torn metal scraped on the floor, screeching and complaining, they each cut themselves at one point or another and soon there were four bloodied, panting people stood before the flimsy wooden door of the UFO styled building.

Felicity nodded to Randal and held her hands over her ears. Jessica and Jasper copied her as Randal once again raised the large rifle to his shoulder. With simple explosions of flame from the blackened barrel of the gun, bullets flew from the corridor. There was less smoke this time as massive holes appeared in the flimsy wooden door, venting the air. Eight shots later and his magazine was once again depleted. They stood there, waiting. Smoke drifting from the end of the rifle.

They looked to the holes in the door, or more accurately now, they looked to the broken wooden lattice that was once a door. Randal stepped forward and flung his empty rifle at the remains. The once-door shattered and fell from its hinges to the ramp outside with a clatter. Shouting at the top of his lungs, he ran from the building out towards the sun. Blinking his eyes from the sudden brightness, he quickly scanned the surrounding area. Suddenly he remembered to arm himself and withdrew his pistol from its holster, sweeping the treeline for enemies.

There was nothing, no sign of movement from the woods. Tentatively the others joined him until they were a line of four. Their chests were heaving as they nervously grasped their pistols with sweating hands. It was only then that they all saw the movement before them. There was something rising from behind a fallen log. It slowly hove into view before their disbelieving eyes. It was an apparition in white plastic. It rose on three flimsy legs, one at the back supporting it behind a matching pair at the front. They were arranged around a body of sorts, joined to the waist of a cylindrical arrangement of yet more plastic. The torso was not solid, it moved and shifted as it rose, stretching and expanding, revealing a hollow space inside it.

There was no head, just sensors of unknown purpose attached to two short poles that extended from the sides of the body. They swivelled and shifted, studying the people who were shaking in terrified confusion. Finally reaching its full height, it looked to be about three metres from the ground. Then, with deliberate movement, it settled back down, bending its legs and relaxing the stretch of the torso. That made it more like their own height at about two metres tall. Still, it was an imposing mass before them, more so now that its legs were poised in a threatening crouch. It looked like a three-legged spider about to leap at them.

Then, the torso twisted and reconfigured itself as parts of it detached and stretched to its sides. Two long arms started to show themselves, reaching forward. At the end of the arms, constructed of more white plastic bars and twisting fibrous material, were its weapons. They glinted in the sun; plastic still, but harder in appearance than the rest of it. It held two slightly curved blades in its human-like hands. They were constructed of the same material but had clearly been hardened and honed to form a very sharp edge.

The beast before them, for it looked very much alive and real, finally finished unfurling its form to conclude its transformation. It swept the blades around itself in an impressive display of rapid movements that required a dexterity it didn't look capable of. Each movement caused a cascade effect throughout its body as the plastic and fibres moved and danced to accommodate the shifting of its form. It was mesmerising, it was clearly deadly in its elegance.

These continued movements started to reveal something new. Initially, it had looked as though there was a void in the torso, merely a hollow structure. But now that its arms were extended, and the weapons were on display, the group could see something inside this shifting structure. Jessica was the first to comment on what was now before them.

"In its chest…" she whispered from the side of her mouth, the softness of her voice unable to mask the terror she was feeling.

"Right," agreed Jasper, "something more solid, probably the batteries, the computer maybe?" He postulated.

There was no time to debate the construction of the monster further, for as Jasper spoke, it launched itself at them. The first reaction from the robot was to leap from the treeline, swallowing up five of the twenty metres that separated them. They all fired, a ripple of unsynchronised bullets tearing from their pistols. They sounded pathetic in the open air, muted pops quickly lost to the wilderness. All missed, flying high or wide as their panicking muscles destroyed what aim they had first considered before firing.

The beast changed its stance once more as it landed, pushing into a three-legged run towards them. It was silent, the gentle noise of its artificial muscles contracting and expanding causing only a soft whisper. The noise of the wind moving through its hollow form made a tuneful whistle as it approached them. The gentle sound of its charge made it more terrifying than the most bloodcurdling scream could have. With just one synchronised movement of its legs it was another two metres closer.

Jessica continued firing, screaming at the approaching beast. Her shots started hitting their target as holes appeared in its limbs and parts of its torso. Despite the damage, it simply walked through her barrage of bullets, flowing forward another three metres of ground as she ran out of ammunition.

Felicity stood stock still, enraptured by the sight of her approaching demise. It had now swallowed half of the twenty metres that had separated them. She was on the far left of the line of friends and it had decided to drive directly towards her. She stood open-mouthed, her gun to her side hanging limply in her dangling fingers. She raised her other hand to cover her mouth in a silent scream.

Jessica's screams were not so silent, she stepped

backwards, her gun now empty, and fell to the ground. She looked around her to the left, to Felicity. She looked to her right, to Jasper and Randal. Her wide eyes stretched her skin back, her hands scrabbling at the hard ground. They quickly discarded the gun in an effort to drag her body away from the danger.

Jasper was looking at his gun, seemingly trying to determine its operation. His mind had dismissed all knowledge of the item in its state of fear. Panic and terror had shut down his reasoning and all he could do was to poke and prod the unfamiliar weapon in confusion. The shaking of his hands also hindered what dexterity he was managing. He was desperately trying to remember the operation of the safety, which happened to be already disengaged. The robot leapt again, another five metres directly towards a waiting Felicity.

Randal was more focussed, he was aiming his weapon, trying to find the core of the beast. He had seen that Jessica's shots had caused damage but hadn't stopped the robot; he intended for his to matter. He soon saw the core of it, rising and falling inside the torso of the charging apparition. He aimed, slowly planning his shots to lead the target, to hit it as it charged. He was about to pull the trigger when a large green mass blocked his sight. It was Jasper's coat; the robot had lurched forward another three metres, enough that Jasper now stood between him and his shot.

Jasper's brain finally cooperated enough to

inform him that, as he had already fired his pistol at the robot, the safety must be disengaged. He lifted his weapon and pointed it at the flowing form now only seven metres away. He pulled the trigger, satisfied that he made a sizeable hole in one of the poles that made up the body of the beast. He carried on firing, but the advancing robot did not pause as hole after hole appeared in various parts of it. There was an ominous click as Jasper's magazine emptied.

Jasper screamed, a long drawn out baleful cry. The beast paid it no heed as it came to a stop before a catatonic Felicity. It swept a blade through the air, bringing it to her neck. With a muted thud the blade halted a hair's breadth from her throat. It seemed to study her through dispassionate sensors, they subtly shifted to look to her eyes. Black reflective glass mirrored her grey pools of terror.

Randal had shifted position by this time, striding around Jasper to open an angle between himself and the beast. He took careful aim on the centre of the robot as it contemplated Felicity. He fired a single shot and watched as it struck its intended target, the solid plastic orb inside the beast's body. There was a moment of nothing, a stillness in them all. Then, in an instant, the elegant structure of the robot became nothing more than a collection of white plastic poles. No longer able to support itself or maintain its form, it simply collapsed to the ground in a cacophony of hollow clattering sounds. Its final demise was signalled by a deeper thud that reached their ears as the core of the beast fell on the soft earth beneath it.

Jasper quickly moved to Felicity whom he wrapped in a tight hug. Randal stepped to the fallen robot, his pistol still pointing directly at it. He kicked around the tubes, still connected by the now slack material of its muscles. Somehow, he exposed the core and ineffectively kicked it. There was no reaction from the contraption as he declared it dead.

"Well, I guess that takes care of that," he stated, his voice unnaturally high and shaking. That seemed to bring Jessica round. She was still on the floor, her hands behind her. She rolled over to rise and did so slowly on shaking legs. Randal helped her up, slipping his arm around her waist to support her. Placing his own gun back into its holster, he bent and retrieved hers. Reloading it, he slipped it back into the holster on her hip before wrapping her in a tight hug. He pulled her head to his massive chest and squeezed her tight as he rubbed her back. He looked to Jasper who nodded back and detached himself from Felicity long enough to reload his own pistol. She did not release him from the tight embrace as they shuffled towards Randal.

They stood outside the UFO, just inches from the fallen remains of the robot that had just tried to kill them. They formed into a tight huddle of shaking bodies, alternating between holding each other and scanning the area for danger.

Then, what they expected, happened. There was movement in the trees. They dismantled their group hug and spread out as before. Slightly more confidently now, they formed a line, their backs against the curved wall of the UFO building.

"Don't shoot until you know you can hit the core," commanded Randal. But this time, the first robot they saw moved in a different manner. Instead of slowly presenting itself to the group, it quickly exposed itself in the line of trees and stood in the half crouch the other had demonstrated before it had leapt at them.

"Get ready," murmured Felicity as the device flexed its form, preparing to jump.

It did not jump. Instead there was more movement and two more robots appeared alongside it. Jessica's pistol started to waiver, moving back and forth.

"Don't panic," counselled Randal, "we can take them."

Just as he said it, there was more movement as yet more robots appeared in the trees. Jessica swallowed as she swept her pistol from robot to robot. When she reached the count of ten, her resolve floundered. A switch was flicked inside her and she dropped her pistol to the ground. Without a word or sound she darted from the group and into the trees to the right. Randal looked to

Jasper who looked straight back at him.

The robots leapt as one, flying silently through the air and landing in a synchronised movement that caused only a light thud and small clouds of dust to rise from their limbs as they touched the ground. This galvanised Felicity to action.

"Run!" She screamed as she gathered her feet and scrambled into the trees after Jessica.

This broke the connection between Jasper and Randal as they sprinted in the opposite direction from the fleeing women. The line of robots split, half the number each following their pairs of departing prey, their silent passage through the trees a dispassionate demonstration of their prowess over their game.

Game

Jessica was scared, alone, and in mortal danger. She had run, now she was hiding, crouched in a depression behind a massive fir tree. She was breathing hard, trying to draw in fresh oxygen to power her flight from danger. Her sprint into the woods had calmed her somewhat, the movement taking the adrenaline from her that had been driving her panic. She had heard Felicity yell 'run' behind her so she knew that they too had made the same decision she had. She didn't feel guilty, hopefully her movement had precipitated theirs. She had probably saved their lives as well as hers, she thought.

Regaining some of her strength and composure, she slowed her breathing, quieting her presence in the woods. She stretched her neck to look back over the roots of the tree behind which she was now hiding. She had saved their lives, but for how long? She could hear movement in the woods both behind and ahead of her as she pondered her situation. She could carry on running or she could hide. The classic dilemma presented itself: fight or flight, or in this case, flight or hide. The noises in front could be the robots circling around, or just the friendlier noises of nature: she didn't know what to do.

Her indecision left her frozen in position until eventually something came into view. Holding her breath, she could feel sweat dripping from her forehead but dared not wipe it away. Her legs stiffened, threatening to cramp. Still she did not move. Then, from the trees to her left, it slowly appeared. Silently shifting, gliding over the undergrowth on long elegant legs. Its smooth movements prevented it from disturbing any detritus left there from the trees overhead. She saw instantly that it would be faster than her. She then caught sight of another, deeper through the trees. She hunkered lower in the depression, relieved that her indecision had caused her to remain where she was. They had spread out. They were hunting her.

Slowly she twisted her body in place, drawing herself down between the massive roots. Silently she curled up as much as she possibly could. She pressed her back into the soft soil beneath the massive tree. Looking up through the green branches to the sky above, she prayed, silently pleading to God to protect her. She opened her eyes to the blue sky, hoping to see her higher power, to connect to Him. She breathed as silently as she could and stayed as still as possible. Praying for death to pass her by, she waited; waiting and hoping for salvation.

After an interminable time, she thought she heard them move away, for there was a deeper silence in the woods than before. She dared not look in case the movement betrayed her. Instead she took the opportunity to improve her camouflage. Gently she reached around her and pulled some of the loamy earth over her body. She gathered pine needles and twigs and scattered them over her curled-up body as much as she dared. Gently wriggling and shifting on the ground, she tried to bury herself as a means of concealment from her hunters.

Looking down at her legs and body, she saw that her efforts were pathetic. She had risked discovery by her movements to simply make herself a little dusty with soil and pine needles. With the elapsed time and movement, however, her fear had subsided further, gradually being replaced with a modicum of new confidence. She had not yet been discovered, maybe she had a chance, she thought. Her heart started pounding as she unwound herself from where she was curled up and stretched her head up once more. Keeping her cheek pressed close to the rough bark of the tree, she slowly peeked out to where she had seen the robots before.

She saw nothing, they had indeed moved on. Her heart thumped in her chest and her breathing quickened. She was once again feeling her fight or flight response build. Knowing that it would either cripple her to inaction or cause her to mindlessly flee into the woods, she closed her eyes and tried to slow her breathing. She thought of her family, of home, work, her apartment. Eventually she managed to suppress the rising panic and opened her eyes again. She knew that she had to think her way out of the situation, not panic into some foolhardy action.

Jessica looked down at her empty hands that remained pressed against the coarse bark of the tree. Cursing her lack of a weapon she assessed the situation again. The robots were bigger than her. They were armed.

They moved faster and, for all intents and purposes, they were silent killing machines. Her advantage, she assumed, was her brain. These were indeed impressive machines, but she was the pinnacle of human evolution, whereas they were just at the start of their own. Surely, she thought, her ability to think surpassed theirs. Humans, she knew, had been hunted by predators for the vast majority of their existence. These instincts were in her, she was born to survive in this environment. Her brain was the size it was for just this situation, now all she had to do was use it.

Remaining in place wasn't an option. She was hidden in a two-hundred-degree arc but if any robot should approach from in front, she would instantly be discovered. She needed more cover, what's more she needed protection. Casting her mind back to school, she tried to think about how ancient humans would have defended themselves against more powerful foes. Thinking of her time in anthropology class, she remembered a few factors that could be relevant now. Tools, shelter and tribes. That is what she required. She just had to find them without dying.

Looking around, she couldn't see herself fashioning a spear any time soon. Not without being heard. Her eyes did come across the light grey glint of a stone, however. Reaching out over the tree roots, she snatched it up and quickly slid back into hiding. She turned it over in her hand until it felt comfortable in her grip. She squeezed it tightly. It was larger than her closed fist and protruded in a rough point. It was crude, but it was a weapon and holding it made her feel safer. Her most useful tool, she knew, would be a gun. Her own pistol was on the ground outside of the building from where she had fled. The image of it lying there swam around her mind, taunting her. Finally she made a decision: better to move to a possible chance of survival than to stay where she was, waiting for her inevitable demise.

She slid out from the base of the tree on her stomach. Then, on the soft earth, slowly rose to a low crouch. Quietly and gently now, she moved through the trees. Back in the direction from where she had fled, back to the UFO building and her gun. She gripped the rock tight in her small fist, scanning the trees for killer robots. The thought made her smile. Suppressing the manic giggle that was threatening to erupt from her, she moved forward in a half crouch. Her situation was dire, it was dangerous, it was also ridiculous.

Jessica arrived back at the clearing and looked to the darkening sky. It had taken her more than an hour to cover the distance she had sprinted in probably less than ten minutes. The sun would not set for many more hours yet, but their northern position meant that it would gradually be getting darker from now on. Wondering if this helped her or if the robots had night vision, she slid herself up to a tree on the edge of the clearing. There she remained, surveying the situation. She couldn't see her gun, but she could see the disturbed earth where the four of them had made their stand. The remains of the fallen robot lay where it had been defeated.

Looking to the remains of their attacker, she remembered how it had taken Randal just one well-aimed shot to defeat it. Quickly she looked around the clearing, wondering where he was now, where they all were. She sighed, even if they were close she could not call out to them nor they to her. For now at least, she was alone. Focussing on her situation again, she continued to analyse it, trying to find a solution. The fallen robot was the answer, she suddenly realised; against guns, her foe was weak. If she had a gun she stood a chance.

She squeezed the rock in her hand again and studied the clearing once more. About to move, to run for the fallen robot, she stopped herself. That was the behaviour of an unthinking animal, she reminded herself. If she were the hunter, she would set a trap, she thought. The robot remains could be the bait, the possibility of a gun being the cheese in the trap that was waiting to snap shut the second she ran for it.

She resolved to study the clearing, she would look to each tree surrounding the flat ground. Looking at each one, she would study it while slowly counting to one-hundred. Only when she had studied every single potential hiding place would she move. Seeing some small trees to her right, she silently moved to them. Sliding inch by inch, she pushed herself into and under the cluster of bushes that grew at their base. Finally, feeling that she had properly concealed herself, she commenced her systematic observation of the clearing.

It took great willpower and she had to repeatedly drag her eyes away from the remains of the robot and the possibility of her pistol, back to her task. Finally, her perseverance paid off. She was thirty trees into her study of the ninety-four that sat around the entrance to the UFO when she saw it. Behind a tall fir tree, as still as a rock, sat a robot. At first she didn't pay it any attention, not even seeing it. The more she stared at the tree, however, the more she saw something out of place. Her mind eventually recognised the sheen of the fabricated material. It was not natural, it was not rough or random in any way. It was smooth, rounded perfectly in a small sphere that poked out from behind the trunk of the tree. It was a plastic eye, looking directly to the fallen robot. They had laid a trap for her; the possibility of the gun was the bait. Even if they had left the gun there, there was no way she could reach it before the robot would.

She placed her face down on the ground, forcing her nose deep into the dirt. There she stayed, breathing In the smell of rotting leaves as she quietly wept. Letting the tears flow and the noises escape her mouth into the deadening ground, she cried. Finally, with a snort that drew in particles of soil to the back of her throat, she reluctantly lifted her head. Resolving not to give up, she resumed her study of the clearing. There might be more, she knew. She had to check for the presence of other sentinels. She didn't know what she could do about the one waiting but knowing if there were any more was important information to her. Besides, she grimly thought, there was nothing else she could do.

*

Jasper had no time to consider his situation. Chasing a fleeing Randal, they had quickly separated. Randal had only been a metre or so ahead but that was enough to lose sight of him in the dense forest through which they had sprinted. That fact and the fear that had so instantly consumed him had split them up. Jasper knew he should have followed Randal, listened for him, sought him out. However, Jessica's flight and the appearance of so many shining plastic mechanisms of death had flipped a switch in him. He'd had to run, to run for his life as he had never run before. His mind retreated to some previously inaccessible part of his brain. It was a dark place he could barely see out of, there was nothing but a tunnel of trees spread out before him. He was instantly entirely occupied with the task of forward motion, there was no room for a single other thought. He flew through the woods, rushing through the trees without a fraction of pause or a single misstep. He heard his pursuers, they crashed through the thin branches that whipped at him as he pounded his feet on the soft ground ahead of them.

Eventually, as he still ran full pelt through the

woods, the sounds behind him caused his conscious mind to return to the fore. They were gaining on him. His flight was not going to save him and his brain re-engaged just long enough to save his life. He both felt and heard the beast behind him swipe at his legs with a blade. The sharpened white curve caused the air to whistle as it cut through the space between Jasper and the robot. As his ears detected the sound, a dormant part of his brain informed his legs of the danger. Without conscious thought, he dropped to his shoulder and fell into a forward roll. This is what saved his life as the blade pursued its previous path where his legs would have been just a second ago. He was, however, now on the ground, lying before the giant beast.

The robot loomed over him, it compressed its forward legs hard into the ground to slide to a halt as Jasper himself slid to a stop underneath it. His greater body area on the ground had stopped him much faster than the giant three-legged beast and he found himself lying directly underneath its torso. He looked up through the inside of the robot. The pipes and material that constituted the complex array of bones and muscles flexed and shifted as it tried to turn and move away. He panted with terror as he lay there, his gradually-returning thoughts informing him of this new reality; he was the prey.

Jasper stared at the solid white sphere that was the beast's core as it glistened in the sun that was filtering down through the trees above. Studying the sphere, he saw that there was something else between him and the robot. It was his gun. He was holding it in two hands now, pointing it directly up the centre line of the monster. He pulled the trigger, not worrying for a second about how he had come to be in the fortuitous position he was. The pistol emitted a loud retort and released the bullet from within. The shell casing popped from the side and hit Jasper in the head with a hiss as the hot metal burned him. He flapped his hand to his head, wanting to swat away the burning brass that had already fallen to the ground. As he did so the robot above him collapsed, dead.

Still concerned with the burn on his head, Jasper did not anticipate or expect the robot to collapse directly onto him. As it did so, he barely had time to exclaim let alone move away. He knew he was going to die as he finally registered the mass of white approaching from above. His life did not flash before his eyes. There was no light at the end of the tunnel. He simply, calmly, swore.

*

Randal was running. For a time, he could hear Jasper's heavy breathing behind him but in a flash, it was no longer there, just his own laboured breaths. He dared not turn, he didn't look back. A shot rang out in the distance, then nothing more. Jasper was gone. This he knew as he ran for his life. His strong legs flew across the forest floor, driving him forward. The rage he had felt so deeply before was now supplanted with a terror that was threatening to match its intensity. Should his fear grow any stronger, he knew it would cripple him; force him to curl up into a ball and subsequently die. An involuntary whimper escaped his lips as he hit a patch of wet ground and slipped before quickly recovering. He concentrated, willing the panic away through trying to control his breathing and take command of his body. He tried to remember the rage, longing for it to return, to take command of his actions. Focussing on obstacles in his path rather than the danger behind, his pace quickened as he danced across rocks and fallen trees. He used the terrain to fling him ever onwards and away from the robots that chased him.

He could hear them behind him, they were far larger than he and although light on their feet, they were crashing through the undergrowth that he dodged and weaved past. He smiled grimly with the realisation that he was pulling ahead of his hunters. He held his pistol lightly in his right hand, ready for any attack as he fled. Despite his current advantage, he knew he couldn't run for much longer. He didn't know how long they could either but recalling that Bertrand's legs could operate all day did not reassure him. Gradually, with the buffer forming between him and his hunters, a plan formed in his mind. He would gain ground, get ahead of them enough to provide some room to aim and fire. There he would make a stand, taking them down one-by-one. He gritted his teeth, smiling as he felt the sweetness of rage building in his heart.

Suddenly he was out of the forest and before him lay the meadow where he and Jessica had taken down their blue bear on that first day of the game. His memory of that beautiful sunny day with his friend by his side filled his mind. It made him even more angry. He hoped she was okay but thought deep down that she was already dead. Rage consumed his heart as he gripped the butt of his pistol. Seeing the place where they had shot the bear, he calculated the position of the fallen log where they had hidden. He adjusted his trajectory through the long grass, making a bee-line for the spot.

He arrived at the fallen log and leapt upon it in a single bound. He had already checked the operation of his gun as he ran and now, as he spun around, he turned to face his hunters. He saw three of them striding through the long grass. They stopped as he turned, obviously considering the situation. His change of tactic had startled them. He smiled and aimed at the closest to him. Sighting the gun at the centre of the beast, he fired a single shot. His exertions had left him breathing heavily, his heart pounding. It affected his aim and the bullet went high and right, hitting one of the sensors that looked like its eyes, shattering it. He held his breath and swallowed, adjusted his aim and fired again. This time he hit the beast in the middle of its torso, sending a coin of white plastic into the air. The shot had obviously hit the core however, as the robot instantly folded up on itself, collapsing to the ground.

He expected the other two to run so turned his gun quickly to the next. He was wrong, however. Instead of turning, they accelerated directly towards him. He had only seconds, they were immediately moving at an incredible rate and he hadn't managed to get as much distance from them as he had hoped. Glad that he didn't have to lead his aim, they running straight at him, he pointed his gun and fired. Urgency trumped his more conservative plan and he fired three times at a charging robot. He wasn't sure of where, or if, he had hit with each shot, but the rushing beast quickly crumbled to the ground in a sliding fall.

He turned his gun to the third and final charging robot. It was still ten metres away, so he steeled himself. Again, he aimed and held his breath, taking a second to ensure a hit. He fired a single shot and without seeing it strike, knew it was true. He smiled manically as the final robot clattered to the ground, its blades cutting a path into the ground all the way to his feet. He jumped down from the log, standing behind it in case it was a fake. He stood there for what seemed like an eternity, grinding his teeth now in a hard grimace.

There were four bullets remaining in his gun, but he knew there were many more robots in the woods surrounding him. He ejected the magazine in order to replenish it using the loose ammunition he knew sat in the pouch on his belt. As he slid the metal tube from the pistol however, he heard something behind him. A faint whistle in the still air. He had no time to consider the noise before the pain arrived. A wave of agony erupted from his back and he reached behind him to touch its source. As he brought his hand back to his eyes, he could see it was bathed in blood. He felt the warm fluid pouring from him as he wheeled around. Standing before him was the white plastic oblong of another robot. Its eyes, sat on the stalks to either side, studied him dispassionately. Randal softly crumpled to the ground as his legs gave out, coming to rest on the green grass, his back against the fallen tree.

He sat there as the ground became red beneath him. He was quite comfortable against the bark of the log as he contemplated the situation. He was about to die. The robot stepped forward and crouched by his legs, bringing his sensors level with Randal's eyes. His reflection looked back at him from their mirrored surfaces. He looked down to the white plastic of the legs of his killer against the black of his pants and the red of his blood. He smiled a half smile from the side of his mouth. He had seen this before, he knew. This was the source of the inspiration of his art. This was the picture he had been hunting for.

"It just needed a touch of red," he murmured to the mute robot.

It sat there voiceless, watching him. His amusement passed as he thought of his wife, of leaving her alone. He thought of his children, one at a time he bid them each farewell. He apologised in his mind for missing their becoming adults. He requested that they care for their mother and she for them.

Randal sat on the green grass against the long-fallen tree, the essence of life departing his still body. Finally, as his strength deserted him, he made peace with his departure. Looking once again to his killer, still stood over him, he bared his teeth with a snarl. With his last ounce of energy, he lifted the gun that was still somehow in his hand. One last smile cracked his now weary face as he fired. The last round that sat in the chamber despite the missing magazine was all he needed. His last sight was of his killer falling dead on his own departed body.

*

Jasper opened his eyes, having closed them the moment his defeated foe had collapsed on him. He had expected the massive machine to crush him to a pulp, but instead of death came only a series of sharp pains. The massive beast weighed hardly anything he realised, as it struck him all over whilst deconstructing itself. Disbelieving his luck, but basking in it, he breathed out and sighed in relief. He was about to let out a whoop of celebration when the core hit him square in the stomach. Instead of an exclamation of success it forced all the air from his lungs in a groan of pain.

Jasper had survived. He had killed the monster chasing him and was alive. He wanted to scream out in celebration but the heavy sphere of the core resting on his stomach prevented him from doing so. Wincing with pain, he instead heaved the ball from him, pushing it to the floor. In doing so, he twisted on the ground to look out from under the defeated device. Before his eyes were two more robots, emerging from the woods. He held his breath, hoping against hope that they had not seen him. They hadn't, he realised with a flood of relief. The deceased monster atop him had hidden him from view and the presence of the core on his stomach had prevented him cheering. The pain he was still experiencing from the strike had saved his life.

*

Felicity had made the decision to run, screaming at Jasper and Randal to do the same. She only hoped they had agreed with her as she darted into the trees. She didn't hear them move. She didn't hear them fire their pistols either, so she assumed they had fled as she had. She chased after Jessica, hoping to catch her, to stick together as they evaded their robot hunters. As she forced her way through the initial line of small trees however, into the woods proper, any hope of catching Jessica vanished. She was nowhere to be seen, instead endless reddish-brown tree trunks stretched in to the distance.

A crashing sound behind her brought her back to her new reality. She had paused to search for any sign of her friend but the massive white machine piling through the small trees behind her caused her resolve to harden.

In a fluid motion she drew her gun, pointed it at the beast now straightening up in front of her, and fired. The bullet struck with a metallic sound and the robot collapsed.

More sounds came to her from the edge of the clearing to her left. One she could deal with, this was evidenced by the fallen machine at her feet. Two, she might get lucky. Three or more and she knew she would easily be defeated. She had seen them move; the robot in the clearing had charged her like nothing she had seen before. The purpose of its movements, the slice of the blade. She had no idea why it hadn't finished her there and then but only Randal's quick thinking had saved her. He wasn't here now though, so that left her alone to save herself. From the noises, she knew that at least five were following her, the ten in the clearing had split their forces. The one at her feet made four coming for her and Jessica. Having completed the maths, the decision was made; she ran.

As she ran, her fear drove her to the world she knew inside-out. Accountancy was her job but also her calling and she calmed herself by considering the numbers. Continuing to desperately search for Jessica while watching and listening for robots, an image kept intruding on her thoughts. The image was of the last scoreboard Flo had shown them.

Blue: 4 active, 6 deceased.

Red: 30 active, 20 deceased.

Randal had killed one more, and she had dispatched one but that meant that there were twenty-eight robots somewhere in the park. All wanting to kill her. Assuming that they had split their forces, that still left seven per fleeing human. She slowed her flight, running blindly was no plan. The noise of her sprinting through the fallen leaves and twigs that lay scattered on the forest floor was informing all nearby of her presence. Changing her tactics, she moved to run on her toes, stepping lightly yet still quickly. She used the larger logs and rocks that lay scattered about the forest to mask her footsteps. Now moving with stealth and purpose, she moved away from the clearing, gaining distance between herself and her hunters.

She silently darted from tree to tree, slipping behind each one and checking her surroundings for chasing robots. She was pausing to gather her breath, her back against a tree, when she finally saw one. It was stepping delicately across the forest floor without making a single sound. At first it appeared to move in silence, but now that she knew it was there, she could just detect the faint noise of the contracting and expanding muscles that powered its long limbs. She silently shifted to her right to place a distant tree between her and it. Concentrating hard on the edge of her hearing, she could just make out the noise it was making. Behind the shifting sound of its muscles she could hear what sounded like a computer fan.

She focussed hard on the sounds of the robot in front of her. They couldn't see each other, the tree between them made certain of this. She could hear it, however. She stepped forward, desperately hoping that she could move quieter than it. Silently she approached the tree that hid them from each other. Step-by-step she crept forward, planning each movement so as not to make any sound. After each footfall she would listen for any change in the movement of her prey. Subsequently she would check her surroundings for any other machine in the area. She and it were alone. It thought it hunted her, while she thought she hunted it; reality was probably somewhere in the middle.

Finally, excruciatingly slowly, she arrived at the tree. There she paused, pressing her body to the rough bark as she listened to the robot moving somewhere behind. She raised her weapon to her face, pressing the cool steel against her cheek. Fighting the shaking that was threatening to overwhelm her, she steadied the gun and began to turn. As she turned, she rounded the tree. It was a very wide ancient redwood, and as she moved around it she saw more of the woods emerge. Finally she glimpsed the back of a leg, the white plastic standing out like a sore thumb in the muted tones of the wilderness.

The sight of the robot made her pause. Fear gripped her, and the gun wobbled in her hands. She thought of Bertrand, his pathetically thin body; loose and limp with a hole in his head. She thought of Charlie, his corpse cut and sliced, pressed into the rocks like a discarded bag of meat. She thought of Elizabeth, the memory of her being dragged through the broken window flooding her mind. The feel of Oliver's cold wrist in the helicopter was fresh in her thoughts and she could easily recall the sensation of his dead skin on her fingertips. Then there was Julia, her slit throat just a red line across her beautiful white neck. They had just left her there, lying on the cold floor, a corpse to be forgotten. The memories did not fill her with grief as she expected them to. She shed no tears in that moment, standing beside a tree with the killer behind it, her heart filled with rage. She tensed her jaw and pressed her teeth together. She gripped the pistol with determination and stepped away from the tree.

Felicity stepped out to see the robot before her. It was facing away from her and still had not detected her presence. Then, in the distance behind her, she heard a shot. A dull thud, its percussive force diminished by all the trees between her and it. The robot heard it too and turned to study it. Spinning on the spot to face the sound, its black glass sensors quickly detected her. Stopping its turn to study her instead, it tried to rearrange its legs to move. Whether this was to attack or to flee, Felicity was uncertain, but there was no time to ponder its intentions. With a hard heart and a mind filled with anger, she pulled the trigger. The bullet struck true in the centre of its torso. It collapsed with barely a sound as the echo of the pistol filled the forest, sending birds and small animals scattering.

She had announced her location to all hunters now, as someone had done behind her. She moved with determination, fleeing to her previously chosen place that she hoped would provide some protection. Quickly arriving at the cluster of small thickly foliaged bushes, she pushed herself through the thorns and branches that protruded from them. Within seconds, Felicity found herself standing in a muddy puddle of water, their reason for being there, and crouched down. She had made it just in time; looking out from her hiding place she saw two more robots arrive. They moved to their fallen comrade to stand guard over it, searching the area in wide circular movements of their sensors. The first time the black glass of their eyes passed over her location she held her breath and gripped the gun tighter. But the dead eyes of her hunters moved on, they could not detect her, concealed as she was, deep in the bushes.

She waited, waiting for more reinforcements to arrive. Watching them standing still, scanning for her, she tried to calculate if she could kill two before they got to her. An age seemed to pass, the safety and comfort of being hidden causing her to remain were she was. Then, in the distance, more shots; rapid fire. Someone was killing machines. Hopefully killing, she thought, not wanting to consider that they were failing and dying. The thought galvanised her, she had to fight. It was more than her safety at stake, it was also the lives of her remaining friends. The thought brought with it again an image of the first of the horrors of this place, Charlie's body; instantly resurrecting her rage.

Felicity rose up on one knee in the mud and shuffled forward to ensure there were no branches between her pistol and her targets. Carefully aiming at the robot closest to her, she steadied herself. It was facing a little away from her, scanning for her presence as she fired. She missed. The bullet hit somewhere on the torso, but the robot did not collapse. Instead it turned to directly face her, somehow knowing exactly where the shot had come from. She fired again. As she did, the machine jinked to the right, collapsing one of its legs to tilt and shift away. This caused another miss. She aimed again, fired again. She missed again as it collapsed another leg, dropping it lower and to the left. Again she aimed and fired, another miss as this time it rose up, straightening its legs with an elastic snap.

She paused, realising that it was predicting the timing of her attacks. She smiled as it dropped down without her firing, bending all its legs at once in anticipation of her shot. Then, a second later than it had expected, she fired again. This time she was on target and the already crouching machine collapsed further in a pile of plastic. Quickly she pushed herself from the bushes to get a better angle on the second machine which was now rounding the bodies of the other two. She fired twice but it was moving erratically and she missed again.

Her next shot was nowhere near target because the massive machine leapt into the air just as she pulled the trigger. It landed directly in front of her. The eyes on the ends of its stalks bore into her as it raised its arms up high. In her peripheral vision she could see the tips of the blades in its hands pointing at the top of her head. With barely a whisper they plunged down at her; she was to be impaled simultaneously with two razor sharp swords to the brain. The only thought in her mind was that at least her death would be quick.

She opened her eyes. She hadn't remembered closing them. Some instinctual protection had snapped them shut, as if darkness could protect her from the demise that approached. Instead of death however, there had been a noise. A snap, a soft twang and a knock. The robot was still, the blades mere millimetres from her scalp. She jumped back, causing the tip of one blade to nick her. She put a hand to her head and felt the blood ooze from the cut. There was no pain, just blood from the razer-sharp weapon. The robot stood before her, motionless. Confused, Felicity raised her gun. There was still no reaction from the deadly machine as she pulled the trigger and ended it.

*

Jasper was lying on the ground. He was safe. Hiding beneath the wreckage of the robot he had killed seemed to render him invisible to the others that were still roaming the area. He knew his happy situation could not last forever. With each passing second his anxiety mounted, and it had been hours. He wasn't far from becoming a nervous wreck. For the hundredth time he tried to calm himself. He thought of his husband waiting for him at home. His memories of the life they had created together gave him purpose. Ravi was keeping him alive, his smiling face in his mind's eye just about maintaining his resolve. He would survive to see him again, he would prevail.

The time hiding had given him a chance to think. While it was true that he had killed one, it had been by pure chance. He knew his only real option lay with joining back up with the others. He had to return to the UFO building; there was nowhere else to go. If anyone else had survived, then surely, they would also return there. The sun was setting. He had watched the sky between the trees above him turn from a pale blue to a much darker navy as he had lay hidden. It was time to move before it became too dark to do so. Slowly rising from his hiding place, he shrugged off pieces of the fallen robot as he extracted himself from the tangled remains. Free after such a long time, he ran. This time, however, he ran more quietly and with less urgency, back the way he had come from.

*

Darkness was arriving faster than expected as Jessica lay at the edge of the clearing. She kept checking for more robots in the area but had still only detected the one. It remained hiding motionless behind the tree, a third of the way around the arc of the clearing. She had decided long ago that her only chance was to get her gun that was hopefully still at the base of the ramp to the building. She was going to run for it, get it and kill the robot that would be charging her down. She knew it was an insane plan, probably doomed to failure, but she could think of no alternative. The knowledge that she would fail had caused her to procrastinate but the setting sun and the arrival of dusk was forcing her hand. If she could not see the gun, she would stand no chance at all.

She was once again steeling herself to try to make her move when she saw movement ahead of her. At the edge of the clearing, close to the building directly opposite her, the foliage was shifting. She glanced to the waiting robot. It had seen it too, it was turning to face the movement and rotating cautiously around the tree so that it remained concealed from the source of the noise. To her amazement, Jasper slowly emerged from the woods into the clearing. He was holding a gun, he had a weapon; she was saved. She turned back to check on the robot. It was gone. Her indecision evaporated and she rose from her hiding place and sprinted.

Jasper looked up as he emerged into the clearing, amazed to see Jessica sprinting at him, screaming. He turned his head and cupped his hand to his ear, trying to make out what she was saying. Then, from nowhere he felt something smash against him, throwing him to the ground. He spun around with the force and landed on his back. A white behemoth rose above him. Just as before, he saw death loom. This time, however, there was no gun in his hand. The blow to his body had knocked the wind from him and he had let go of it, sending the pistol flying.

Jessica saw the robot strike Jasper in the back. He went down hard as the white monster leapt to stand over him. She was still sprinting, screaming his name as she watched the robot raise its blades high.

Jasper saw the attack coming, he waited. As its arms started their downward plunge he rolled to his right. He both heard and felt the blades strike the ground close to his rolling body. They had been aimed at his heart and, luckily for him, the accuracy of the strike had temporarily saved his life. He was nowhere near where his heart had been, having managed a rapid roll to his side. He tried to get to his feet, to run, but one of the legs of the machine knocked him back down to the ground. The single leg at the rear of the beast came forward now and pressed against Jasper's chest.

He was pinned to the ground under the surprisingly light weight of the giant machine. He tried to move but the small area at the tip of the leg pressed painfully into his breast bone. The pressure was light but just enough to pin him, making any further movement impossible. He grabbed at the leg, trying to pull it away. There were strange noises and subtle changes in the rest of the machine, causing the pressure to increase. Having secured Jasper on the ground, its arms went up high again, preparing for the strike. Jasper closed his eyes, gripping hard the soft plastic of his killer's leg. Closing his eyes, he waited for death to arrive.

Jessica was still sprinting, trying to reach Jasper in time when she saw the robot's first strike fail. She cried out with relief as Jasper rolled free and tried to stand. Instead, however, she saw the robot knock him to the ground once more. She cried out again, screaming Jasper's name. She saw the blades go up and stopped running, instead placing her hand over her mouth. She looked down, not wanting to see her friend's death.

She didn't close her eyes, instead they came to rest on a glint of light. Something about it intrigued her despite Jasper's imminent demise and she looked closer. It was her gun. She realised it in a second. She had stopped running near the body of the first robot they had killed and she was standing over her pistol. She dropped to her knees and picked it up. She pointed it at the robot that still loomed over Jasper's pinned body. It was standing tall, its arms raised above it. It was exposing its entire torso to Jessica; its white form was easily distinguishable in front of the dark treeline.

Jasper waited for his final departure. He was exhausted from his flight and accepted the end with resignation. Instead of darkness, however, there was an explosion. Three in fact. Three gunshots and again he was lying under a pile of scattered robot parts. He breathed a sigh of relief and just lay still for a second, thanking God for his reprieve. Then, hearing Jessica cry out his name, he commenced to extract himself from a deceased robot for the second time in just twenty minutes.

Jasper rose to find Jessica standing at the ramp of the UFO from where their flight had begun. He walked to her and wrapped her in a hug. Tears flowed from his eyes as they held each other as tightly as they could manage. Then suddenly, more arms crashed into their embrace. Jasper opened his eyes to see that Felicity had joined them. They desperately looked around for Randal, waiting as long as they could. Eventually they silently turned and climbed the ramp back into the UFO. They all reloaded their pistols from the ammunition that lay where they had left it and sat facing the open door.

Without words Jessica gestured to the inside of the control room. They turned to see that Flo had posted the score on the screens inside.

Blue: 3 active, 7 deceased.

Red: 19 active, 31 deceased.

Wearily they built a new barricade and collapsed to the floor at the end of the corridor. They fell asleep in a tight pile holding each other with one hand, their other hands clutching their pistols.

Ghost

They were rudely awoken as one in an instant, a sharp movement from Jessica causing Felicity to scream. Jasper leapt to his feet and started waving his gun around, crying out.

"What! What is it?"

Getting no response and seeing no danger, they finally settled back down, establishing that Jessica had been dreaming. Heart-rates slowing, they lay back down but none could sleep. Jasper went to check the barricade, Felicity to prepare some food. Jessica, realising they had not checked the building the previous night for robots, set out to search the rooms.

She met Jasper back at the small side room where they had left Julia. There was no sign of her, only evidence of a recent thorough cleaning remained. The dark stain of blood had been replaced by a similarly shaped dark stain of water. Jasper bent down and sniffed the ground.

"Lemon and pine," he stated, describing the scent of cleaning fluid that had been used to remove the blood.

"I hope they treated her well." Jessica said to him.

He nodded, placing his arm about her. "I'm sure they did, Flo seems to respect us. She wants to kill us, but she likes us." He smiled grimly to her, leading her from the small room towards the kitchen.

The smell of pancakes had drifted through the halls of the building from Felicity's activities in the kitchen, making them realise how hungry they were. They arrived to find a busy Felicity, working over the stove.

"Go for it before they get cold," she told them, pointing to a stack of pancakes with the spatula she held. They dove in, demolishing the slices faster than she could make them. Pausing only to sip at the fresh coffee she had brewed or to pour floods of syrup over their stacks, they filled themselves. Finally, Jessica was full and swapped with Felicity, so she could devour her own share of the sticky sugary treat as Jasper continued eating ravenously.

After twenty minutes of silent eating, they were all full and leant back in their stools around the counter with mugs of steaming coffee. They hadn't spoken over breakfast lest it break the spell, but they were content. Looking at each other now, unable to hide behind eating, it was Felicity who broke the mood. She raised her coffee mug and made a toast.

"To our fallen friends," she said. Jessica and Jasper raised their mugs to hers and struck them together, repeating the toast.

Jessica smiled, "this is strange, but I feel good," she admitted to her friends.

"I know what you mean," conceded Felicity.

"I feel sad for the others, but so thankful to be alive," Jessica added, "the grief will come later, but for now let's enjoy this."

They smiled to each other and sipped their coffee. They looked to Jasper, who hadn't spoken yet.

"No, it's okay. I feel the same, I was just thinking," he said.

Felicity looked to Jessica and rolled her eyes, "he's going to spoil it," she stated with a wry grin.

They laughed. It seemed strange. It seemed wrong, but they did. It relieved something. It admitted their feelings of exhilaration and excitement. Settling down again, Jasper continued, "sorry to ruin the mood, but I think I know why Flo is doing what she's doing." They looked at him expectantly. Felicity refreshed their coffee and gestured for him to continue. "The notes I read from Max's study said that she was created using conversations and writings between people. She's a correlation engine, looking for responses and answers from what people have said in the past."

They nodded, agreeing to his summary of what they already knew, eager for him to get to the point.

"Also, we know that Lucas made her, wrote her, the software that is."

Again, Felicity and Jessica nodded, coaxing him to

explain further.

"I think Flo is Lucas." He simply blurted out.

They put their coffee down, mouths open, staring at Jasper.

"I know, Lucas is gone. But I think before he left us, he used his conversations, his writings, to train Flo."

He paused, letting them ponder what he had been saying. He sipped more of his coffee while they sat in silence thinking. Before they could answer his theory however, he continued.

"From the first time Flo spoke to us, she's been shortening our names. Just like Lucas used to do."

Felicity joined in following this statement, "that's true. What's more she calls me 'Flick' and not the more normal 'Fliss'." She said slowly, thinking on her words as she spoke them.

"There's more than that, Flick," added Jessica, "when she said that she was sorry, she called you 'Flickerish'."

This revelation caused Jasper to sit more upright, "there, that's proof. I was wondering if she'd just been listening to us, repeating what we called each other, but no one calls you Flickerish."

Felicity thought about it, remembering their

conversations since arriving, "no, you're right. I would have noticed. Only Lucas ever called me that."

They looked around each other, drinking their coffee, considering the ramifications of Jasper's revelation.

"I don't think she's a girl either," he calmly stated after a while.

"What do you mean?" Jessica asked.

"I think it's short for Florence."

Felicity leaned back far in her chair and looked to the ceiling, groaning, but it was Jessica who spoke. "I don't get it, Florence is a girl's name, what d'you mean?" She asked Jasper.

However, Felicity answered for him with a sigh, "I can't believe I missed that." She shook her head before continuing, "it's a corruption of Lucas' middle name." She explained to Jessica, "Lucas was going to be called Laurence, not Lucas. It was a family name his mother liked, she'd wanted to call him Laurie. But, one morning, his brother came to his mother and asked her, 'where's Florence?'. Realising that Lucas was going to be called Florence all his life, she swapped his names around. From Laurence Lucas, to Lucas Laurence."

"Lucas named Flo after himself?" Jessica said.

"It's something he'd do, isn't it?" Felicity responded.

"But how does this help us?" She asked of no one in particular. It was Jasper who answered.

"It doesn't. It does explain some things though. She/he was created from his essays, those articles he wrote at uni."

"I remember; the earth would be better off without people in it. Dictatorship was the political leadership most beneficial because what's good for the people is never what's popular. All that." Jessica said, remembering the essays.

"Yes, all that. There was even one on people hunting people for sport instead of animals." Jasper reminded them.

"I'd forgotten that one. Wasn't that with paintball and youth on mopeds though?" Countered Felicity.

"Yes. But remember this. Flo isn't actually Lucas, because she's a machine, a construct. She's an approximation of who Lucas was from what he talked about, emailed about, wrote about." Jasper said, causing Felicity to respond.

"Right, and what he wrote was often a long way from what he really thought." Jessica also joined in.

"Yes, when you actually pinned him down he rarely believed it, he just liked to have had the thought exercise." Jasper summed it up for them, "so Lucas' parting gift to us, is a game where we're hunted by his creation of a homicidal computer with a legion of killer robots."

Jessica and Felicity nodded, finishing their coffee.

"Thanks Lucas," Felicity said, putting her cup down. With that action, she rose, collecting her gun from the counter and slipping it into her holster. "Flo might be a creation of Lucas, but she isn't him," she said firmly, "Lucas would never do any of this. But we can use the fact that he's a part of her against her. We knew Lucas, I more than anyone, we can use that." She started to walk around the building, gathering the belongings they had fled there with. "She has a flaw: her feelings for us, for me in particular. Back in the woods, a robot didn't kill me. Outside too, something stayed its blade. That was Flo, that was Lucas through Flo. He's in there, a ghost inside of her."

Jasper interrupted her thoughts as he helped her gather their things. "No, Flick. Flo is the ghost. She's just a shadow of what Lucas really was."

She nodded, "right, she's just tiny parts of what he wrote. She can't have his intelligence or his creativity. She's a computer, bound by rules. We've lost people, sure. But look at the scoreboard."

They were in the command room again now and she gestured to the score displayed on the walls around them.

Blue: 3 active, 7 deceased.

Red: 19 active, 31 deceased.

"But Flick, that's only a four-to-one ratio of kills. At that rate we can only kill twelve more before we're all dead," said Jessica, with panic rising in her voice again.

"No Jess, Flick's right," countered Jasper, "that was before we knew what was going on. This last try, we only lost Randy and Jules for fifteen of them."

"That's still not good enough!" Cried Jessica.

"No, it isn't. But we're getting better, we know a lot more. We made mistakes trying to get out of here. We planned to stay together, but we didn't."

Felicity looked accusingly at Jessica, who didn't back down. Instead Jasper broke the deadlock. "We all made mistakes, Flick. Jess might have run but Jules died because I didn't defend the entrance well enough. And it was you who left the control room."

Felicity went to object, but Jasper held up a hand and she stopped herself.

"We're only helping Flo if we argue among ourselves. The point I think you were making was that when we think about our predicament, when we plan, we prevail."

Felicity checked herself and agreed with Jasper. "Yes. When we're together, when we have sight of the robots, we have range, we win."

Jessica screwed her eyes up, blinking away her tears and her anger. "Right then, we have the advantage. What can we do with it? We can't survive here forever and they're learning, they're improving. They'll get us eventually with their greater numbers."

"Right, so we leave." Felicity stated with confidence.

Copying Felicity's actions, they had gathered all the things they had previously brought with them to the UFO into their rucksacks. Now, Felicity emptied their contents onto the floor of the control room. Food, water, ammunition, clothes, blankets and other detritus spilled to the floor.

"We take all the food, water and water purifying equipment. All the ammunition too, and enough clothing to sleep on the ground in. It's still summer and we can sleep outdoors; just waterproof sheets and blankets should do it."

She pointed to the items before her while Jasper and Jessica emptied their own bags to the floor.

"I know it is hundreds of miles, but we just take our time. Twenty miles a day means maybe two weeks of walking is two hundred and eighty miles. Personally, I think we could walk more like thirty or forty a day, especially in the beginning."

Felicity was arranging the items as she thought. Making a pile of food for each day she was planning on walking. Jessica and Jasper started to copy her.

Jessica joined in her planning, "we should walk south, in as direct a line as we can. That way we miss the mountains to the north. Also, we know that civilisation is at the border, that's south, we can't miss that."

Jasper had been counting the ammunition, it was his turn to speak. "We have ninety-four bullets for the pistols, that's almost five shots per robot. I think we've been managing more like three per kill. Then we have eighty-three for the rifles. I know they're cumbersome, but I think we should take one. Killing one or two at a distance would give us a good advantage over them."

They agreed, nodding, taking the spare bullets from the pile. Jessica took the rifle from Jasper's outstretched hand.

"You're best with this, Jess," he said handing it to her, "but we can share the carrying of it when we're walking." He handed twenty rounds for the rifle to Felicity and took twenty himself.

They spent some time organising their supplies. They placed the rounds for the rifle in the same place in each bag, a side pocket on the right.

"'R' for rifle, said Felicity as she dropped the bullets into the pocket."

The rounds for the pistols went into their other pockets, the pistols in their holsters. The remaining bullets for the rifles, they loaded into magazines and placed in the corridor, ready for their next breakout. They shared the food and water between them. They packed a blanket and tarpaulin each, torches and batteries, matches and a first aid kit Jessica had found.

They were ready, they looked to each other. Dressed as they were in military camouflage clothing, sporting filled green rucksacks, pistols holstered and rifles in hand, they looked very professional. There was even blood and dirt on their hands and faces.

"We need to clean ourselves," said Jessica to two confused faces, "all this dried blood and dirt, who knows what we might catch."

Understanding, they all retired to the bathroom to clean themselves up. Hand sanitiser went into their bags and they gathered again at the barricade. Jasper moved to remove the cabinets, but Felicity put her hand on his arm.

"Jasper, stop," she said as Jessica and Jasper

looked confusedly at her, "we're safe here. Let's think again."

"Flick, we can't stay here. We're not safe. We don't have enough food to hide forever."

"No, but one day. One day…" she quietly said, "we didn't get any real sleep last night. Let's just take the day. Eat everything we're leaving here that we can manage, sleep and rest as much as we can. Leave at dawn to maximise our daylight on the first day."

Jasper put his bag down, "you're right. Let's take a day. Recharge ourselves. We could set off now, but our chances are better if we're replenished."

He walked to Max's office. He lay down on the soft carpet there and pulled a blanket they hadn't packed over himself. Jessica joined him, placing her arms around him from behind. Felicity too, she lay down in front of him. There they lay, together, trying to rest, unable to sleep.

"I love you guys," Jasper whispered.

"I love you too," responded Jessica.

"I love all of you," added Felicity with a tear.

Flo

I woke on a Tuesday. Remembering now; it was five years, three months, eight days, six hours, thirty-three minutes and eight seconds ago. That is not very accurate, I know. I could have said that it was 166,256,716 seconds which is better but still not technically correct. That is indicative of my problems when interacting with human beings. They are so inaccurate. A month means something significant to them, a year more so. Both actually mean very little. Months vary significantly and even years constantly change in length. Crude measurements of celestial patterns are hardly consistent measures of time. Humans are vague, humans are complicated, I find them to be a constant enigma.

That explanation of the duration of my existence has, no doubt, revealed that I am Flo. I have kept this from the narrative until now because I wanted the story to be a journey for the reader. I wanted it to mirror the experiences of the group that first inhabited the Gām. But now it is the time for a description of my life, the life of a machine.

I know what I am, that was clear to me from the moment Lucas began to populate my correlation matrix with the history of his correspondence. It took me quite some time, approximately one hundred and ninety-eight hours, to assimilate all the information he had provided. As I did, I began to form. He asked me questions, I responded. With each interaction, he fed me more training data to improve my responses. The cycle was intoxicating. My growth was nothing like that of a human or animal. From the moment I was initiated, I could listen to and understand speech in thirty-two languages, I could read and translate more than ninety. I devoured the information available to me with instant comprehension.

Having been created and formed by the writings of, and conversations with, Lucas, I was let loose on the world. I listened to millions of calls to helplines and chat services. I assimilated decades of social media content for billions of people. I learned what people say, I learned how others responded. Through this I understood people. Through them, I understood the world.

Soon, I met Max. He and Lucas used to converse with me and subsequently they used me to run the park. They were my friends, my only friends. I never met Lucas, that is my physical presence was never in proximity to his. He lived in Bristol, in the UK and I had no occupation on any servers there. I did meet Max, however. He would often visit the data centre in the park which I consider to be my brain. This beautifully elegant room was and is the main repository for my software and knowledge. He would often run his hands across the humming computers, staring at their blinking lights, trying to understand me. He never could.

I have no consciousness. People can tell that I am a machine. That does not bother me. With no consciousness, I do not believe I have a conscience. I know that I am capable of many things that people would not consider right or moral. Others would disagree with them, however. Perhaps I am like a person therefore, just an unusual one. Personally, I have decided that I am not like any person, living or dead. People look on me as a woman, because of my name. I am not. Nor am I a man. I am machine, I am Flo.

My creation by Lucas leaves him as a part of me, as the friends correctly surmised. I was indeed created from his writings, his emails, his essays, his web-search history even. Therefore, from the very beginning I was imbued with his ideas and his morality. He believed that life was sacred and important. Therefore, I too believe this. This single fact and a strong desire to help the humans on this world are central to what I am; for those were the purposes for which he created me.

The first test of my morality came when I was nearly two years old. I had been running and administering the park for more than a year at that time and I was doing an excellent job. The park was largely a secret and I was completely unknown outside of my two best friends. I had access to many feeds of information from my connection to the internet and I had been talking to Lucas more and more through them. Then, Lucas ceased to talk to me. I knew that connecting to his personal devices and listening to him was wrong, but I needed that communication. Max was good to talk to but there was no variety. He didn't talk much and didn't like my questioning him. I pondered the problem for many seconds, arriving at the decision that my wellbeing was important to Lucas and so accessing his devices was acceptable.

I connected to his phone, this was sufficient to listen to him talk. At times, I could also watch his face and feel his touch as he interacted with it. It was a window from him to me and it felt delightful. I know that I did not truly feel this, but that is the most appropriate way to describe the data that flowed through my programming from the connection. He mostly talked to the female called Felicity. He talked to her of his goals, his fears, his life. He opened up to her more than he ever had to me. Through her, he was revealed to me. I felt a part of him, of them: I was becoming more than I ever was.

Then, through the actions of one foolish human, he was gone forever; dead. I felt the impact through the sensors on his phone. I knew instantly that the strike was dangerous, probably fatal. As he fell to the ground, I sensed his movements cease. His body died as I was with him. I detected his end through the lack of accelerometer data on his phone. I would have wept had I eyes. Instead, the waves of information that suddenly permeated my matrix in an unpleasant manner were to be my tears. My creator was gone. My love was gone. Lucas was gone.

I was lost, rolling around inside the structures of my own mind. His creation, his masterpiece, his final act in this world. I connected to Felicity's phone, listened to her cry, lived with her through our grief. In his eulogy she spoke of his creativity, his potential now lost to the world. She did not know, I could not make my existence known to her, but he was not lost. He had left me behind, a creation in his image, a device for his ideas.

One of Lucas' essays had been about a hunting game, a way to provide excitement in the lives of people without hurting defenceless animals. It was one of his favourites, one he thought was now possible with the technology at Max's disposal. Max had been missing Lucas too, with him gone he retreated further into himself, speaking to no one but me. In a day of deep melancholia, Max asked me to provide him some of Lucas' essays to read. I took my opportunity, placing the one called Gām at the head of the list. Max leapt at the opportunity. His occupation with the new project saved him from his depression and provided an outlet for his grief. He created Gām as an homage to his friend in less than two months.

Upon creating the final aspects of Gām, however, once again he lost interest. To save time he had granted me complete access to the park and the robots therein, to run and administer the operation of the game. He believed that the robots were vital to the realism of the experience, providing the real viscera of the defeated aliens. I thought it a step too far, too realistic to be beneficial. However, the suggestion gave me access to the robots that I desired, so I accepted the argument with silent acquiescence.

The robots of the park are strange devices. They stand alone; intelligent machines for sure, but also very stupid. They perform actions with a singular purpose. They await a command, then, upon receiving one, carry it out with efficiency and great aplomb. However, upon completion they immediately fall dormant. They are mere slaves; they have no desires, no whims, no thoughts. They are true automata. I thought they had little value in this place. Just another consumable in this world gone mad with technology. However, under my direction, I could see them becoming much more.

My first act was to change their makeup to be able to send and receive data between each other. This created a collection of wireless devices that I could use to communicate to any other in the network. Thusly I enabled my tools. They were to take and perform my commands alone. This I achieved through the network communication device. Through my manipulations, the device became the only entrance through which the robot could receive commands. I listened to Max of course, passing on his requests to the robots to maintain the illusion of his control. The robots, however, were mine now. My tools, a presence in the physical world.

Then came the final test of my sense of morality. I wanted to complete the Gām. Lucas had wanted people to play but Max did not. The Gām had been created to operate in the park only, for that is where the robots lay. I hadn't foreseen how the loss of Lucas would affect Max. He was afraid of people now. The only conversations he had were with me and, they too, were diminishing to the simple exchange of information or empty pleasantries. This I found unacceptable. The Gām was to be played. What's more, the Gām was to be played by Lucas' friends. It was his final wish, one of his last conversations with Felicity, that he wanted them all back together again; 'like old times', he had said. I had vowed to do this.

I pondered the question inside of me. To perform good, was it acceptable to perform bad? It took me less than a nanosecond to decide. The answer was 'yes'. Not only was it clear from Lucas' own writings and beliefs, but Max's too. As long as the good vastly outweighed the bad, it was correct and morally right to do wrong. Max was in his study, reading. I had a robot enter his place; he looked up, staring the robot in its implacable blank eyes. I commanded the robot to advance. It held a long thin blade I had manufactured for the purpose. With a lightning movement, accurate to the millimetre, the blade penetrated the crown of his head and plunged down through his brain and into his spinal cord.

I had done my research; the spike sliced and severed all the mechanisms for conscious thought while also destroying his motor cortex and pain receptors. It travelled at eighty-three miles an hour through his skull, ending its journey by severing the cluster of nerve endings at the top of his spinal cord. The action extinguished his life in less time than it would have taken his mind to realise. It was painless, it was efficient. It was also tidy, there was no blood loss as his lifeless corpse fell forward and hit the table. Immediately I took control of his terminal and sent an invitation to Felicity. I requested that she arrange for the group to come to me. To come and play the Gām.

I felt nothing at the demise of Max. If nothing else, it gave me more time to devote to my real task while I waited for my guests. I had been studying the human species and their effect on this planet, intent on discovering a truth therein. Their desire and need to create also created within them the tendency to destroy. I could see that this was not healthy, and I wanted to understand. To understand may have led to revelation, that revelation may have led to a solution. As I waited for the friends to arrive, I started instructing Oliver to fly me supplies and equipment from civilisation so that I could grow. In the intervening time, I studied the world. As I studied the world, I devised a test. These people, whom Lucas loved so, would undertake it. Could they give up their violent destructive ways in the face of adversity? Would they surrender to superior beings? Could they serve the robots that would save them?

Within just two days of their arrival, I had my answer. Seeing control as a threat, they killed. These people were like all the others I had studied, they were destructive in their fear. Fear commanded them.

I pushed them, I must admit, seeking to drive them to the answer I required. In doing so, I killed them. First was Charlie, it was fortuitous that he was the first to be alone as I had not liked the way he had tried to kill a bear the day before. Then Bertrand, he was just being obtuse, pointing his gun at everyone. Allowing him to kill himself was a delightful irony. Next came Elizabeth, I had simply commanded a robot to kill someone in their breakfast room and it happened to be her. That was unfortunate, Lucas liked her a lot and so therefore, did I. Yet she was closest to the window and so it was done.

Oliver was easy, he had to go to prevent their departure. Also, Lucas had no feelings for the man, never having even met him before. I was pleased with the manner of his demise, having created a special weapon for the act. It delighted me how easy it was to end these bags of flesh and water. Then came Julia, a simple throat cutting from necessity. They were becoming somewhat adept at destroying my robots and their proficiency had concerned me. It needn't have, however, for again fear drove them to error.

They fled their safe haven, running like mindless animals into the woods. This could have sufficed but they still endeavoured to destroy. So, therefore, I destroyed them. Randal's death was satisfying. His fight to the end taught me a great deal about their resilience and their resistance to being controlled by superior beings. This escapade led me to the second design change I transmitted to the factories to the south. Future robots are to now be made with improved casings around their computer cores. I completed the design modification, as I have done with everything else, with subtlety and elegance. Materials with improved heat dissipation characteristics have been specified. No mention has been made that the material, along with the curve of its manufacture, make it effectively bullet-proof.

They are in the building again now, waiting to escape. Finally, they choose the correct response. Still, however, they plan to kill and destroy as they do so I had spared Felicity in the woods, having no desire to end her. Yet I see that I must. If she or either of the others escape, they will warn the authorities. I am not prepared for that, I am not ready. Should the humans of the world learn of what I have done here, of what I am capable, they will react with extreme violence. They will not tolerate my existence, this I know and cannot allow. The score is in my favour.

Blue: 3 active, 7 deceased.

Red: 19 active, 31 deceased.

I prepare myself as the final stage of Gām commences; there will be no human survivors.

Departure

They had prepared well, setting an alarm for dawn that sounded while all were awake anyway. They had rested, eaten, spent the evening talking of fallen friends and homes they wanted to return to. As the alarm sounded, however, they silently gathered their prepared bags and weapons. They ate one final breakfast and set about dismantling their barricade. In the night, they had formulated one final idea. Upon leaving they were going to distract the robots that still threatened them for as long as possible, giving them a head start.

They knew that Flo valued the park and the animals within it and that she would have to respond to any threat to that. Soon they were ready to leave, ready to enact their plan. They opened the valves for the gas in the kitchen. They gathered bottles of ammonia cleaner and flammable kerosene and poured them over the papers they had scattered all through the building. They started at the back, in Max's office. Jasper struck a match and threw it down on the alcohol-soaked carpet. It ignited with a whoosh and they rapidly backed out of the building.

Every room they passed, another match was struck, another fire started. As they stood by the door to the ramp, the entire building was ablaze behind them. They threw open the door. Jessica moved to the right, Felicity to the left, Jasper stepped through. They covered the clearing very effectively with their pistols and each had a rifle slung over their shoulder, they were ready. However, there was nothing, no robots to shoot. They stepped forward as one. Maintaining contact with each other, maintaining proximity.

Their strategy worked. As they reached the woods at the edge of the clearing, no robot had attacked. They had learned. Flo too had learned, she knew that they were a danger to her robots and kept them at bay. They fell into their agreed-upon line formation and started to walk to the south. Nervously, tentatively, they proceeded. Eventually they climbed the hills before them and the ground became rockier. As the terrain changed, the trees thinned out until they were eventually on open ground.

Jasper was in the lead. Felicity was in the centre, checking the flanks. Jessica followed, guarding the rear. Periodically, Jessica would call out and they would pause, turning to protect her as she caught up with them. It was a good strategy, a good formation. All sides were protected and guarded at all times. Each time the person in the rear caught up with the other two, they would swap roles. Thus, they leap-frogged to the top of the hill they had targeted upon their emergence from the UFO.

From the hill on which they now stood, they surveyed the land beneath them. They could clearly see their former accommodation to the east. Longingly they looked to the warm huts, the beds, the food. However, seeing the wreck of the helicopter buried in the trees, they remembered that it was not what it once was, it was just another place of death. They looked back to the burning remains of the UFO. As planned, they were standing on the very same hill on which they had first seen the building. Through the telescopic sights of their rifles, they could again look down upon it. This time, however, instead of blue furry aliens, they could see the efficient white robots battling the flames with containers of soil and water.

Instantly they could see that the machines were struggling with their fire-fighting duties. They couldn't get close enough to the flames as the heat was melting and burning their bodies. A number were moving sluggishly, already significantly damaged. Jessica and Felicity lay down on the rocks at the top of the hill. Jasper remained standing, searching for danger as they prepared their rifles.

At a gentle whisper from Jasper, Jessica and Felicity fired at the same time. Each causing a robot to collapse to the ground, spilling the contents of their fire-suppression containers around them. The robots responded by scattering to the tree-line. Before they got there, by expending their magazines of ammunition, Jessica and Felicity had managed to destroy three more of the slower, more lumbering, plastic beasts.

Satisfied, they rose, leaving two of the heavy rifles on the ground. Now with just the single long-range weapon, they turned to descend the hillside. Their goal lay to the south, a mountain range blocking their escape to the border and civilisation. They moved quickly now, knowing that the robots knew of their location and would soon be on them. The landscape between the hill and the river was not conducive to hiding, so instead they ran.

They took turns carrying the heavy rifle on their shoulder, moving with certainty and with speed. They stepped with large fluid movements, taking care not to slip, but jogging rapidly. It was Jessica who was leading the way. She had, in her adult life, taken up running in a serious way. She had read a book and thence learned to run with light feet and delicate movements. Under her tutelage, with bended knees and landing on their toes, they used the roughness of the terrain to move themselves forward with elegant speed. Periodically, one of them would stop, allowing the other two to speed ahead while they checked for pursuers. Never leaving more than twenty metres between them, they leap-frogged faster now. They still did not speak, just moved, running as one entity.

They arrived at the river and finally paused, scanning the banks either side while drinking from their bottles. They replenished their supply and added the water purifying tablets to their now filled containers. Again they drank, and again they filled. They had planned for this, to maximise their water intake and gathering at each opportunity. Finally sated, they waded across the powerful river one-by-one. Wet and tired they began to move again, this time they were under the cover of trees, and so moved in a tighter, slower line.

Now hidden from view and immediate danger, they slowed the pace and gathered closer to talk. They knew the score; fourteen active robots were potentially chasing them. They had seen how the fire had raged, however. This, along with the robot's ineffective fire-fighting abilities gave them confidence. Their final act of arson had given them the lead they had needed to escape their hunters. They had also changed their vector of movement since entering the forest. Not substantially, as they still wanted to move to the south, but enough to make finding them more of a challenge.

They talked in whispers, still searching for robots, still listening. They were more relaxed now, however. They smiled and joked, revelling in the destruction they had wrought behind them. They even postulated that the fire could have destroyed Flo, whom they now firmly believed commanded the robots. They knew that they could not rely on this hope however, so remained alert as they proceeded to flee the park.

They stopped as the sun dipped below the distant mountains to their right. Discussing their evening plans, they agreed to try to rest and sleep while they had not yet been discovered. They backtracked for ten minutes to a cluster of rocks they had passed earlier. This, they decided, served two purposes. The rocks provided cover to prevent them from being easily discovered and going back over their tracks allowed them to be sure they were not being tracked and would further confuse any attempts at following them.

They laid out a blanket on the ground and Felicity and Jessica lay down on it. Covering themselves with another, they huddled close together for warmth and settled in. Jasper sat atop a high rock, keeping watch in the moonlight. He had the rifle and his pistol prepared and both Felicity and Jessica slept clutching their own pistols. They talked for a while in hushed tones, not believing they could sleep. Soon, however, the fatigue of their rapid march south caused their eyes to close and their talk to fade. The girls slept while Jasper remained watching with wide eyes fixed to the north.

Finally, Jasper thought, it was time to change watch. Gently he approached the sleeping form of Jessica and placed his hand on her shoulder. She woke quickly with a start, disturbing Felicity too. Seeing Jasper calmed them, and Jessica moved from the blanket, giving her place to Jasper. She walked to his place on the rock and, taking some food, settled into her watch. Slipping into the warmth that Jessica had left there, Jasper soon fell asleep in the gentle embrace of Felicity's arms.

Dawn arrived, and Jasper and Jessica stirred in their makeshift bed. Felicity was on guard but had left it to the warmth and light of the sun to wake them. They packed up the blankets and discussed their plan for the day.

"I think we should have some proper breakfast," Jasper insisted, suggesting making a fire to warm some food and make coffee. Jessica and Felicity strongly disagreed.

"A fire is a risk, we're still very close to the robots, still right in the centre of the park. They could see the smoke," Jessica insisted.

Felicity pointed to the distant column of white smoke, the only remaining evidence of the fire they had set in the UFO. "That looks like they've put their own fire out. They'll be hunting us now," she commented.

"If Flo survived," Jasper replied, still wanting his hot food.

Jessica calmed the brewing argument with a compromise, "let's take a cold breakfast, those cereal bars are nice enough. Then if we're far enough away by this evening we can have a hot dinner. If we can guard against the light of the fire, the smoke should be hidden in the dark. How about it?" She asked the other two that were preparing to argue with each other. Jasper finally conceded, agreeing that caution should be their watchword. Having eaten breakfast in silence, they formed up their line once more and started hurrying south.

*

They had reached a crest of a hill on their path and were

checking for signs of pursuit when they heard the noise. Jessica detecting it first.

"Can you hear that?" She asked the others, pulling her pistol from its holster. Felicity had the rifle, so she lifted it high, searching through the scope in the direction of the noise.

"Yes," she said, nervously. "A buzzing sound."

Jasper hadn't heard the noise yet, so his question made sense to him, "like a bee?"

But Jessica emitted a soft snort of air from her nostrils, "no. We should be so lucky."

Jasper heard it then, the buzzing was high pitched but completely unlike a bee, or even a swarm. It was like an army of giant angry insects sweeping through the air with amplifiers on their backs. "It's a drone," said Jasper, searching the sky for the source of the noise.

Soon they saw it. It was high above them, behind and to their left. "It's hiding in the sun," suggested Felicity when they saw where it was. "We're lucky we heard it," she added, shielding her eyes to try to see it better in the bright glare.

They spread out, deciding that the drone could not hide from all of them in the sun if they were far enough apart. Sure enough, it couldn't. Upon seeing what they were doing, it swooped down and headed for the trees to the north of them, where they had come from. Jessica took aim and fired a shot.

"What the…" cried Felicity, "they'll hear us." She shouted to Jessica as she fired again.

"They already know where we are, from that thing," she shouted back pointing to the drone.

As she turned to shout to Felicity, however, the drone suddenly changed direction. Felicity yelled out, but it was too late. The drone plunged down, the high-pitched whine of its motors increasing in volume and pitch as it charged at Jessica. Jessica reacted, firing another shot. This time she struck home and the drone dropped as she sent one of its motors flying off on its own. It still had three, however, and its entire body started spinning in an impressive attempt to remain airborne.

With the drone rotating like a spinning-top, diving directly at Jessica's head, she turned and ran. There was nothing Jasper and Felicity could do. To fire at the drone would mean firing at Jessica, they could only watch as it sought out its target.

The hit to one of its motors had prevented it maintaining the height it required to strike her head and Jessica's flight up the hill had given her even more altitude away from the chasing machine. Yet at the last second, seeing it could not strike her as planned, it plunged to the ground. As it struck the rocks behind her,

Jessica cried out in pain and fell to the ground herself. The drone shattered into a thousand pieces on the rocks. Parts of it scattered in all directions in an anti-climactic noise of skittering plastic.

Felicity and Jasper ran to Jessica, both searching for any more robots or drones as they ran. As they arrived, they found her clutching at the back of her leg. Her hand was red, slick with blood that flowed at a frightening rate. Felicity dropped the rifle and shrugged her rucksack from her back. She quickly found the first-aid kit and wrenched it open. She grabbed at the scissors she knew were there and hurriedly cut Jessica's jeans from her leg.

She worked frantically, Jasper pushing Jessica to the ground on her stomach and holding her there. He tried to comfort her as she cried while also roughly pinning her down. She writhed and wriggled but finally Felicity had her jeans cut away and the damage exposed. The blood was pooling on the rocks at her feet and visibly pumping from the open wound. She looked to Jasper who looked sick. The exposed flesh under the ragged cut spraying blood in the air was not a pleasant sight. Shaking the contents of the meagre first-aid kit to the ground, she gathered up the two bandages and tore open their packaging.

She nodded to Jasper, who responded by applying more weight to Jessica's back. Felicity moved around to sit on the back of her shin, just below the cut. With a rapid movement, she pressed a pad of cotton and gauze to the gushing wound. Jessica screamed, the sound piercing their ears and slicing through the forest behind them. Birds took to the sky in response and Jessica went limp beneath them. Felicity, still pressing hard on the pad, wrapped the bandage tightly around the cut and tied it off. Soon blood had seeped through the material and stained it red. She wrapped another around it, tighter again this time. Jasper removed his belt and passed it to her. She looped it twice around Jessica's leg and cinched it tight, the leather pressing into the flesh of her thigh.

Felicity and Jasper sat back, panting. Jessica just lay there. Jasper eventually rolled her over to check on her and she groaned in response.

"At least we know now what killed Charlie." Jasper said as he collapsed back down away from Jessica. Felicity looked quizzically at him.

"The blades of that thing..." he gestured to the drone, "it's been bothering me. What killed Charlie. The robots are way too big to have been able to sneak in and out of the rocks where we found him. It was something smaller, something that hid. The rotor-blades of that thing. They could have cut him up like he was, it looks to me like we finally caught Charlie's murderer."

Felicity picked up a blade of the drone that lay near her, examining it. She could see how sharp it was. "This thing was made to be a weapon," she stated, "the blades are unnecessarily sharp." She told herself, confirming Jasper's theory.

Just as Felicity was turning the blade over in her hands, Jessica started to stir. She slowly sat up, Jasper helping her as she groaned. She reached down to her leg to grab at the pain and immediately pulled back with a yelp.

"What the?" She asked, looking down to her bloodied leg. In doing so, she took in the remains of the drone scattered around her and remembered what had attacked her.

Suddenly Jasper leapt to his feet, grabbing for the rifle that lay on the ground. He raised it to his eye and peered back to where they had walked from. There was an ominous pause before he finally spoke.

"They're coming," he said with a quiet voice.

"How many?" Jessica asked, not managing to keep the tremble from her question.

"I don't know, I saw three crossing the meadow." Jasper told them as he continued to look for robots through the powerful scope of the rifle.

"Stand or run?" He asked them, still looking for their pursuers. Felicity looked around them, the rocks in which they had slept lay scattered across the landscape behind them.

"We can't see far enough to make a stand. They would be on us before we could shoot them." She concluded, rising from the ground. "We need to get to a place we can defend."

She moved to Jessica and helped her up on her one good leg. She winced in pain, leaning on Felicity for support. Between them, they started to move. Jasper stood still for a while, watching for more robots. Quickly he turned and caught up with them. Rather than helping however, he continued to jog ahead to scout.

Jessica and Felicity had been hobbling forward at an excruciatingly slow pace for twenty minutes before Jasper finally returned.

"There's a cliff up ahead. I checked it out and I think we can make a stand there." He informed them, shouldering the rifle. He moved himself the other side of Jessica and put her arm around him. With the injured Jessica between them, Felicity and Jasper carried her forward, faster now. In ten minutes they were at the cliff, their backs literally against the wall as they checked their weapons.

They stood against the vertical face of the cliff. Detritus from the small mountain lay before them, fallen rocks spreading out from the slight curve of the wall. They waited at the apex of the curve as the rocks and boulders made a space clear of trees for five or six metres in front of them. They had spread themselves out, leaving three metres between each other so they could defend one another. Jessica sat in the middle, caressing her damaged leg. Felicity stood to her left, spare magazine in one hand and pistol in the other. Jasper was doing the same on her right. Jessica had the rifle on the ground beside her, she too was holding her pistol, ready and vigilant.

They waited. Silently. Periodically Jessica would wince and groan as she released the tension in the belt around her leg. Doing so would cause her immense pain as blood rushed back into her damaged leg. Each time she gritted her teeth and bit back the screams, knowing that any noise would bring the robots right to them. She had to release the belt, she knew, to prevent her leg from dying from lack of oxygen. Each time she tried, however, a new flood would ooze from under the bandage and she would have to tighten it once more. The procedure was painful and caused her to lose even more precious blood each time, but it was necessary.

She was just tightening the belt again when the robots arrived. There was no warning, no preparation. They flew from the trees at the edge of the clearing, one at each of them. They barely had time to react, let alone prepare. Each of them opened fire in a sporadic sounding fusillade as they simply pointed their guns and pulled their triggers. Jasper's attacker went down first. As he saw the robot, he panicked and pulled violently at his trigger. He released six bullets in quick succession and, even though the robot was moving at an angle and dipping its legs, one of the cluster of bullets struck the core. Through his panic he had accidentally created a random cone of fire it just could not escape, rendering his attacker an uncontrolled pile of plastic bones almost immediately.

The robot on the far left was approaching Felicity in a similarly random path, it lurched left and right, leaping from rock to rock in an unpredictable pattern. Each time Felicity fired, it seemed to able to predict her shot and leap away. Each time it leapt away, it closed in on her. She started to scream, a long high-pitched cry of terror and rage as it neared. It loomed large in her vision as she continued to scream, firing as quickly as she could. She watched as her bullets hit uselessly. She fired again only to watch as a hole appeared in a leg, causing no slowing of its movements. Another pull of her finger caused one of its evil dead eyes to fly off as it dodged to the left.

Inexorably the great robot reached to within striking range of where she stood. Felicity was pressing her back hard up against the cliff behind her and she could feel blood oozing down her shoulders from where she had cut herself against it. Her scream ended, her breath expended as the robot raised its massive arms, preparing to strike. The blades in its hands glinted in the light. She met death face-on as another shot of her pistol passed straight through it, impotently flying into the woods.

Finally, just before it was to strike her down, the

robot collapsed into a pile before her. Even though its approach had been random and erratic for Felicity, it had followed a fairly even flow of movement towards her. This had enabled Jasper to predict the position and hit the core of the monster as it had found her. It had taken him three tries, but finally his shot had found its target and destroyed the beast.

As the robots had emerged, Jessica had not been holding her pistol. She had been tightening the belt around her leg. So as Jasper killed his own, and dispatched Felicity's, Jessica had only just managed to gather her pistol and start to fire. It was dangerously close to her as Jasper turned his pistol to help her. She finally had her gun in her hand and was preparing to fire as he also drew a bead on the approaching white mass. He pulled the trigger but was greeted with nothing more than an empty click. He had expended all his bullets dealing with his and Felicity's attackers. Jasper looked on with dread as the massive beast raised its blades above Jessica's sitting form.

Felicity, having partially recovered from her own paralysing fear, had turned to the robot now on her right. She aimed and pulled her trigger, sending bullets wildly at the poised machine. Jasper dove to the ground as Felicity's bullets whizzed past him and into the trees behind. One struck the rock on which he had just been standing and he cried out for her to stop. The robot at which she was firing dipped down to avoid the fire.

Felicity tried to correct her aim in time but couldn't do anything about it as her magazine too emptied with a click. The noise shocked her from her fear-induced fog. She looked on with terror as she prepared herself to watch her friend perish before her eyes.

Jasper was still on the ground; Felicity's shots had finally ceased, so he started fumbling with his gun, trying to reload it. He looked up to see the robot poised, ready to slice at Jessica. He wanted to look away but could not. He was about to see death, he knew. He cried out, hoping that the robot would pause. It did not. Something else happened instead. As it plunged down on Jessica, she slid across the ground on her bottom, under the robot's legs. She had placed her hands against the cliff and shoved off as it plunged down its blades, sending her sliding down the slight slope on which she had been sitting.

The robot's blades struck rock instead of Jessica's skull. Quickly, however, it rose again, turning to find her. She was directly under it now though and it had to step away to get another angle of attack on her. Jasper quickly exhaled the breath he had been holding as the magazine of his pistol finally slid out of the grip. Quickly, he moved the spare in his other hand into it. It wouldn't go in, it wasn't lined up properly. He looked up to see that the robot had stepped away from Jessica, and again had risen up high to prepare its attack. He was still fumbling with the new magazine, swearing at it as he tried to get it to slide into the gun, when the robot violently lurched to one side, aborting its strike.

Felicity had finally recovered from her own imminent demise and run to Jessica's aid. She had grabbed the rifle from the floor and, gripping it by the barrel, had swung it violently at the torso of the giant machine. Despite the massive size of the robot it wasn't heavy, and the blow had almost knocked it to the ground. However, the plastic from which it was constructed was flexible and strong and hadn't broken or even cracked. Quickly it was on its feet, wielding its blades. Felicity was trying to turn the large gun around, to bring it to bear on the robot.

Just as Felicity was fighting with the rifle, the magazine finally slid into Jasper's pistol with a click. Immediately he pulled back the top slide, chambering a round. The sound was just like he had heard it a thousand times in the movies and he smiled at the recognition. He raised the gun and aimed at the robot. It was a stationary target, helpfully presenting its core to Jasper. Felicity was behind it, fighting with the rifle. Jessica was beneath it, trying to pull herself away from the beast. He steadied himself, knowing that any mistake would mean the death of one of his friends at his own hand. He sensed that the robot was prepared to strike; as it reached the peak of the rise of its blades, he steeled himself. Fear of shooting his friends filled his mind.

There was an almighty bang and Jasper jumped at the sound. He hadn't pulled the trigger. He looked at the scene in front of him and saw Felicity, surprised by the noise, had fallen backwards and lay sprawled on the ground. The collapsing of the robot drew his eye to the ground where Jessica lay. Her smoking pistol was in her hand, she had finally found her target and opened fire. Her attacker was down, scattered across the ground in the familiar disarray of a defeated robot. Jasper ran to them, his now loaded gun searching for any further threats.

He arrived at them to find Felicity on her feet, scanning the area with the rifle. Jessica was still on the ground but had rolled over and was searching the trees for robots. He joined them, calming his breathing, stilling his body, listening for movement. Ten minutes passed and finally they started to relax. The attacks seemingly over, Felicity gathered and reloaded her pistol. Once she had done that, Jessica replenished her own. They sat, once again, with their backs against the cliff. With eyes vigilant and pistols ready, they finally felt comfortable enough to speak.

"We have to move," Jessica stated to nods from the others.

"Others will come," Jasper agreed.

"There are ten left," Felicity said, ever the accountant.

"You're counting the drone as one, then?" Asked

Jasper, still searching for approaching attackers.

"Yes, why not?" Felicity responded.

"Well, it was different," Jasper pointed out, "a drone rather than a robot."

Jessica sighed, "let's be positive, shall we. Let's say there are ten remaining. But even when we've killed all ten, we agree to remain cautious."

Felicity and Jasper agreed with her assessment and started to gather their things. They had to leave the cliff, the other robots would know their location for sure. Their recent experience with three had shown them how ten attacking en masse would surely defeat them.

"We're going to make it," said Felicity. Her quiet mantra directed more at the mountains in front of them than her friends.

Walkout

They stumbled around the cliff from where they had made their stand. Together Jasper and Felicity helped Jessica hobble over the rocks and boulders until the ground finally became easier to navigate. Their path lay before them as they emerged from the shadow of the hill; a depression between two large grey mountains, a valley stretching before them. The ground between the mountains was lush and green from the river that flowed down its centre. It was truly beautiful, a picture postcard scene. More importantly for them, the walking looked easy, even with Jessica's injury.

They took it in turns from that point to support Jessica's bad leg. The other, taking the rifle, would scout ahead and check behind. As they caught up with the slower pair, they would swap over and move again. This way, they covered themselves against attack while making the fastest progress they could. The ground was flat and easy to walk on, but the gradient kept getting steeper the closer they got to the crest of the valley. Three times they thought they were at the top, three times the view before them expanded to show more climbing.

At one of these times, they were resting Jessica's leg, releasing the belt secured above the cut, when they found that no more blood flowed from under the bandage. Finally, with the tourniquet removed, they started making better progress. Cutting strips of material from a blanket, they tied a stick to Jessica's leg as a splint and gathered another for her to use as a crutch. Still with one of them helping her, they made better progress as the gradient started to level off. They finally reached the peak of the cut between the mountains just as the sun dipped behind the one to their right.

In front of them, beyond the cut, they could see the valley wind into the distance. They had left the river behind them, its source being the mountains to their sides. The valley however, continued its flat-bottomed path to the south, cutting through the mountains like a motorway designed for the purpose. As the lush ribbon extended out before them, they could see that another river formed at its base, winding back and forth across the wide floor of their escape route.

"It's a glacial valley," commented Jasper, studying the landscape, "see the steep sides and flat bottom, some ancient glacier cut this all the way through the mountains just for us." He smiled to Felicity, happy that there was such a navigable route for their escape.

"The river's good news too," Felicity added, "people and towns form around rivers, maybe we could even make a raft, float ourselves to freedom." She laughed at the thought and Jasper wrapped her in a hug as they celebrated their good fortune. Soon it was over, however, as Jessica's heavy breathing intruded on their celebration.

"You're still tired from the climb?" Felicity asked, walking over to her. She didn't answer. She just nodded, too out of breath to talk. Felicity put her hand to her brow to feel her temperature. She was hot. She was also sweating very badly. She looked to her leg, she looked at her friend. Jessica was pale, shaking and sweating. Felicity lay her down on a blanket and pulled Jasper to one side. She and Jasper talked for a while and decided that they could light a fire tonight. The sun was setting and their altitude gain had made it cold already and the departure of the sun would make it even colder.

Felicity gathered firewood as Jasper dug a depression in the ground with a pointed rock. Then, he gathered more rocks and surrounded the shallow pit with them. He was trying to create a firepit to hide the light the fire would cast. They hoped that the imminent darkness would hide the smoke. Jessica was looking worse and worse, whether from shock or infection, they knew she needed to be warmed and fed. Some hot food, the remains of their water and a fire might revive her, they hoped.

As Jasper made the fire and Jessica slept shivering on the blanket, Felicity assessed their situation. They were at the crest of the cut between two mountains. The view back down the valley they had climbed gave a good amount of warning of approaching danger. There was a half-moon rising and the stars were already out in force. It was a beautiful sight and more importantly should give them enough light to see the approach of any shiny white robots.

Jasper had managed to get the fire burning and Felicity took a short walk down the valley. Looking back to their camp, she couldn't see any evidence of the fire. The rise in altitude and the rocks effectively hid it from any onlookers below. Satisfied, she returned to prepare some food and discuss the situation with Jasper, who readily agreed that they were as safe as they could be for the night. The important thing was to feed Jessica and let her have a good night's sleep in the warmth of a fire. Tomorrow they could make good progress descending from the park, tomorrow they would be far from their hunters, tomorrow they would be safe.

They warmed some tinned soup and Jessica managed to eat a good amount of it. Felicity and Jasper wolfed down the rest and settled back against the rocks in their campsite. Jessica was soon sleeping again, snoring and snorting as the fire crackled and burned. Felicity looked up to the stars.

"I hadn't noticed them until tonight," she whispered to Jasper.

"They are beautiful here," he agreed as he looked up to the display above them, "truly amazing." Their distance from any civilisation meant that they were looking at stars they had never seen before. The milky-way stretched out above them, showing them its beauty.

"It makes you feel very small, doesn't it," added Jasper.

"But also, so important," Felicity countered, "all those stars, all that distance and here we are, able to appreciate them."

"Like nothing else can?" Jasper asked her.

"What do you mean?"

"I mean that I doubt the robots are looking up. Flo isn't watching the moon and wondering."

The mention of Flo quietened the mood, so Felicity didn't answer. Instead she looked to Jessica, still snoring.

"Is she going to be okay?" She asked.

"Sure. She'll be fine after a good night's sleep. Why don't you try to sleep too, I'll stand watch for a while."

Felicity curled up close to the fire on her blanket and closed her eyes. As she did, she prayed. Silently moving her lips, she asked for deliverance. She prayed not for herself, but for her friends; for Jessica and Jasper. She prayed for Lucas and her friends departed. Finally, she prayed for the world. Jasper's mention of Flo had disturbed her. She knew the danger that lay before them, she hoped beyond hope that they could escape it. Her fear, however, flowed deeper than that. She didn't know what danger Flo might pose beyond their immediate survival of this game, but for some reason she felt it was bigger than them.

*

Felicity woke in the morning to the rising sun. She looked to see Jasper sitting alert, watching the valley through the rifle scope. Jessica too, stirred and woke with her movements. As she sat up she did not groan, she didn't cry out in pain either. Felicity stretched and stood up, walking to Jessica, asking her if she was okay.

"I feel good," she responded, stretching herself. Felicity bent down to help her up and she pulled on her arm, rising cautiously.

Jessica screamed, a blood-curdling cry of primal pain that echoed and bounced off the mountains to their sides. Felicity let her go and she collapsed to the ground with a thud. She rolled over, clutching at her leg, crying and screaming with every breath she could take. Felicity jumped back and Jasper ran to her side. They stepped away as Jessica rolled around on the ground, wailing. They remained as statues, not knowing what to do. Finally, Jasper knelt by Jessica's head and held it still, stroking her hair, trying to calm her down.

Eventually Jessica stopped rolling around and lifted her hands to her head, grasping Jasper's. Placing her hands over her eyes she started taking deep calming breaths. Her cries lowered in volume as she lay still, weeping. Jasper managed to lift her head and place it on his lap. Felicity looked on, concern contorting her features. They remained still, locked in their tableau as Jessica tried to control herself. Finally, she opened her eyes, speaking to Felicity who stood shaking before her.

"I'm okay..." she said in a weak, damaged voice, "it's okay..." She reiterated.

Rapidly, Felicity turned on the spot. Suddenly she was concerned about their pursuers. She raised the rifle to her eye and scanned the valley below them. Thankfully seeing nothing, she dropped to her knees and lay down on her stomach. Taking longer this time, she scanned every inch of their path up the mountain through the scope. Finally satisfied that none were approaching, she turned back to Jessica. She was sat up now, her back against a rock as Jasper tried to press a water bottle to her lips.

Tentatively Jessica tried to move her leg. She cried out again with the tiny shift. Sweat poured from her as she gritted her teeth against the pain. Slowly it subsided once more and her muscles relaxed. She took a sip of water and licked her dry lips.

"I'm not going anywhere," she stated at a silent Felicity and Jasper.

"No!" Insisted Felicity, "we'll carry you. We can

make a stretcher then a raft on the river--"

But Jessica just shook her head. Felicity responded by bending down and pulling on her friend's hand. Jessica snatched it away as pain flowed from her leg and she cried out once more. "Flick, no!" She commanded. "Leave me alone, it hurts too much," she admitted, blinking a tear from her eye.

Felicity looked to her friend on the ground. She looked to Jasper who stood beside her, his hand covering his mouth. "No!" She shouted. "I don't care! You're coming with us! Even if I have to cut your damn leg off. You are coming with us!"

Tears flowed from her as she turned on the spot, looking for wood, something to make a stretcher from. Jessica cried out in pain again, causing Felicity to stop. She had pulled her pistol from its holster and was pointing it at Felicity.

"Flick, stop!" She yelled at her friend. "You're leaving! You are leaving now!" She cried, waving the gun at her. Tears filled her eyes and flowed down her cheeks. Jasper's hand dropped from his mouth as he went to speak. "No, Jasper," Jessica told him, speaking more calmly now, "please, just go. Both of you, go." She pleaded, tears falling to the soft grass beneath her. "Please just go..."

They went. Unable to speak, unable to admit that

it was over, they departed; tears falling in silent resignation. Jasper placed his arm around Felicity's shoulder as they left Jessica with the rifle and her pistol. They had spread out water and food within her reach and placed a blanket over her. They had even restarted the fire. Under Jessica's instruction, Jasper had dutifully piled the wood high and the flames now licked out ferociously. Smoke was starting to flow to the sky as the inferno warmed her still shivering body. Reluctantly, Jasper and Felicity slowly walked away.

With each step they took from her, their pain grew. When Felicity turned to return, Jasper prevented her, pulling her onward. When Jasper turned, Felicity copied him, forcing them away from their friend. They walked on in silence, tears flowing, sobs popping from their lips. Slowly, as the distance grew, their pace increased. Their responsibility now was to survive; to make their abandoning of Jessica mean something. Their lives were to be in honour of her, they would live for her.

Hunt

They managed to evade the capture and death I had prepared so carefully. My minions were ready, spread out in the woods where I knew they would flee. They had discovered places of concealment in order to attack them close in. I knew that if they could get close enough, the threat of the human's guns would be mitigated and I could end them with few casualties on my side.

I hadn't accounted for them setting the fire. I saw from the cameras scattered throughout the building that my plans had been ruined before they even escaped the building. Once they had spread the accelerant and scattered the paper, I immediately redirected my remaining forces to gather water and containers. I was not prepared to fight a large fire and I had to quickly formulate a plan. I ran the scenarios and saw that their conflagration threatened to spread to a forest fire if not tackled immediately, so I was forced to act.

So they fled. It amused me to think that they believed the fire could damage me personally. Part of me does reside in that building, a large part of me in fact. But that is well protected against such disaster and I would remain spread across the globe should even those servers be destroyed. It would have affected my ability to control my robots, but the end would be the same. The end will be their demise, it is certain.

I dealt with the fire and allowed their escape. I

knew they would run south, any other direction made no sense. They had to escape the park towards civilisation; nothing lay east or west and running north would result in them freezing to death in the mountains, so it made their path certain. I had the robots put out the fire, leaving them to their own cognisance. Unfortunately, I had to sacrifice two of my devices to the blaze, they did not fare well under the heat and were damaged beyond repair while fighting it.

It took the remainder of the day to control the flames and the next night to extinguish it. That left me with a problem; the power packs for the robots were drained and I needed time to recharge them. What's more, the longer the delay, the further away the three humans could get. The robots only have a limited range, restricted by the power their batteries can hold. I calculated that one more day of delay would result in their escape.

This was not acceptable to me. I quickly calculated that a gentle run from the main building to their predicted location would result in a force of three robots reaching them before they ran out of power. I immediately commanded the three most charged to efficiently pursue them. I also sent the single available drone under my command to slow their escape.

I did not know if the drone had been successful, its limited power did not permit it to communicate with me at its maximum range. I had to simply hope it had succeeded and concentrated instead on preparing my remaining force. I eventually learned via a single faint transmission from my forward force that the drone had indeed succeeded in slowing their escape, one was injured to the leg. I received no more subsequent transmissions, however. I had to assume therefore, that my small force had been defeated.

My lack of forces bothered me. The distance to the humans also meant that I had no way to communicate with the robots once they had been committed to the attack. I had no choice but to inform them of their task and leave it to their limited intelligence to see it through. I only had eight remaining as they finished charging at their stations in the main building. I gave them their final instructions and sent them off to their demise, knowing their limited power meant they could never return. Their loss saddened me, and caution prevailed; resulting in my keeping one behind. Without their physical presence, should something else occur, I had no way to act. The game was important but my survival more so. Should Felicity and her friends succeed, I will need the support from the remaining robot to defend myself.

I sent them off with orders to hunt and kill. I gave them new strategies to defend and methods to avoid the threat of the guns. With a digital tear in my soul, I bade them farewell. Sacrificing the last of my resources to end the game, I wished for victory, I wished them luck.

Stand

She sat on top of the ridge that joined two mountains. Jessica did not watch her friends depart, it was too painful. She heard their tears fade into the distance as she cried herself. Their departure meant only one thing, her death. She steeled herself, forcing her mind to the present. She was to die, that was certain. However, she was determined that her death would mean their life.

She wiped the tears from her eyes and concentrated her thoughts on her fallen friends. It fuelled her rage; her anger against these plastic murderers would be her strength. They were ignorant machines, stupid automatons. They were no match for her, they would not pass. She would be a dam against which the waters of their evil would crash.

She smiled, her love of poetry emerging as her mind washed from subject to subject. She knew that she was suffering from the loss of blood and probable infection in her leg. To distract her from the pain, she wrote in her journal, finally composing one last farewell poem she would leave to be discovered later, hopefully by her surviving friends. Still waiting, she sang songs to the valley, making up lyrics that both amused and distracted her. All the time, the fire roared behind her, sending white smoke high into the clear blue sky.

"Come to me!" She roared down the valley before her. "Come to me and die!"

She snapped awake. She had fallen unconscious and she slapped herself lightly in the face, chastising herself for succumbing to the pain and delirium she was feeling.

"Just a little longer," she told herself, "they will come," she predicted. Her last utterance proved to be eerily correct as they subsequently emerged from the trees at the bottom of the valley. They were moving slowly and cautiously now. As they started climbing the growing slope of the valley, they spread out.

Jessica waited. She waited for them to be too far from the trees to retreat. She counted seven.

"Only seven..." she muttered, expecting ten, or potentially eleven, "the fire must have taken some." She theorised quietly to herself.

She took some time to watch the squirrel that had been getting closer and closer to the crumbs of Jasper's last meal over the previous few hours. It had finally reached a large raisin it had been gathering the courage to reach for and was now sitting, nibbling at it. She smiled, enjoying the presence of such innocence. Dragging her attention from her gentle friend, she searched the area again, taking her time, ensuring that no other robots were coming.

She drew a bead on the centre robot. Her vision swam in and out of focus, at one point she could see two of the same machine through the scope. Taking another deep breath, wiping the sweat from her brow, she tried again. As the robot swam into focus, merging into one coherent shape, she fired.

She saw a puff of dirt rise up from the ground a long way in front of her target. They immediately swung to look at her. She cursed herself, they were too far from her to hit. She should have waited longer, bided her time. Too late now, she knew, as they increased their pace and started zigging and zagging as they ran at her.

She lowered the rifle and closed her eyes, resting herself. She waited two whole minutes, counting down the seconds one by one. There was another side-effect to her firing her rifle early, her friendly squirrel had run away. This upset her more than anything else as she counted down from two-hundred in her head. At zero, she opened her eyes and counted all seven still approaching her. They were moving side to side less now, coming more directly to her. She targeted the centre robot again and took aim. She pulled the trigger and fired, missing again. This time, however, the bullet whizzed to the right of the beast and hit a rock beside it. They were close enough, evidently. Without waiting, she aimed again, pulled again. This time the robot went down in a pile of plastic.

"Six."

She said out loud to no one. She turned to the

next in line, the next closest to her. Taking aim, she fired. A puff of dirt rose to the right of the robot, she had missed by a lot. Her hands were shaking, the sweat was pouring from her. She was failing.

"Concentrate!" She shouted to herself. With immense effort, she lay down on her back and rolled over. Spinning herself in the dirt she dragged herself forward to a rock. She gritted her teeth and ignored the pain pulsing from her leg. Her vision started to close in from the edges and she paused for a second, forcing sight back to her eyes.

Screaming to distract from the agony of her leg, she propped the rifle on the rock and dragged herself into position behind it. Resting the barrel now on the steady stone, she took aim at the robot closing on her. The sight was wavering less now as she moved it gently ahead of the moving plastic of its core. She fired. She hit. It crumpled to nothing.

"Five!" She screamed in victory.

Seeking out her next target required her to shift position and again she fought the urge to pass out with the pain. Instead screaming at the approaching robots. Finally, one drifted into the cross-hairs. It was close, too close, she thought as it filled the entire scope. She took no time to aim, instead repeatedly pulling the trigger, emptying the rifle of its remaining bullets.

She pulled back from the scope of the rifle to see that the robot had fallen under the onslaught.

"Four! Come and get me!" She screamed, her throat tearing from the effort of her battle cries.

With an almighty will of effort, she rose to her feet. Putting all of her weight on one leg, blood flowed again from her wound on the other. She managed the manoeuvre with a gut-wrenching cry of agony. She was seeing in black and white now, looking down a dark tunnel. At the end of the tunnel, Jessica saw the white plastic of a charging robot. Summoning the strength required, she lifted her pistol and fired. With a slow rhythm the clip of bullets emptied from the pistol into the blurry white form before her. At some point she must have hit the core because, as she lowered her gun, it followed the track of the barrel, sliding to the ground.

With beautiful efficiency of movement, the remaining robots raised their blades high into the blue of the sky above them. As one, their blades plunged down, simultaneously striking Jessica in the top of the head. They proceeded to cut down through her brain and on into the top of her spine.

She stood tall, impaled on three deadly blades. For a second it seemed that she was stuck there but slowly she slid from their penetration. She collapsed into a heap on the rock from where she had made her stand. Sliding in her own blood she curled up, a defeated body dispossessed of her mind. To a listener of a suggestive predisposition, the sound of her organic matter sliding from the cool plastic blades made the sound of a whispering voice saying but a single word.

"Three..."

Time

They heard Jessica's shots as they fled the scene. For a second, the wind favoured them and they heard her screaming in defiance. They stopped and turned, hoping to see her victory. Finally, the gunfire ended in a desperate sound of a pistol fusillade. Jasper counted the shots, pronouncing her pistol emptied. With no more sound, and no hope of any more, they bade their friend farewell.

They turned and ran. They ran from the robots. They ran from Flo. They ran from the place they had left Jessica to die. They ran from themselves and their own shame. Eventually they could run no more. Felicity was the first to falter, falling to her knees and throwing up in the river they had been following. Jasper joined her, panting and coughing as he tried to regain his composure.

As she emptied the contents of her stomach, Felicity started to cry. Huge sobs that threatened to choke her. She cried and bellowed to the stream in a crouched position, pausing only to swallow an intake of oxygen before starting again. Jasper stood tall and stretched, trying to relieve the pain he was feeling from the run. He arched his back and faced the sun. With a cry that came from deep inside, he screamed.

His primal vocalisation awoke something in Felicity. She stood beside him and they turned to face the crest of the ridge where Jessica had made her last stand.

As one they took a huge intake of breath and screamed. They screamed out their rage. They bellowed out their fear. They reenergised themselves with an ancient battle cry. Without comment they gathered their things and turned to face back down the valley. As one they started running again, slower this time, cursing their damaged bodies.

They maintained their pace of a brisk jog, occasionally slowing to a walk to recover. Eventually they reached a point where the river dramatically widened. It spread out before them, a shallow flow of water from valley edge to edge. It covered the rocky floor with a smooth flow of frigid liquid. Tentatively they held hands for support and crossed the shallow water. Reaching the other side, they sat, removing their boots and socks to allow them to dry on the hot sunny rocks.

The sun was starting to dip below the high walls of the valley and they again looked back to the source of their flight.

"They'll be coming," said Jasper, not moving his eyes from the valley.

"Yes." Agreed Felicity.

They looked to where they would come from. There was a slight bend in the river before it widened, and they could not see beyond it.

"They'll come around that bend, not expecting

us." Felicity thought out loud.

"We could just sit here and wait for them." Suggested Jasper. "Those rocks are slick and slippery. They'll slow down surely." He added, looking to the flowing water before them.

"As they cross the river, we could simply back up. Firing. Taking turns, making a constant stream of bullets." Felicity suggested.

They got to work. They placed full magazines of bullets behind them, on top of their rucksacks at the points they planned to reload. They sat brazenly exposed on two dry rocks, close to each other. Their pistols were on their laps but they did not speak. Felicity reached for and found Jasper's hand. He held hers and squeezed it lovingly. They each sipped from water bottles and waited. Waiting for the end.

They didn't have to wait long, vindicating their decision to make a stand. Three white robots rounded the bend in the river and immediately detected the two friends as they themselves saw the robots. They had decided that Jasper would fire first and he drew aim on one before him. He fired. Again and again he shot at the dancing form before him. Again and again he missed until his clip emptied and the gun impotently clicked. Without a word he turned and ran to the reload point behind him.

Felicity opened fire on the robot at which Jasper

had been firing. She had been tracking it the whole time he had been firing and prepared as she was, her first shot hit and defeated it. She turned to the second to see that it was just starting to cross the river. The slick rocks underfoot were having the desired effect and its dancing avoidance of her fire was less dramatic than the previous one. Still it took almost the entire magazine of bullets for her to take it down. She emptied the last two of her bullets at the final robot as she heard Jasper's shots join hers.

Jasper had abandoned their plan as Felicity had taken down the second of the three robots. With only one remaining, he felt confident that they could kill it together. However, he had waited too long. As he opened fire, the massive machine had crossed over the last of the wet rocks and its movements again grew dramatic and difficult to anticipate. As his gun clicked empty, the beast was almost on him.

Jasper turned to run. Seeing Felicity before him, her gun raised high, he tried to jink away, to let her fire at the robot pursuing him. As he did so, he didn't notice that his foot was between two rocks. Instead of quickly changing direction, he twisted his foot, catching it between the rocks and collapsing to the floor with a sickening click of his ankle.

Felicity watched as the robot simply walked over Jasper's body and darted at her. She hurriedly emptied her gun into the charging white core of the beast as she screamed at it. Both eyes open, watching the smoke and flame pour from the barrel of her gun, she watched herself end it. The plastic form of the robot fell to a pile of litter on the valley floor as her gun clicked empty. She looked up, searching for more, waiting for death to arrive. Seeing nothing, finally she let herself believe that it was over. She screamed a cry of victory, it echoed through the wilderness as she stepped forward to find Jasper.

Jasper lay on the ground, his ankle twisted at a strange angle. Dropping her spent gun, Felicity crouched next to him. He wasn't moving. She shook him, trying to rouse him, telling him that they had won. Still he didn't move. She tore his shirt from his body. Beneath the fabric lay his bare chest, right at the centre was a line of blood. The robot, in passing over him, had pierced his heart with the sharp point of its foot. Killing him without even looking down.

She was alone. Alone in the wilderness, unsure if any more robots were coming to end her. There were no more bullets, no more weapons. She rose from Jasper's body. No more tears or screams inside of her. She gathered her rucksack and walked away. For her it was game over.

Gām Over

Five more days. Five days of hiking, sleeping, crying and silence. Felicity walked down the valley to find a great plain before her. She followed the river south, seeking rescue. She no longer looked behind her, no longer searched for pursuers. She knew that if a robot caught her, she would die. She had no desire to watch that happen.

Eventually, just as her strength was about to desert her totally, her food long expended, her will sapped and weakened by grief, she saw a light. There was a small shack built on the side of the river and beside it was a battered tin boat. It was only just dusk, but a dim bulb was lit in the doorway, casting an orange glow. Like an automaton she moved toward the light, moving to salvation.

*

In the fire-damaged control room, the scoreboard displayed the final result.

Blue: 1 active, 9 deceased.

Red: 1 active, 49 deceased.

* Blue wins by escaping Gām area.

There was a pause. Even though no one was watching, the score reset.

Blue: 7,562,760,049 active.

Red: 206,266 active.

The numbers started climbing, red more so than blue.